# RUNNING INTO THE FOREVER

A novel by

J. W. BECKER

J. W. Becker

# Running Into the Forever
Copyright 2012 by J. W. Becker

Published in the United States
ISBN-13: 978-0983853824

## DEDICATION

I come from a military family. My father served in the Navy,
my brother in the Air Force, and my husband in the Army.
This book is dedicated to every man and woman who has served
in the United States Armed Forces.
Thank you for your service to keep this great country safe
and to help ensure the freedom that we enjoy.
God bless you all.

J. W. Becker

# ACKNOWLEDGMENTS

To Carol von Raesfeld (The von Raesfeld Agency)
for her editing skills, her encouragement and her endless
support.

J. W. Becker

# 1

The false sense of spring left abruptly with an icy blast of winter. It was late March and the cold winds of winter made an abrupt about face to rejoin them. The bright sunny day had turned dark and cloudy, bringing with it a foot of new snow. It was mid-afternoon, but dark as night with the north winds howling as temperatures dropped. Floating on the wind was the ever-present low moaning, ending with the high-pitched howl of the Beast. The sound entered and floated throughout the house, bringing with it icy fear. They were all used to the Beast's noise, but this was somehow different. It seemed closer—not in the distance as it had always been. It sounded like it was right outside their door.

Trevor struggled out of bed. He was still recovering from a recent injury, but managed to limp over to his rifle. He moved slowly, his belly burned, and his leg throbbed with the dull ache that always seemed to be there. He stopped to take a deep breath, pushed back a lock of long black hair that had fallen into his eyes and grabbed the gun. There was an urgent sense of danger so he ignored his pain and looked around for Keeley. He called to her, but when she didn't answer, he went to look for her. He made his way down the hall to the front of the house. Silently, he nodded at his brothers. George and Tommy were standing at the front windows, Elliott stood ridge at the front door. Only six year-old Taylor and Daniel were still missing. They all knew the drill because they'd been though this many times before.

"Where's Doc?" Trevor asked almost casually.

"Took the girls to his office," George replied, never taking his eyes away from the window.

"Sounds close," Elliott whispered to Trevor.

Suddenly, the howling stopped, leaving behind only the sounds of the winter winds ripping through the trees. The boys stayed where they were and waited patiently. It was always a waiting game with the Beast and Trevor was sick of it. Cat-and-mouse and they were definitely the mice. No one moved. They didn't even look at each other as they waited to see if one of the Beast's monsters would appear. Trevor hoped that if it came, it would be a mudskin. He hated those bastards with their horrible smell and ugly brown color. Let them show their one red/one brown eyed hideous faces and he would be obliged to kill it. He listened carefully, but there was no telltale clicking or that stupid giggling that they all knew so well. He started to relax. This appeared to be just another false alarm.

"Damn it! Shit!" Elliott yelled.

George looked disapprovingly at his little brother. "Elliott, stop swearing."

It was all Elliott needed. He set his rifle down and jumped George, landing a right cross to his eye. Trevor grabbed Elliott by the collar and pulled him off of his brother. He put his arm across the boy as he had done so many times before and pulled him solidly against his chest. He tightened his grip so Elliott couldn't break free. "Stop it! Now!" This was also something Trevor had said many times when Elliott felt it necessary to attack his brother.

At that moment Daniel strolled in with rifle in hand. He saw Trevor restraining Elliott and sighed. Trevor shrugged and continued to control the boy who was struggling to escape.

"I'm a lot bigger than you, bro, and I'm not letting go, so just relax."

"What's going on here?" asked Daniel.

Trevor grinned. "Just brotherly love, Doc."

"That son of a bitch is always trying to tell me what to do!" Elliott screamed, trying to take another swing at George, but with Trevor holding him, no harm could come to either of them. It was an empty threat.

"Hey! Don't we have enough to do dealing with the Beast and all those creatures of his? Do I gotta fight you too?"

"Let me go!" Elliott yelled, struggling to get free. Trevor merely smiled and gently tightened his grip around the eight year old.

Daniel came over to stand in front of Elliott. "Elliott, if you promise to behave and not try to hurt your brother, Trevor will let you go."

"Fine, I won't hurt his ass."

Trevor reached down to retrieve Elliott's rifle and released his grip slightly. He watched Elliott glare at his brother.

Daniel stepped in front of him. "Elliott, calm down."

"I am calm!" Elliott screamed, feeling some of his anger dissipate.

"Why did you jump George this time?" Elliott shifted uncomfortably, refusing to look at Daniel. "What the hell's bothering you?" Daniel asked him.

Elliott glanced up at Daniel, but then returned his gaze to the floor. He felt sick, numb, and scared. The vision of Daniel's death had done that to him. He'd seen it more than once in his nightmares and was trying desperately to control it. The last thing he wanted was for Doc to see his fear for him—a fear that was making him angry and aggressive. His constant swearing was a symptom of his pain and George was always his target of release.

"Elliott?"

"He's still looking for you. He's still after us. The Beast is near. I can feel it. He's trying to find you, Daniel and I don't know how much longer I can fight him." Elliott said in a flat, helpless tone.

Daniel felt his anger burn. Their whole situation made him angry and his children were suffering because of it. He spoke in a hushed voice. "You listen to me, Elliott, the Beast is far away and if we have to we'll run and stay ahead of them."

"Are you sure?"

3

"I'm sure. This is over. It was just more noise to scare us. Let's all go back to bed."

Sam placed a blanket over Elliott and bent down to kiss his cheek. Daniel leaned against the doorjamb watching his beautiful wife as she tucked the blanket tighter. She looked over at him.

"When will it end?"

"It may never end. Let's make sure the rest of the kids are in bed and then let's go to bed. I'm tired."

Daniel took Sam into his arms. He covered her mouth with his and caressed her lightly as he pressed her against the door. She felt him press into her, rotating his hips to place himself firmly against her. "I need you."

"The children," she whispered.

He released her and together they moved along the hallway, where they met George. Daniel turned his head to the light.

"You're going to have a black eye."

"It's okay, Doc, it's not my first. Is Elliott okay?"

"He will be after a good night's sleep."

"Guess I'll go to bed too."

"Everyone should turn in," Sam said as she moved Taylor toward his bedroom. *Thank God the girls didn't wake up this time.*

It took about thirty minutes to get everyone settled before Sam and Daniel retired to their bedroom. He walked over to the crib where their daughter Katie slept. The five month old had his black hair and deep blue eyes. He pushed the hair off of her face, leaned down, and kissed her gently.

"Love you, sweetheart. Only good dreams."

Sam came out of the bathroom with her robe hanging open, she had nothing on underneath. He watched as she went to check on Katie. When she leaned over the crib, he saw the contour of her breasts and felt the heat rise in his body. He wanted her. He slipped up behind her and pressed his body to hers. She smelled good and her softness felt good against him. He reached under her robe and squeezed her butt.

"Nice butt," he mumbled.

Sam turned around and molded herself to him. He kissed her deeply pushing his tongue into her mouth. He picked her up and carried her to the bed, then laid her down gently. She shuddered at his touch and he smiled down at her.

"Don't talk. Let me do everything for you tonight. I want to please you."

Daniel slowly stripped off his clothes and then removed Sam's robe. Rolling on top of her, he cupped her breasts in his hands and covered her mouth with his. He gently nibbled at her lower lip. She touched him tenderly and he moaned. He didn't want her to stop, but he wasn't done with her. Giving her a goofy, lopsided smile, he eased between her legs and then very slowly slid inside her. He felt urgency and began to thrust hard and deep. She started to climax and waves of pleasure enveloped her as he continued thrusting until his release came. Daniel rolled off, collapsed, and pulled her close to him. They fell asleep in each other's arms.

## 2

Daniel woke Sam later that night and made love to her again. He felt like he just couldn't get enough of her and as he pulled her close, he whispered, "I love you so much. You keep me strong. Tomorrow we have to make some serious decisions about where we're heading. I'll need your help."

"Where are we headed?"

"Away from here. It's not safe anymore and as soon as winter takes a break, we have to leave."

"What about Keeley? She'll be going into her sixth month if we leave here in April."

"And you'll be in your third," Daniel said softly.

"What?"

Daniel leaned over and kissed her. "Honey, my professional opinion is that you are about six weeks pregnant right now."

"How can that be? How did this happen? I don't..."

"Honey, I'm sure you know how it happens, but if you want me to, I'll explain it."

Sam playfully slapped him and they both laughed. "Remember the night I told you that just because you were breast feeding didn't mean you weren't ovulating? Well, you were and I probably impregnated you that night." He leaned over and planted another little kiss on her.

"I should have listened to you. Are you sure? I don't feel different."

"I am, but I know you aren't. Tomorrow we'll do a blood test and an exam."

Daniel studied Sam's reaction and was somehow unnerved by it. She didn't seem happy with the whole idea of being pregnant again and deep down he couldn't blame her. He wasn't exactly happy about it happening so soon after Katie was born—not to mention the fact that they were plagued by a bunch of blood-thirsty monsters that had invaded the earth and were now searching for them.

"Are you okay?" he asked.

"I don't know. This whole world is so uncertain and now we're being forced to move again. Another baby? How are you with all this?"

Daniel pulled Sam into his arms and leaned her against his chest. "I love you, Sam. This baby is a part of our love. I will love him as much as I love both you and Katie...as much as I love all our children."

"If I'm pregnant..." she said.

"Doubter." Daniel snickered. He had to admit that a big part of him was elated. "That's what you get for being so damn irresistible."

# 3

Five year old Rusty was up early. It wasn't quite six, but she was wide awake and wanted company. She looked over at Emma who was sleeping soundly next to Brady, so she decided to go see Sam and Daddy. She walked down the long corridor leading to Daniel's office with her little cat Spot following close behind. She had a bottle of soda in her hand. The bottle cap was fighting her and remained unopened. She pushed the office door open and walked through to the bedroom. She pushed that door open and found Daniel and Sam, who were both still asleep. She peeked in the crib and saw Katie. She pulled Katie's bottle from underneath her hand and took it.

Rusty was afraid and wanted comfort, but everyone was still asleep. She shrugged and tucked Spot under her arm before quietly walking away. She shushed the cat. "Quiet Spot, Daddy and Sam are sleeping." She went back into the office and crawled into Daniel's overstuffed chair. She liked his chair because it smelled of leather and her Daddy. She curled up and with Spot safely tucked in her arms, closed her eyes, and fell asleep.

Daniel woke shortly after seven and went to check on the baby. She was still asleep. He walked back to the bed and sat down next to Sam, watching her chest slowly rising and falling with each breath. He placed his hand on her stomach. He knew that he wouldn't be able to feel his child yet, but somehow couldn't help trying. He loved Sam and wanted them to have lots of babies together. He felt that this pregnancy was badly timed and that he should have insisted they use protection. He was a doctor, for God's sake and knew the risk of her becoming pregnant again, especially now because they would be moving again.

"*Damn it!*" Although he'd whispered, it was just loud enough to wake Sam.

"Good morning," she said. "Don't tell me the baby is kicking already?"

"Funny. Come on, sleepyhead, get yourself up. I want your blood and I want to do the pelvic before the troops start to stir."

"You're so romantic in the morning, Doctor."

Daniel leaned down and kissed her. He moved his hand up to her breast. He wanted her again. She had a way of doing that to him instantly. He stopped.

"God, you're beautiful, but I can't do this now, not when I have to do a clinical exam on you, but I'll take a rain check," he said with a smile and a wink.

"Now who's the coward? Give me ten minutes to get cleaned up and check on Katie."

"I'll be in the office. I want to write a few notes on the kids."

Daniel kept a detailed record on all the children, probably a throwback to his intern days, but it was also a good reminder. He regretted that he couldn't have spent the entire morning just enjoying his wife's body. He sighed, forced himself up, and dressed quickly.

Walking into the office, he discovered Rusty. He lifted her into his arms, kissed her cheek, and carried her to Katie's crib where he snuggled her next to the baby. Rusty immediately curled closer, put her arm around Katie, and then inserted her thumb into her own mouth. Daniel gently pulled it out. She cried out, trembling at his touch. He rubbed her back until she settled back into a fitful sleep.

"When are you going to give up? I don't think you're going to break the thumb-sucking habit."

Daniel looked up and continued to rub Rusty's back. "Do you want a teenager who sucks her thumb? I'm going to talk to her about it again."

Daniel took Sam's hand and led her into the exam room. He closed the door quietly behind them. "Is she having nightmares again?" Sam asked.

"She's scared, Sam. The nightmares do that to her."

"Like Elliott?"

Daniel shook his head in agreement. He smiled and pointed. "Table."

"Daniel."

"Don't make this difficult. Get up there."

Reluctantly, Sam eased up onto the exam table. "Can't this wait until after breakfast?"

"No, lie down."

Sam let out a deep breath and eased back on the exam table. Daniel put the tourniquet on her arm and prepared to draw her blood. "Relax your arm, honey."

"Do you call all of your patients honey?"

He gave her a big smile and winked. "Only the one's I impregnate. Now hold still." He drew the blood. "Okay, let's check the baby, bend your knees and quit squirming."

"I don't squirm," she shot back at him.

Daniel did the pelvic exam and found everything was going along fine. He could feel the fullness of her uterus indicating that she was indeed pregnant.

"You are pregnant, Mrs. Bryant," he said in his most professional voice.

Sam scrunched her face. "Are you sure?"

"I'm sure. I was there when it happened and I can feel the difference in your uterus. We'll need to check your sugar levels carefully and make sure you don't get gestational diabetes again."

"Great, more needles."

"Now you sound like Trevor. Humor me. Even I deserve some fun around here. Let me listen to your heart." Daniel took down his stethoscope from its hook and gently placed it on Sam's chest.

"Daniel, what..."

"Shush. I can't hear."

"Hi, Daddy."

Rusty ran over to Daniel and raised her arms so he would pick her up. He gave her a big hug.

"Hi, Sam," she said. "What's you doing on Daddy's table? You sick?"

"No, I'm fine. Are you hungry?" Sam asked as she jumped down from the exam table and buttoned her shirt.

Rusty shrugged. "Maybe, but I don't think I know."

"I think I know why you're not hungry, Miss." Daniel threw the little girl into the air and eased her onto the exam table so he could talk to her. He pushed her mop of blond hair off her face and looked into her troubled blue eyes. God, he couldn't get over how much this kid got under his skin. He loved her unconditionally. She made him happy. She made him laugh. He loved the way she said things backwards and wrong, and made up answers, usually blaming her cat for any trouble she managed to get into. It tickled him and sometimes it was hard not to laugh at her, but right now he needed to be stern. She had to understand that he was not happy about her stealing Katie's bottle.

"How did this bottle find its way into your pocket?"

"I think Spot gived it to me," she whispered, not daring to look up at him.

"And why did Spot give it to you?"

"Because he didn't want it no more, so I was holding it and it sort of fell into my pocket."

Sam tried to keep a straight face as she listened to their conversation. Daniel was leaning against the exam table, one hand on each side of Rusty's knees.

11

"Buppy, you're a big girl now and big girls don't drink from baby bottles."

"Not when the monsters come and make me shake inside. I get really scared, Daddy."

Rusty lowered her eyes and put her hands in her lap. She started to tremble. Sam shook her head and quietly left them. Daniel lifted her off the table. He sat down in his chair with Rusty on his lap and wrapped his arms around her. She was just a baby, his baby, and as he held her against him, he felt her vulnerability. She shook as tears ran down her face and all he could do was hold her tight. He spoke in a quiet voice, reassuring her that he would always be there to protect her. He rocked her gently. "Tell me why you're so scared."

"Monsters. They never go away."

Daniel leaned back thinking about the monsters that were frightening Rusty. Monsters definitely existed in their world. They had all seen them...been hurt by them. He placed her head against his chest next to his heart. "Tell me about your monsters?"

Rusty pressed her face against his chest and talked into his shirt. He gently lifted her chin so he could hear what she was saying. "The monster that hurt Trevor. It pointed at me and laughed."

"Trevor's much better."

"Not today, Daddy, he gets hurted later," she sniffed. She snuggled closer so she could listen to Daniel's heartbeats.

"Close your eyes and rest for a little while."

"You won't go away?"

"I won't go away."

"Good." Rusty adjusted her position and placed her hand over Daniel's heart. She started to quietly hum, making a low continuous sound as she drifted into sleep. He cuddled her like he did Katie, always making sure she could feel his closeness. He hated that the world had gone to shit.

Rusty was restless. Her entire body twitched with short involuntary jerky movements as her dreams snagged her in webs of fear. Daniel attempted to reduce her tension by repositioning her so that her ear was directly over his heart. He wanted her to be able to relax listening to its steady beat. She sighed deeply and shuddered until she finally became quiet. Daniel leaned back with Rusty nestled in his arms murmuring reassurances to a child trapped in a world that had been destroyed and no longer cared about them.

# 4

Sam went to the bedroom to check on Katie. The baby looked up at her from her crib. "Hello, sweet pea. Come on, Mommy will change you. How does lunch sound?"

Sam wanted to continue breast feeding Katie for a while longer. It would make the next move easier. The baby made loud noises as she suckled. Once Katie had her fill, she fell asleep in her mother's arms, still making little sucking motions with her mouth. Sam chuckled at her piggish little daughter.

Daniel had been standing in the doorway watching her. He walked over and lightly touched his finger to Katie's mouth. She made a little sucking motion, opened one eye for a second, and then instantly went back to sleep.

Daniel bent over and gently shook Rusty. "Daniel, don't wake her."

"I promised that I wouldn't leave her alone. I also have a few more things to discuss with her."

Daniel took Katie's bottle from his pocket as he shook Rusty again. "Buppy, time to wake up." Rusty yawned and smiled up at him. "We haven't finished our talk yet, little one."

"Spot did it."

"Spot is an innocent victim. I want you to stop taking Katie's bottle and keep your thumb out of your mouth," he said sternly.

"What if it just falls in by itself?"

Daniel didn't want Rusty to see him laugh, so he caught her up and threw her in the air, stood her upright and gave her a little swat on the butt to move her along. "Go get dressed—and remember what I said."

"Okay, Daddy."

"Good luck with that," Sam said. "Wave bye-bye to Daddy, sweetheart."

After Daniel finished his charting, he strolled over to join everyone in the kitchen.

"Morning all," Trevor said as he walked in. Keeley went to help Sam get breakfast ready. Daniel was sitting at the counter, looking at her very carefully. He wasn't happy with what he saw. She was almost five months pregnant and had a nice little budge showing, but she appeared tired and drained. He got up and casually picked up her hand to feel her pulse. He looked into her eyes.

"Are you sleeping alright?"

She sighed. "Restless, I guess."

Daniel put his hand on her belly. "How's the little one? Is the baby the reason you're not sleeping well? Are you still having problems with your stomach?"

"It's not too bad."

"Most mornings, Doc," Trevor chimed in.

Daniel leaned over and kissed Keeley's forehead, she didn't have a fever. "Come see me after breakfast and I'll have a look. Maybe I can help you feel more comfortable."

"Mornin' y'all," George said as he energetically entered the room. "Doc, whatever you gave Elliott could you do it again? He hasn't tried to clobber me in hours."

"Is Elliott up?"

"Still sleeping like a baby."

Trevor grinned. "Better watch that baby stuff, George, or he will clobber you."

The three little girls came in with Taylor trailing after them. Emma, Brady, and Jamie were still in their pajamas.

"Doesn't anyone get dressed around here anymore?" Sam asked, eyeing the girls.

"I do," Rusty yelled and jumped up so Daniel could lift her into his lap.

"I can see that. Where are your shoes?"

"I think they're hiding under Jamie's bed."

"You need to go and find them and put them on. What happened to your shirt? It looks crooked."

"The buttons hate me. They make me do it all wrong and Spot wouldn't help me." Rusty looked accusingly at the cat who was ignoring everyone.

Daniel sighed. Rusty had a running battle going when it came to putting on her clothes and ninety percent of the time, she lost. She leaned back against him as he re-buttoned her shirt. He wrapped his hand around her foot.

"Your feet are ice cold. Go right now and find you socks and shoes. I don't care who's hiding them."

"What if they went away?"

"Now!"

"Okay." Rusty held up the bottle of soda she'd been carrying around all morning. "Daddy, I can't get this damn bottle to break."

Daniel raised his eyebrows at her profanity, but said nothing. He took the bottle from her and held it in his hand. "Why do you want to break the bottle?"

"I want to drink the damn thing," Rusty said in frustration.

"Oh, so you want to open it, not to break it."

Rusty solemnly shook her head while Daniel showed her how to open the bottle. "Why do you keep saying the word 'damn'?"

"Elliott does it."

As if that was enough of an explanation, she said no more. Daniel patiently exhaled. "Elliott shouldn't be saying it either and I don't want you to use that word or any other word that you know you shouldn't say, even if Elliott does. Do you understand?"

"Why?"

"Because it's a bad word and I don't want you to use it."

"What if I do?"

"Then you and I will have a problem. Now, go find your shoes."

Rusty giggled, jumped off Daniel's lap, and headed for her bedroom. She stopped to peek into the room where Elliott was sleeping. He was still there, so she went over to the bed and climbed up next to him. "Are you asleep?" she whispered in his ear.

"No."

Rusty wiggled under the blankets next to him. She snuggled up against him and made herself comfortable. "What're you doing?"

"Thinking."

"About what?"

"Rusty, do you feel like something's wrong?"

"They're coming," she said quietly. "I seen them last night in my head. His monsters. They're going to hurt my Trevor."

"I think I saw it too. What did they look like to you?"

"Like us, sort of, but really tall. Taller than Daddy. They gots eyes like Ethan."

"I saw the red eye and brown eye too. They walk funny, stiff like, and they've got six fingers."

Rusty nodded her head. "They hurted all those peoples. They called them inside peoples. They're like us, the real ones. There are lots of them."

"I saw that too," Elliott said. "Some of the kids, they left the place where the Beast keeps them. They're running."

"I know," Rusty whispered. "They're running to us. The monsters scare me."

When Rusty started to cry, Elliott wrapped his arms around her. "I'm scared too, but I can't tell 'cause I have to be brave all the time."

"Rusty mumbled. "I seen them when Daddy was holding me."

Elliott held onto Rusty and moved as close as he could to her, hugging her tight against his chest. He was as scared as she was. Spot jumped up to join them and made himself comfortable on top of them.

"I'll try not to let them hurt Trevor," Elliott mumbled. "I promise I'll try and keep our brother safe."

# 5

"Doc, I need to talk to you. It's important." Trevor got up from the chair and flinched with the pain that ran though his leg. Daniel grabbed his arm as Trevor's leg threatened to buckle under him.

"Your leg bothering you?"

"No, I'm okay, just a twinge."

"He's lying." Keeley scowled. "He cries out at night because of the pain."

Trevor gave Keeley a look of disapproval.

"Why are you hiding it?" she asked.

"It's not all that bad," he mumbled.

"Keeley was annoyed by Trevor's stubbornness and refused to look at him. She turned to Daniel. "That's why he couldn't sleep last night."

"Hold on, kids," Daniel interrupted. "Let's not have another war going on right here in the kitchen. Let's go to the office and we'll discuss this further."

Trevor and Keeley stood their ground. Daniel looked at Sam, but she just shrugged her shoulders. "Well, I'm going and I would be delighted to have the both of you join me."

The staring contest between Trevor and Keeley ended when they both started to laugh. Keeley gave him her sweetest smile. "Don't be so stubborn."

"Okay fine," Trevor conceded. "Let's go face the music."

When they entered the office, Daniel had already set up the exam table for Keeley. He was concerned about her and wanted to check on the baby just to make sure everything was going well before they made the next move.

Trevor leaned against the wall to help support his leg. "Doc, I really need to talk to you."

"Good. I always enjoy talking to you, but first I want to check on our girl. You go sit on the overstuffed chair and behave yourself. This won't take long."

Trevor reluctantly gave in. He knew it would do no good to protest once Daniel had his mind made up. He fell into the chair and was actually glad to get off his leg. It had been hurting for days and wouldn't let him rest. He thought the stomach injury would be his undoing, but the old leg injury was what was acting up, and as much as he didn't want to admit it, the pain and constant ache was starting to become a problem.

Daniel gave Keeley a reassuring smile as he helped her onto the exam table. "Keeley, we need to check on the baby, just to make sure everything is coming along as it should."

Daniel looked over at Trevor and frowned, but said nothing.

"Hell Doc, don't go looking at me like that."

"What's going on with your leg? Pain?"

Trevor gave him a cautious look and grumbled. "Yeah, it just hurts some."

Daniel squatted down next to Trevor and felt along his leg. He flinched involuntarily and pulled away. "Hurts just a little, huh? You're next, right after I finish with Keeley. I want to get a closer look, so don't plan on moving from that chair."

Daniel went back to the exam table and gave Keeley his full attention. He did a blood draw and then a pelvic exam. He spoke softly to put her at ease. "Just relax and let me get a feel of this baby."

The baby felt good. Secure. The uterus was firm and it was at least a five-month fetus. Daniel suspected she might even be a little farther along than that.

"Everything feels right," he smiled at Keeley. "Get dressed and I'll run the blood work. I'm sure it will be normal, so don't worry. A slight change in the medicine should help your stomach."

Keeley kissed Daniel. "Thanks, Doc. Love you. I'll be right back." She eased off the table and went into the other room to get dressed.

Daniel pointed at Trevor and then the exam table. "Strip."

"Doc, it's not..."

"Stop! No arguments. Pants off now or I'll come over there and do it for you."

Trevor mumbled under his breath as he unbuckled his belt. Stripping off his pants he limped over to the exam table and stood there.

"Up, please," Daniel said.

"Up, please," Trevor repeated with disgust. "I'm doing this under protest."

"Objection noted. Get on the table."

Trevor eased up on the table and pain shot through his leg. He closed his eyes briefly. Daniel helped lift the injured leg onto the table. "Go ahead and lie down, tough guy."

Keeley came back into the room and went immediately to Trevor's side. She took his hand and he squeezed it. He smiled at her. "Are you okay?" he asked.

Keeley gently patted her belly. "We're both okay."

Daniel had been probing Trevor's leg. He knew it was tender and was being careful so he wouldn't cause him more pain.

"Trevor," Daniel shook his head. "You've managed to get an infection. There's also an open wound right here."

Daniel continued to work as he talked, cleaning the infected wound and applying antibiotic ointment. He bandaged the area and leaned over Trevor.

"You're my star patient. You keep me on my toes because you're constantly getting injured and/or wounded. You are the most stubborn, hard-headed patient I have ever had to deal with. Do you remember that I told all of my children to come to me if

21

J. W. Becker

they are sick or hurt? That includes you, my son. Now, can you explain to me why that plan doesn't seem to work for you?"

"Ah, Doc, you know I come to you when I can't stand the pain anymore. I probably had at least a day, maybe two left on this one."

Daniel pushed Trevor's black hair away to feel his forehead. He had a fever brewing as well as an infected leg. He shook his head. "You make my job harder when you wait so long. Now you get to stay in bed for a week. Ah, don't argue." he cautioned. "Not one word. One week, not six days, not five, one whole week off of your feet. And just for fun, I'm going to give you antibiotic injections every day, so I can clean up your infection."

"A whole week? Needles! But...but..."

Daniel held up his finger. "No! No! You are not allowed to talk back. You are only allowed to listen. One whole week! Daily injections! If you don't stay in bed I will..."

Trevor sighed and finished the sentence for him. "Sedate me."

Daniel held up a syringe and smiled. "Ready?"

"I suppose you want my butt."

"That would work."

Trevor didn't argue. He knew when he'd lost and arguing wouldn't do any good, so he rolled onto his stomach. He snorted. "You and those needles!"

"Get used to them and me behind them. You are now my favorite pin cushion. Keeley, would you please get me a blanket. Trevor has the honor of staying with me for a while longer."

Trevor's eyes followed Keeley as she exited. When she was gone he tried to get up.

"No!" said Daniel. "You need to stay right there."

Reluctantly, Trevor eased back down on the exam table. "I need to talk to you."

Trevor's expression was both worried and serious. Daniel went back to the exam table, rolled the stool up to it and sat down.

"You'll be fine and Keeley's doing well. Your leg's going to take awhile, but the infection isn't anything I can't handle. It must have been brewing for awhile and it could have been cleared up faster if I had known, but you don't need worry. I won't let anything happen to you."

Trevor leaned back. His voice cracked as he started to talk. "I know that, Doc. I'm not worried about my leg. It's Ethan."

"You had to kill him or he would have killed all of us."

"I'm okay with that. I made him talk before I killed him. I made that Patrick/Ethan kid talk. I want you to know how it went down. I confronted Patrick. I told him I knew he was really Ethan." Trevor relaxed, moving his sore leg slightly, trying to find a more comfortable position. Daniel brought over a pillow and placed it underneath his leg. He sighed deeply and gave Daniel a verbal play-by-play of that night.

*Patrick: "All right, I'll tell you. I am Ethan—the Ethan you thought you killed. I wasn't dead because you hit the wrong eye, stupid. The Beast has powers you don't even know about yet. He changed me and made me look different to you."*

*Trevor: "If you want to live, you'd better start talking. Tell me all of it and don't try to lie."*

*Ethan: "Sure, why not? There are more of us. I'm not the only one and there's more than one of the Beast. You can't win, so you might as well give up now."*

*Trevor: "How many more? How many more Beasts?"*

*Ethan: "There are incubators and they're growing. His kind. My kind."*

*Trevor: "How many Beasts?"*

*"When Ethan didn't answer, I shoved the rifle barrel into his right eye—the red eye. I leveled my rifle and pulled the trigger back and told the bastard to talk. His words turned cold, as cold as he felt."*

*Ethan: "Three. They're in hibernation."*

*Trevor: "Where are they?"*

*Ethan: "I'll tell you.  In fact, I'll be glad to tell because it isn't going to matter.  Brighton Ridge, near Clayton Canyon.  You're going to be the Beast's slave."*

*Trevor: "How many mudskins are left?"*

*Ethan: "I don't know.  There's captives.  Your kind.  Mostly kids, but there are some grown women. The Beast wants you and Daniel.  He needs breeders."*

*Trevor: "We're supposed to impregnate those women?"*

*Ethan: "Yeah—and the others when they age. Hell, you should enjoy it. All that fucking should be fun for you, especially with the under-aged."*

*Trevor: "What are you talking about?"*

*Ethan: "When they first bleed.  After that you get to breed them.  The Beast needs more feeders."*

"I couldn't stand it anymore, Doc.  I was furious with Ethan and backhanded him."

Jumping away from the memory, Trevor shivered and shifted on the table. He wanted to get up, but Daniel gently pushed him back down.  He was alarmed at how warm Trevor felt.

"We need to take your temperature."

Trevor grabbed Daniel. "Do you understand what's going on here, Doc?  That bastard's looking for us. Ethan was just a scout— a searcher and there's more of them after us. He found us here and so will they. We have to move on.  It has to be very soon…like right now."

Daniel turned to the window. A light snow was falling.  "We can't move now, at least not until the weather breaks and you're feeling better. Ethan was the only trouble we've encounter so far. I think we can chance it.  If Ethan had told them our location, they would have been here by now."

"My leg will be better in a week, then me and Elliott…" Trevor stopped talking and thought briefly about Elliott. "Maybe I'd better take George or Tommy.  Elliott's been through enough.

24

We'll go ahead and find another place. It'll be better if we know where we're going. If there is no trouble within the week I'm laid up, it should hold for awhile longer."

"Trevor, it could take longer. You have a fever and the infection will take time to heal."

"It can't wait, Doc. I'll be fine. Keeley's got to have a safe place to have our baby."

"So does Sam," Daniel said softly. "About six weeks. It was a mistake on my part. I shouldn't have gotten her pregnant so soon."

Trevor smiled slightly. "Then I'll find a place for them both. Our babies will be born in a safe place."

Daniel helped Trevor up. "I can do it."

It wasn't a total lie and Trevor was actually grateful for Daniel's help. Suddenly, Trevor pulled Daniel into his arms. Trevor needed Daniel's touch. Father and son embraced. The love they had for each other was unspoken between them, but deep.

"Let's get you to your bed. Keeley can sit on you for awhile and if that doesn't work I can always send Rusty to help her."

"Can I stay here for awhile? I'll use the bed over in the corner."

"It would be my pleasure to have your company."

Daniel made Trevor comfortable on the bed and then took his temperature. It was an even 102. He got a cool cloth, placed it on his forehead and told him to close his eyes and try to rest. He was asleep in minutes.

Trevor slept peacefully until the nightmares of Ethan filled his fevered mind. He was with him again, killing him again, and re-living the deaths of every family member, the loss of his wife and his unborn child. The Beast had planted these false memories in his mind the day Trevor killed Ethan. They were coming back to haunt him. He jumped from the bed screaming.

Daniel dropped the book he'd been reading and went to him. "Easy, Trevor, you're alright. You're safe at home."

Daniel held the boy in his arms, leaning him against his chest. He rocked Trevor as he did Rusty when her nightmares terrorized her and like Rusty he placed Trevor head against his chest next to his heart.

"You're safe."

Daniel reassured him like he had all those months ago when Trevor would wake in terror and was surprised to find that he was still alive.

The nightmares were always so real to him. Nightmares he was re-living over and over, but it had been a long time since he'd awakened screaming and Daniel wondered what it was at this moment that had brought all of it back to him. *Maybe it was nothing more than the fever.* He held Trevor until he lapsed back into a restless sleep.

"God," Daniel said out loud. "We need to leave here. It truly isn't safe anymore."

# 6

Jamie and Brady watched the snow fall. The ground was turning a clean white. "Want to make a snow guy?" nine year-old Jamie asked.

Brady got a big smile on her face. "Sure. Let's get Emma and Taylor to help us."

The two girls found the other children in the kitchen. All four raced outside to construct what turned out to be a reasonable snowman. Sam called them in when she felt they had been out in the cold long enough and made them hot chocolate. They sat in a semi-circle around the fireplace, laughing and talking. Elliott sat down to join them and Rusty plopped down into his lap. A few minutes later she managed to spill the chocolate down the front of her shirt.

"I'll go get you a clean shirt," Emma said. "Brady, help Rusty take off the dirty one?"

"Come over here, Rusty."

Brady was helping Rusty with the buttons when it started. The low moan quickly became the howl of the Beast. All the children became instantly quiet. Rusty put her head in her hands and started to cry.

"Elliott!"

Elliott leaned down and whispered into her ear. "Stay with Brady. I'll be right back."

"Not again," Brady huffed. "That damn Beast."

It was a brief sound that echoed into the house, which somehow seemed to stop and hang there, and then it ended as quickly as it started. Rusty bolted from Brady and ran behind a chair, pushing herself into the corner. Elliott came back and moved to the window, his rifle ready. George seemed to appear out of nowhere and joined his brother.

"See anything?"

Emma was unable to move. She stood with Rusty's shirt in her hand and her entire body began to shake. Sam took Emma into her arms. "It's okay, Emma. It's just noise."

Tommy entered the room and placed two rifles down next to the door. George went to position himself between the girls and the door. Daniel came in armed with his rifle, joining Elliott at the window and they all waited. After fifteen minutes, Daniel broke the silence. He winked at Sam. "It's over. Nothing is going to happen. We could all use something to eat."

"I wish he'd stop screaming at us," Brady said and headed for the kitchen to help Sam.

Daniel directed his attention to Elliott who stood stiffly, sweat running down his face. He never moved or diverted his eyes from the window. Daniel walked over and gently put his hand on Elliott's shoulder. Startled, Elliott spun around, his weapon pointed directly at Daniel's heart. He didn't move as their eyes met. With trembling hands, he slowly lowered the gun. "Sorry, Doc."

"It's over," Daniel said quietly.

"It'll never be over. They'll never stop looking for us," Elliott said and walked away.

"Emma, where's Rusty? You're holding her shirt," George asked.

"She was here before the Beast called."

When they found Rusty, she refused to come out. Everyone tried, but she refused to move from behind the chair. Finally, Daniel moved the chair so he could get to her and gently tapped her on the back.

"It's Daddy, baby girl," Daniel said.

The look on her tear-stained face was one of abject terror. Daniel lifted her into his arms. She clung to him. "It's all alright, Buppy." He picked up a blanket from the chair and wrapped it around her. She buried her face in his chest and shook uncontrollably.

Daniel carried Rusty to Trevor's and Keeley's room. He knocked and Keeley opened the door. He went directly to the bed and Trevor looked up at him. "What happened to Rusty?"

"She's upset and needs a little love and reassurance, so I brought you some company. She's a little beaten soul who needs some big brother comfort."

"The howling," Trevor said with disgust. We heard it. That bastard never gives up."

"That's part of it, but Rusty's had a rough day and could use some special attention."

"Come here to me, baby girl."

Rusty crawled in next to Trevor and threw her arm across him. She hugged him and burrowed close. Trevor put his big hand across her back and nestled her against him, her little body shivering.

Daniel got another blanket from Keeley and covered both Trevor and Rusty. "Don't worry, Buppy, your brother is going to take good care of you."

Trevor tightened his arms around her. He leaned down and whispered in her ear, telling her all the things a five year-old needed to hear to feel safe and secure. He shifted her against his shoulder and chest, so she would feel completely safe.

Daniel explained to the other children that while the Beast's voice was unsettling, it had never hurt them, so there was no reason to fear it. "It's just noise to try and frighten us, but it's far away from here."

This seemed to satisfy them for the moment—everyone except Elliott, who clutched his rifle as he turned and walked silently back to the window.

# 7

Daniel was in his office and watched as Sam put Katie down for her nap. She had been changed and fed, so he was hoping the crankiness she had displayed all morning would leave her. He wondered if the howl of the Beast was affecting her too. He gently rubbed the baby's back as her sleepy eyes tried to stay open. She finally gave in, rolled over, and put her thumb in her mouth.

"Great, another thumb sucker," Daniel laughed. He went back into his office, picked up his book and concentrated on Pediatric care.

"Doc," Elliott stepped in. "Sam said you wanted to talk to me."

Elliott moved Daniel's desk chair over and curled into it pulling his legs up to rest his chin on his knees. Daniel leaned forward and looked closely at the little boy.

"What's going on? What's frightening you?"

"The Beast speaks to me. He comes in my dreams, but they're not really dreams. There are others out there. People like us. The Beast calls them 'To-Pans,' the inside people. He has them and won't let them go. He drinks from them, but worst than what Ethan did to Emma. Elliott's voice dropped to a whisper. "He reaches out to touch me. I've seen the people he hurts."

Elliott put his head down on his knees and was silent for a long time. When he didn't move, Daniel reached over and pulled the child into his arms. Elliott let himself collapse into the comfort Daniel offered.

"I don't know why he can touch me, but I do know that he'll never stop. Rusty sees it too and that's why she can't sleep. I think it's worse for her. I want him to go away. Go away from both of us."

Elliott's voice trembled and Daniel pressed him closer. Today, Elliott Shavers was a little eight year-old boy, not the defender of his brother or the slayer of the Beast's monsters. If everything Elliott said was true, they were in bigger trouble than Daniel realized. Moving had just become a big priority. He didn't know what to say to ease Elliott's fears.

Daniel suddenly realized that he too was afraid. The Beast had made him afraid. He held Elliott close and let him know that he wasn't alone.

## 8

Two weeks went by with relative quiet prevailing. The temperatures climbed, bringing sudden warmth that was welcome by everyone. The snow started to melt and the family had started preparations in anticipation of moving on. Daniel worked with both Elliott and Rusty, trying to help them overcome their fears while he tried to quiet his own. The Beast still visited Elliott and Rusty in their dreams.

Elliott sat watching the door as if the Beast was standing on the other side. Trevor sat down next to him. He had his own terrors and understood what Elliott was going through. There were times when he wanted to scream.

"What's up, bro?"

Elliott didn't answer. He slowly closed his eyes and again he saw Daniel's death. He quickly opened them again and froze. He watched as Daniel moved around the room, gathering things he wanted to take with him when they moved. Elliott was so tired he was having trouble keeping his eyes open. He crawled into a chair, leaned back, and drifted into a light sleep.

The Beast immediately entered his mind. Its red eye was fixed on Daniel. The brilliant blue and shimmering yellow colors of its huge hump glowed in the dark as the Beast bobbed up and down in a swift rocking motion. Elliott was unable to move or look away as the Beast hovered over Daniel. He could see its long, curved finger and the huge barbs of its purple tongue shove deeply into Daniel's neck.

Elliott tried to scream, but nothing happened. He couldn't move to help Daniel. The Beast drank deeply of Daniel until his body shriveled and he was no more. When the Beast was done, it let out a hideous howl—the same howl that was often heard throughout their house.

Elliott woke with a start, dropped his rifle, and put his hands over his eyes to block out the vision. "DOC!" he screamed.

Daniel threw the log he was holding into the fireplace and hurried to Elliott. "Are you alright?"

"Those damn nightmares! They seem so real."

"We've all seen horrible things, Elliott, and we'll be seeing more. It's time to let go. Don't let him win."

Elliott got up and went to Trevor, crawling onto his lap. Trevor didn't speak as he held his little brother tight. Elliott couldn't hear the rest of what Daniel said because his mind was filled with the vision of his death.

# 9

The two ten year-olds had a plan. Travis Baines and Harlan Hayes had been in the Beast's captive pens for almost four weeks and it was time to escape. Blond haired, blue eyed Travis surveyed the compound. Harlan moved up next to him. His deep set brown eyes were alert, following every movement in the compound.

The boys had survived a mudskin attack only to be captured and brought to the Beast's camp. Originally there were five of them, but Jobie, Bethany, and Martha were killed during the attack. Jobie had been the oldest at sixteen. Bethany was fifteen and pregnant with Jobie's child at the time of her death. Martha was only thirteen , killed by mudskins and reduced to dust and bones.

The Beast killed the four mudskins at the presentation of the prisoners. When the Beast learned that Jobie had been killed during the recovery, it became infuriated. Jobie was to be saved at all costs because he was a proven breeder. Bethany's pregnancy was proof that Jobie could successfully impregnate a woman. Jobie was necessary for his survival and the Beast went wild destroying the mudskins and sending them into the hereafter with one destructive blow. No questions were asked of the mudskins. They were dealt with swiftly. Travis and Harlan were thrown into a holding area while the Beast's rampage continued. They were labeled as part of the inside group: To-Pans 677432XC.

The boys quickly learned about their jailers. The Beast's guards were called "Exposers." They looked human enough, but walked stiffly, glaring at the insiders with their one red, one brown eye. Exposers also had an extra finger on each hand. Often, they let their actions speak for them. The Inside people feared them and for good reason.

Immediately after his capture, Harlan tried to climb the high fence that encircled the camp. He was caught by an Exposer.

"Get your damn filthy hands off me, you stinking son-of-a-bitch," Harlan said.

The Exposer never spoke to him, but forced Harlan to kneel in the center of the compound. Captives gathered round and spoke quietly among themselves. Most of those who had been at the camp for any length of time were aware of what was going to happen. Other Exposers encircled the insider group. They were going to be forced to watch. With his arms and legs spread-eagled, Harlan was fastened to a large wooden board that was buried deep into the ground.

Without saying a word, the Exposers warned the other insiders not to interfere or they would suffer the same punishment as Harlan. A lesson was about to be taught.

"Fuck you," said Harlan in a sinister voice as he stared at the Exposer with disgust.

The Exposer raised its hand and out of the sixth finger a barbed spike appeared. Slowly, the Exposer inserted the barb into Harlan's carotid artery and injected a purple powder that instantly paralyzed him.

The powder traveled into Harlan's circulatory system like shards of glass grinding against and flowing through his blood stream. The pain increased until Harlan screamed. It felt like every pore of his body was being sliced into small bits.

Travis moved forward to help his friend and was immediately blocked by an Exposer. It trained its red eye on the boy, forcing him to stop. Travis felt pain go through him like a lightning strike. He fell to his knees clutching his head. He was unable to move. He felt cemented to that spot which prevented him from helping his friend. The torture of Harlan went on for over an hour before the Exposer let him drop to the ground in a heap.

The lesson: NEVER ATTEMPT TO ESCAPE!

The moment Travis was released he bolted to Harlan's side and gently rolled him over, placing his head on his lap. Everyone else shied away, ignoring them as they went their individual ways. They were afraid to help.

Travis made Harlan as comfortable as he could and sat waiting for him to recover. Sitting in the big compound, he hugged his friend and let anger seep through him. He wanted to kill the bastards for what they'd done to Harlan.

It was twenty minutes before Harlan started to stir. He groaned, his eyes fluttered open and then closed again. The small boy twitched and groaned louder. Travis rubbed Harlan's arms and legs.

"You okay? You're looking kind of bad. Can you talk?"

Harland grimaced. "Feel like I was burned alive. I hurt all over."

"Let's see if you can get up."

Harlan was unsteady, so Travis kept his arm around him as he helped Harlan to his feet. An Exposer approached them. Harlan made a fist and Travis looked around for a weapon, but there was nothing. He balanced Harlan as best he could, keeping his other hand raised, ready to fight. At least he could try to get the first punch into that blasted red eye. The Exposer simply indicated they should follow him. The boys looked at each other and shrugged. There was no choice, so they followed the smelly thing down a long dusty road. The Exposer pointed to a dwelling. Harlan limped into the small room. It was a round hut with two beds and nothing else. Travis helped Harlan to one of the beds and then turned to face the Exposer. There were tense minutes of staring with neither moving until the Exposer abruptly turned and left.

"I'm getting out of here as soon as possible," Harlan said from the cot.

"I'm going with you," Travis agreed. "We'll need to plan it out. It has to be perfect because we won't get a second chance."

"Hello, can I come in?"

The young girl in the doorway was fifteen year-old Georgia Rose Starling. She'd been at the camp for over three months. Travis smiled. She was pretty with long blonde hair. She had the lightest brown eyes he'd ever seen. They were so pale they looked golden.

"I came to see if I could help. I'm Rose."

Travis and Harlan learned from Rose that there was going to be an escape attempt and she wanted them to join in the plan. The plan was a very simple one. The only problem was that they'd have to wait a few weeks until everything was in place.

Travis liked Rose instantly. She introduced the two boys to Robert Lawson who, for lack of a better word, was the leader.

"Why do we have to wait so long?" asked Harlan.

"It has to be a really dark night, but since we no longer have a moon in the sky that isn't too much of a problem. We also want to make sure the Beast is gone from camp. He leaves every few weeks. It should be soon."

Travis frowned. "Where does he go?"

"Nobody knows," Rose said as she peered at the boy.

"If he follows his usual pattern, the Beast will leave in two, maybe three weeks," Robert said. "Then, hopefully, we'll have a little while before they discover we're gone."

Finally, the weeks of planning were over and the day finally came. Everyone who was going felt ready. Everyone knew what they were supposed to do. They would leave at the darkest part of the night. The weather was cooperating. The snow had finally stopped so it was warmer than it had been in weeks, so the ground was soft and muddy.

Robert found a weak spot in the perimeter fence. He'd studied it for days and worked on making the opening a little larger, and then he assembled his team. The team consisted of not only those going, but many who were staying behind. Those staying were vital to the execution of the plan. They had the

37

hardest part—a diversion that would give the others time to escape unnoticed. It was dangerous because there could be violent repercussions from the Exposers.

The diversion was actually quite simple, but timing was everything. Tonight the Beast would be gone from the camp. It was time for them to escape.

There were six of them going. The oldest was Robert Lawson, age sixteen; Billy Layton, age fourteen; Karen Stafford, age 13; Rose, age fifteen; Travis and Harlan. Robert had lied about his age and made sure he kept a low profile around the camp. They all knew the Beast wanted breeders and it wouldn't be long before the lie was uncovered.

Robert was old enough to be used for reproduction. He knew it was essential that they flee before it was discovered and he was forced into service. Rose and Robert wanted to stay together and decided they'd go at the same time. They had come into camp together and refused to be separated.

The Exposers were confident there would be no more escape attempts since the little demonstration with Harlan, so they'd relaxed considerably. The insiders were pretty much left alone during the daylight hours, only to be herded into their huts at night and almost forgotten. The Exposers didn't bother to watch carefully during the night time hours.

The group that was leaving managed to secure an escape route under the fence without too much trouble thanks to Robert's discovery weeks before. The night before the escape, Karen Stafford was summoned before the Beast and they all feared she would be forced to tell their plans.

The Beast wanted to be fed before he left and Karen was his choice. He held Karen lovingly in his arms and his soft rocking motion mesmerized her. She relaxed and felt completely at ease, even as the Beast opened her shoulder and inserted his barbs to penetrate her body. It drank deeply as the gently rocking continued.

When Karen was returned to the compound, it was obvious she would not be going anywhere. She'd been left with just enough blood so she wouldn't die. It would take a long time for her to recover, much longer than they could afford to wait. They all stood around Karen.

Rose was the first to speak. "Why her?"

Harlan shrugged. "Who knows? It was hungry."

Travis looked down at Karen and shook his head. "This can't change things. We have to go just like we planned."

"Without Karen?"

"I don't see a choice. She'll never make it," Harlan muttered. "I won't stay here any longer."

"Me either," Robert added. "Rose, you're going with me. I won't leave you behind."

"I'm sorry, Karen," Rose said to the unconscious girl.

"Don't you be worrying about her. I'll see to her," Mrs. O'Lipda said as she came into the hut.

Mrs. O'Lipda was one of the older women in camp—age thirty-one. She was from Atlanta, Georgia and had watched the Beast kill her husband and child as it marched through.

"Tomorrow the rest of us will make enough disruption they won't miss you until it's too late. Go on now and don't be worrying about Karen."

The remaining five didn't sleep much that night or the following day. Finally, when darkness came, it was time to leave. Robert tried one last time to convince others to join in the escape attempt, but they were afraid and refused. The escape attempt was common knowledge throughout the camp's prisoners, but everyone kept their silence.

The group stole quietly across the compound. At the fence line, Travis raised his hand and Robert dropped the rock. Mrs. O'Lipda and sixteen young children went out into the compound and sang at the top of their voices. The five escapees slipped quietly under the fence line where Robert had dug out a small rut.

The soft mud made it much easier than anticipated. They shoved mud back under and packed it down, hoping it wouldn't be noticed or that they'd be discovered. They scrambled for the wooded area four hundred feet away. Behind them the confused Exposers watched an apparently mad group of insiders as they jumped up and down, yelling, screaming and singing.

The Exposers stood watching and did nothing because they did not have any orders for this kind of disruption.

Suddenly, the insiders stopped and formed a straight line. Mrs. O"Lipda stepped from the line and started to sing solo. Her sweet voice was caught by the wind and drifted through the wooded area reaching out to the hidden children. They collectively stopped and listened to her. She was singing "Jesus loves the little children."

Hidden by the dark night and surrounded by dense woods, the five children stood for several minutes listening. Robert was the first to break. He looked at each child and then started to run in a straight line. They didn't stop until they were far from the camp. The next day they ran until the light started to fade and darkness was creeping into the sky. They crawled into an abandoned building to rest for the night.

# 10

Trevor made his announcement early that morning at breakfast because he felt it couldn't wait any longer. "It's time. I'm as healed as I'm going to get and the weather has broken. Tommy, Elliott and I are heading out to find a new place."

"Not Elliott. Not this time."

"It has to be Elliott, Doc, he's my backup. I've given it a lot of thought. Maybe it's a good thing for him to go with me. It's important for me to have him with me and it's also important to Elliott. I won't let anything happen to him. Hell, he always watches after me."

Daniel knew Trevor would not only protect Elliott, he would lay his life down for him, but the kid was breakable and he wasn't sure it was in Elliott's best interest to let him face danger right now. *Hell, the whole world as we know it was now in danger.* Daniel wasn't sure if he should let the boy go. He knew Trevor wouldn't question him or argue if he just said no.

"Trevor, he's been through a lot. He needs a break or he might break."

Elliott walked in, looked first at Trevor and then at Daniel. "I'm going, Doc. I need to protect my brother's back."

"I'll go," George interjected. "Elliott, you stay here."

Elliott became instantly angry and was about to pounce on George when Daniel grabbed him around the chest. "Not this time," he said mildly.

Trevor bent down so he was face to face with Elliott. "Maybe Doc's right, bro. You've been kind of crazy lately."

"I'm your back up. I go! Nobody takes care of you like I do." Elliott freed himself from Daniel's grip, picked up his rifle, and stalked out of the room. They watched him leave. Trevor grinned. "Doc, that boy won't take no for an answer."

Daniel decided to give in to Elliott's determination. He would have to hog tie him to stop him and then the kid would just follow at the first opportunity. "Watch him, Trevor."

"Count on it. Nothing will happen to him—not unless it gets through me first."

Trevor was acutely aware of Elliott's problem. He knew about the bad dreams and muffled cries in the night. He knew he was haunted by memories of the Beast. He also knew that Elliott would never let him down, never back away in the face of trouble or danger. He was the toughest little kid he'd ever met and he felt a lot of comfort having him at his back.

"He needs to be with me. Don't worry. Hell, he'll take better care of me than I can of him."

"You watch you don't get hurt again, son," Daniel warned Trevor. "Keeley will have a fit and it won't make me happy either."

"I don't want to make you unhappy, Doc. Hell, that would break my heart, but just think of all the fun you'd have sticking needles in me," Trevor grinned. "I'll be right back. Got to say goodbye to Keeley."

Trevor went to his room and peeked in. Keeley was sitting on the bed, crying. *Damn it! Somehow I knew it was going to be like this.* He put his rifle in the corner and sat next to her. He stroked her hair. She turned her back on him. He pulled her to his chest and held her, not saying a word. He knew how she felt about his leaving, so he just waited. Finally, he knew he had to say something.

"Don't cry, Darlin'. I won't be gone long and this has to be done. I know you're worried, but there's no choice. We all agreed on it."

"I didn't," she said angrily. "I didn't agree. Why you?"

"Because it's what I do. I need to find us a safer place so when you and Sam are ready to have our babies you'll both be safe."

Keeley let out a sob and Trevor eased her back on the bed, kissing her. He took his time. Spooning her, he held her close.

"Be with me before you go."

Trevor undressed her, slowly removing each piece of clothing, and then dropped his clothes next to the bed.

"Let me look at you," Trevor said softly. "I want to see you and our child."

Keeley was in her fifth month and her pregnant belly bulge showed in a small curve. She had a neat little jutting of her belly.

"God, I love you," Trevor said as he cupped her belly in his hands. She rocked with him and cried in response to his gentle cradling of her. He made love to her and soothed her as he continued to move in that protective love. She could feel the heat building and exploded with warm sensual pleasure. He kissed her and continued to hold her close.

When he knew it was time to let go, she held onto him desperately. She whimpered and cried softly. All Trevor could do was hold her tight, stroke her, and hope he brought her a little peace.

"I'll come home to you," he whispered. "I promise."

# 11

Emma went down to Bentley's stall and brought the big horse out. She stood quietly stroking him and waiting for everyone to arrive. Within minutes the entire family scrambled out to the front porch. Brady and Jamie sat in the porch swing while the rest milled around Trevor, Tommy, and Elliott.

Trevor went over to Bentley and put his hands on the big horse's back. He slowly stroked downward checking his legs and under his belly. He picked up each foot and checked the bottoms for any type of sore or cut before moving up to his head. Trevor moved his hands across his nose and checked his soft black eyes. Bentley pressed his nose into Trevor's chest and nickered, playfully pushing him. Trevor gave him a little swat and then kissed his big nose. Only when he was sure that Bentley was sound did he motion to the others that it was time to go. Sam told them to be careful several times before she hugged and kissed each one of her sons.

Taylor went to Sam. The little boy was tired and wanted his mom. "Carry me."

Rusty ran down the front steps and straight into Trevor's leg. Grabbing him, she cried. "Pick me up."

Trevor lifted her into his arms and squeezed her to him. "What's up, baby girl? Why the hurry?"

"I'm gonna go with you," she squealed and kissed Trevor on the cheek. He threw her up on Bentley's back and then turned back to Keeley. He took her in his arms, kissed her gently and again tried to quell her worries.

"I'll be back before you know it. I'm going find you the greatest, safest place to settle in and have our baby."

Keeley hugged him desperately. They kissed for what seemed forever. "I love you!"

"Me too," she sobbed.

George walked over and put his hand in Keeley's. She hugged him to her. He tightened his arms around her and held on. "I'll take care of you until Trevor comes back."

"Come on, Rusty, it's time for me to go."

Trevor helped her down. "NO! Put me back!" she cried, struggling in his arms. "I'm goin' with you."

"Baby, you can't come this time," he said and nuzzled her warmly.

"Come on Rusty. Come with me," Emma urged.

Rusty tightened her grip on Trevor's neck, unwilling to let go. "Nooooo!"

Sam looked at Daniel and shrugged. "Okay me," he said and went to Trevor's aid. "Got a problem, son?"

Trevor sighed as Rusty stayed glued to him, refusing to let go. He looked pleadingly at Daniel who reached out to fold Rusty into his arms. "Come on, little one, you can't go this time."

"I'm got to go with Trevor."

"You need to stay with me and Sam."

"No! No! No!" She screamed and struggled against Daniel, hitting him with her small fist.

Gently, Daniel took her hands in his and leaned her against his shoulder. "Shhh…" he whispered softly as she began to cry. He rubbed her back in small circular motions. Finally, she sighed, shuddered, and then slipped her thumb into her mouth.

Daniel held out his hand to Trevor. "Be careful and keep a careful watch on Bentley, he's an endangered species." Daniel grinned. The big horse and Rusty's little cat were the only animals they'd seen in over a year. Bentley was indeed an endangered species and a valued member of the family.

Trevor was about to mount Bentley when he turned back to Daniel and put his arms around him and Rusty. "Love you." He kissed Rusty and told her he'd be back soon. "I'll bring you something beautiful, baby girl."

Everyone watched until Bentley was out of sight before they resumed their various activities. Sam and Keeley sat down on the porch steps with George lurking close by. Daniel sat in the rocking chair with Rusty firmly secured in his lap. He rocked her gently back and forth until she stopped crying and relaxed. No one spoke. They were all deep in their own thoughts.

Rusty stirred and looked up at Daniel. "Daddy, I have to go with Trevor," she whispered and ducked her head, playing with the button on his shirt. He took her thumb out of her mouth and tilted her head back so she had to look at him.

"Why is it so important that you go with Trevor?"

"The peoples are coming to us and I need to help find them."

Daniel thought as he continued to rock her. She had spoken of other people before and so had Elliott and Emma. She said she saw the inside people crying. Neither child could explain who these inside people were.

"Buppy, you know you have to stay with Daddy because I would miss you terribly if you left me. If there are people to be found, Trevor will find them."

She sighed and stuck her thumb back into her mouth. "I miss Trevor."

"He'll be home before you know it," Daniel assured her. "Let me tell you a story about a flamingo that turned blue when he got cold."

Daniel went into the story and by the time he was finished Rusty was fast asleep. He kissed his troubled daughter. She was deeply disturbed by all the things that invaded her sleep and he was at a lost how to change those bad dreams to good ones. Maybe there were no good dreams left.

# 12

Trevor, Tommy, and Elliott had gone approximately forty miles before they decided it was time to stop for night. The sun was setting early this time of year and it wouldn't be good to get caught in the dark. There were too many bad things that they could run into at night—things they couldn't see.

Tommy pointed to the Southeast. "Look over there."

In the distance, a lone building sat about six hundred feet away. "Let's check it out."

Trevor nudged the big horse in the new direction. Bentley moved toward the house, but about a hundred feet away the horse stopped and refused to go any closer. He reared up slightly when Trevor tried to get him to move on.

"Hey," Elliott yelled. He slid down Bentley's backside, grabbed onto his tail and let himself down gently before he hit the ground. He let out a moan.

"Damn, that was a long way down."

"You okay, Elliott?" Trevor called down to him.

"I'll live," he said picking up his rifle.

Trevor grabbed Bentley's mane and slid down. He reached up to help Tommy down. They stood silently looking at the house. Elliott was the first to break the silence. "Trevor, if you had to find a horse why wasn't it a smaller one?" he complained.

"Tommy," Trevor said. "Y'all stay with Bentley; I'm going to check out that house. If there's a problem or we don't come back, you need to take Bentley and go home. Got it?"

"Yeah, but maybe I..."

"No buts, Tommy, you just do as I say."

Elliott put his hand on Trevor's arm. "I got a bad feeling. Let's skip this house."

"It's almost dark. We've got no choice, bro."

"You're not going without me."

Elliott picked up his rifle and silently followed Trevor. They had done this many times before, but he still felt a cold chill go up his back. They silently moved up to the front porch. Trevor took a deep breath and pointed to Elliott. The boys entered together. Trevor went to the right and Elliott went to the left and as always, they kept each other in sight. The entire downstairs was clear. They approached the staircase, moving silently. There were sixteen steps in total and Trevor gave the signal for them to start up.

Suddenly, green lights flooded the staircase and before they could react two Rhythm Making Teddies were on the top of the steps shooting pointed green glowing sticks at them. They heard the clicking sounds accompanied by a hideous giggle. Their short fuzzy bodies filled the staircase's landing. Each one looked like a large, ugly, stuffed teddy bear, only these bears were lethal.

Elliott swiftly raised his rifle, took aim, and fired at the closest one. Trevor fired at the one next to it. Their shots were true and the two dead Rhythm Maker Teddies tumbled forward, rolling down the stairs. Another Teddy appeared. It threw a green glowing stick at Elliott. Trevor pushed Elliott out of the way and jumped to the side. He chose the wrong direction and groaned as the stick went into his leg.

Trevor went down, the glowing stick protruding from his left leg. He swung the rifle around and shot at the Teddy, but missed. Elliott bent down on one knee, aimed, and hit the red eye on his first shot. He bolted up the staircase.

"Elliott! Damn it! Come back here!" Trevor yelled after him. "Damn it, Elliott!"

Trevor forced himself up and struggled to climb the stairs, the pain in his leg intensifying into an electric fire. The stick penetrating his upper thigh gave off an intense green glow. He sat down and tried to pull it out, but it wouldn't move. Trevor grunted and took a deep breath before he broke off the back piece to make it easier to maneuver the stairs. He realized he couldn't get up, so he began crawling up the stairs.

"Elliott! Where the hell are you?"

"Back here at the end of the hall. I'm okay."

Trevor finally managed to make it up the stairs and limped down the hall using his rifle for support. Blood flowed steadily down his leg as he followed Elliott's voice. The boy was standing over a Teddy and smiling a cruel smile. "Killed the bastard. Last one. Now it's clear."

Trevor grabbed Elliott's shirt and pulled him close. "What the hell's the matter with you? Never, ever, go it alone unless there's no choice. It's the rule and you know better."

Elliott didn't answer as Trevor slowly collapsed down to the floor. He quickly went down to his knees and inspected Trevor's wound. He pulled his handkerchief out and bound it as tightly as possible. "I didn't know you were hurt. Sorry, Trevor, you're right. I should have waited, but I got so damn mad that it shot at you. I just didn't think."

"Well, you better start thinking and do it right now, boy. You could have been hurt or worse," Trevor said through gritted teeth. "Damn! This really hurts. Go get Tommy. I need to get downstairs so we can patch up my leg."

Tommy and Elliott helped Trevor down the stairs and onto a couch. Elliott looked around at the room and thought how it resembled so many others they'd been in. It seemed that most of the farm houses were set up the same way. There was a large fireplace covering most of one wall and the rest of the room was probably used for family gatherings. It had a couch, several chairs, and a couple of tables with lamps. There was a large mirror on the far wall facing down toward a hallway that led to the kitchen. All of the bedrooms were upstairs. The house had two bathrooms, one upstairs and one on the main level.

Tommy settled Bentley next to the fireplace. He went on a search and found what he was looking for—a first aid kit.

Elliott was concentrating on Trevor's leg. "We need to get that stick out. It looks like it went in and got stuck somehow."

"You'd better pull it out. If you can't pull it out, you'll need to cut it out," Trevor said, looking directly into Elliott's eyes. He hoped the kid could do it. "Tommy, go find some liquor. I'm going to need something for the pain. Elliott after you finish patching me up, we need to get those bastards out of the house. I'm not sleeping with them in here."

"Trevor, I don't know if I can do this," Elliott said quietly. "I don't want to hurt you."

"You've got to do it, bro, 'cause there's no other way. The stick can't be left in. It's already burning up my leg."

"I can take you back home and Doc can take this out."

"We're not going home."

Tommy came back with half a quart of whiskey. "It's all I could find. There aren't any drugs anywhere."

"It'll have to be enough."

Trevor took a long, hard drink downing half of what was left in the bottle. He made a face and coughed. "Y'all listen to me and listen good. We can't go back. I don't think I could make it. You can do this, Elliott."

Elliott stood next to the couch and shook his head. Trevor pulled the boy down to him. "You can do this. You've got to trust me that there's no time to get Daniel. It's burning really bad and still bleeding. I can feel junk pouring into me. Tommy will help you. It's probably gonna take both of you. I hate doing this to you, bro, but there's no choice."

Tommy looked worried as he took Trevor's hand and squeezed. "I'll try not to yell or move and I'll try to make it as easy as possible for you guys. I know y'all can do this. The poison will get me for sure if you don't."

"Let's get the damn thing out," Elliott said with quiet determination.

Trevor felt the alcohol burn his throat, but forced himself to finish the rest of the bottle. "Take the knife. You might need it if you can't pull it out."

The two boys helped Trevor down to the floor. Tommy placed a cloth over his eyes and positioned his legs across Trevor's to keep him from moving. Trevor grabbed the leg of the couch.

"I'm ready."

Elliott took a deep breath. "On three, we pull it together."

They pulled with all their strength, but it wasn't enough. Sweat trickled down Trevor's face. Through gritted teeth he said, "Use the knife."

Elliott placed his small hand over Trevor's heart. It was beating so fast it felt like he'd run a race. "I'm sorry, Trevor. I don't want to hurt you."

"Just get it done."

Elliott winced as he put the knife to the wound. He had to cut deeply to release the stick. He managed to extract half of it, but got scared when Trevor started to bleed heavily. He jumped back and looked helplessly at Tommy. All the blood loss scared him.

"Try again."

Trevor felt the stick slowly ease out. It took three more tries before the entire point was all the way out. Trevor only lasted for the first minute before falling into unconsciousness.

Elliott held up the stick. "Damn thing has a barbed end. I ripped his leg pulling it out."

Trevor's leg was bleeding freely now. Tommy cringed. "What do we do?"

Elliott took a roll of gauze and shoved it in the hole. He packed Trevor's leg to try and stop the bleeding and then wrapped it as tightly as he could with additional gauze. He looked down at his shirt and saw that he was covered in blood. He removed his shirt and threw it across the room.

"Tommy, go get some pillows and blankets so we can make him as comfortable as possible."

Tommy came back with all the blankets and pillows he could find. He handed Elliott a shirt. He put on the shirt and found it was way too big for him. He rolled up the sleeves, but that didn't work, so he took it off and using Trevor's knife, he cut off the sleeves. Elliott reached over and put his hand over Trevor's heart. It had slowed down which somehow gave him the comfort he so desperately needed.

Later, as Trevor slept, Elliott and Tommy struggled until they had dragged the Teddy bears out the back door of the house. Elliott shrugged. "Trevor said he couldn't sleep with them in the house. Now maybe we all can rest."

Tommy put his arm around Elliott and he felt a slight tremble snake though his body. "Let's go build a fire."

# 13

The children gathered in the family room. Emma and Brady sat at a small table playing a game that involved cards and marbles. Taylor came in and pulled up a chair to watch them. George was stretched out on the floor, absorbed in a book on airplanes, while Jamie sat placidly gazing out the window. It was a windy day and the wind always fascinated her. She smiled, enjoying watching the trees as they swayed in the breeze.

Rusty was lying in front of the fireplace. She'd been out of sorts all day. The warmth of the fire and her state of exhaustion finally enabled her to fall asleep. In her left hand she clutched her little teddy bear. She was deep in sleep when the Rhythm Maker Teddies attacked and impaled Trevor with the glowing stick. She bolted upright, wide-eyed, although still half-asleep. She screamed as she saw Trevor fall and then she saw the blood.

Sam and Daniel were in the kitchen preparing dinner while Keeley was keeping a watchful eye on the baby. Katie had decided it was time for dinner and let her demands be known.

"You're on your own for about fifteen minutes, Daddy." Sam said, and extracted Katie from Keeley's lap. "Come on, baby, the dinner wagon is open."

Sam offered her breast. The hungry baby didn't hesitate and began to suckle. "Everyone's hungry around here," Keeley laughed. "It seems so easy, Sam."

"It is. You won't have any trouble breast feeding either. The baby instinctively seems to know exactly what to do, but the first time they may need a little direction to make sure they find the right spot. I always rub Katie's back while she nurses because it seems to relax her and she suckles easier. The baby has to really pull to start the milk flowing."

Sam was deep in conversation about nursing while Daniel continued working on dinner. They all stopped when they heard Rusty's blood curdling scream.

Stay here, "I'll go," he said.

Daniel dropped the knife and hurried into the family room where he found George holding Rusty. He was trying to calm her as she fought to get free of him. Daniel leaned over and picked her up, speaking softly to sooth her.

"Easy. Take it easy. You're all right."

The other children sat silently watching Rusty and waiting for what would come next. Taylor became frightened and jumped out of the chair, running to find Sam.

"Mommy!"

The baby was crying, having been deprived of her dinner before she was full. Keeley intercepted Taylor and took him into her arms.

Daniel held the squirming Rusty tightly against him. Sam called out to him. "Need help?"

"No, go finish feeding the baby and I'll deal with Rusty. You children go help Sam with dinner. George, what happened here?"

"I don't know. I was reading. Rusty was asleep by the fireplace. She woke up and started to scream. She was calling for Trevor."

Daniel directed his full attention back to Rusty. Her eyes were closed and she appeared to be entrapped in a nightmare of terror. Daniel sat down in the chair next to the fireplace and wrapped his arms around her, pulling her tight against his chest. She arched her back and gave a deep sob. Daniel spoke to her in a calm, quiet voice. "It's just a bad dream. I want you to try and wake up now."

Rusty was terrified, her little chest heaved and her heart raced. In her nightmare she saw the blood running down Trevor's leg. She felt his pain.

"Don't be frightened, baby. I've got you."

Rusty opened her eyes. Tears fell as she pushed her little body against him. She was exhausted. Daniel cuddled her like he did Katie, hugging and rocking her slowly, giving her the time she needed to recover. He leaned down to kiss her. "Are you alright now?"

"Daddy," Rusty mumbled, looking up at him with pain and confusion in her eyes. "Trevor's hurt bad," she said dully. "He's crying."

Daniel felt a shiver go down his spine. He believed her. Another cold shiver hit him as he silently said a prayer for his son.

# 14

Tommy started a fire in the fireplace and then went to find something for them to eat. Elliott tucked a pillow under Trevor's head and repositioned the blanket he'd kicked aside. His leg was seeping blood, but it seemed to be slower now. Elliott took another pillow and propped it up under Trevor's leg before lying down next to him and placing his hand on Trevor's chest.

"Hey bro," Trevor said weakly.

"How do you feel?"

"Considering everything…great."

"You know Doc's not going to like this," Elliott whispered. "He's going to be downright pissed off. I think I'll just let you explain what happened. Damn it, you shouldn't have pushed me away like that."

"Then you'd be dead. Hell, Elliott, at least it's the other leg this time and stop swearing. Damn it, I hurt. Thanks for getting that Teddy off of me."

"Now who's swearing? No problem, I kind of like killing them, but I'm sorry I didn't get to him faster."

"You kill when you have to, but you shouldn't like it. Course, it's hard not to be glad when they're dead."

"They sure are nasty little bastards. Look at all the times we've been hurt by his monsters."

Trevor leaned back and closed his eyes. He was hurt and very tired. All he wanted to do was sleep. He would welcome the relief it would bring.

"Trevor, this whole messed up world scares me."

"Scares me too, bro."

Tommy eased down next to Elliott. "What's the plan for tomorrow? Are we staying here or going on?"

"I reckon we stay put. He's still kind of drunk and will probably feel a lot worse tomorrow. I really want to take him back to Daniel, but he won't go. He said we have to go on." Elliott whispered. "Tommy, I think he's hurt bad."

Tommy looked down at Trevor. "Why don't we ask him tomorrow? Elliott, I thought they didn't go into houses? I thought they only stayed out in the dark? Why were they in here?"

"They usually don't go inside, but the Beast sends out scouts where he thinks we are and they go in sometimes and hide—at least that's how I think it works…and they're looking for us."

Elliott had been looking at Trevor's leg. He wrinkled his nose and turned to Tommy. "It's still bleeding. How does he look to you?"

"Kind of pale."

"I don't think we can go back now, at least not until we find a new place. Trevor said it's important and every day we stay at the house is a day closer to the Beast finding us. Tomorrow I'm going alone. When I find a place, I'll come back for you and him."

"Trevor won't stand for that."

Elliott stood up and looked toward the door, then down at Trevor. Suddenly he was filled with rage. "Hell, what a fuck up!"

Elliott felt depleted of all his strength. He shook his head and plopped down next to Tommy. "We better get some sleep. Tomorrow's right around the corner."

# 15

Trevor woke up with the world's worst hangover. His head throbbed and the pain in his leg was incredible. His head was only adding to the misery.

"Morning," Tommy said brightly. "How do you feel?"

"I think I'm dead."

"You wouldn't be talking if you were dead."

"Thanks for telling me. Where's Elliott?" Trevor asked as he closed his eyes and put his hand to his head. It wouldn't stop throbbing.

"He's outside with Bentley. He said he needed to graze some. We didn't want to leave you alone."

"Smartass kid. Tell him it's time to leave."

Trevor attempted to get up, but couldn't. He moaned and laid back down. Tommy went to help him but he raised his hand and slowly forced himself into an upright position. Once he got his legs steadied, Trevor limped over to the door, letting out a deep breath.

"You better have Elliott bring Bentley over to the porch so I can get up on him."

Trevor had spent many hours practicing mounting Bentley, but the horse was so huge he always had to find a rock or anything that would provide him with a step up. Bentley had been very patient as Trevor continued to experiment with different ways to mount. Finally, he found if he took a running start he could jump up, grab some mane and lift himself by swinging his leg over the back of Bentley's big butt. Even that had been difficult. Trevor looked down at his leg, realizing that would be impossible now.

He didn't want Elliott or Tommy to know just how much pain he was in. He popped four aspirin into his mouth and chewed them to keep the pain at bay. He found that it worked faster when you chewed them. The taste was bitter in his mouth and he cringed.

When Elliott suggested he go alone, Trevor immediately dismissed the idea. The three boys rode away from the house and continued to head west. They made another thirty miles before Trevor admitted he couldn't go any farther. His head was throbbing in time with his leg. He could see the small trickle of blood dripping from his wound and he felt like he wanted to vomit.

Trevor remained on Bentley while Tommy went with Elliott to secure the house they selected for the night. He was nervous about sending the two boys in without him, but there wasn't a choice. Thankfully, this one was free of all monsters. They spent the next two days at the house waiting for Trevor to regain his strength.

Trevor felt the fever that engulfed his body and downed four more aspirin. Two days became three and each day seemed worse than the one before. Trevor considered turning back, but he knew how important it was to go on. There wasn't a lot of time and they desperately needed a new place. There was no turning back. The Teddys' attack meant that the Beast was close. He could almost feel the hot breath of the Beast on the back of his neck. What Trevor didn't know was that the Beast was actually far away from them and he didn't need to fear a confrontation.

The next morning brought a new horror to Trevor. He had decided to give himself ten minutes and indulge himself with thoughts of Keeley. He felt her flowing brown hair touching his chest as she towered over him, scolding him for getting injured again. Her piercing blue eyes drilled into him as cool hands rubbed gently against his chest. Her hands slid into his pants and his erection jumped into them, hard and willing. She leaned down against his body, moving slowly as rising heat engulfed him. The longing for her hurt, but there also seemed to be terrible physical pain attacking him. Everything was becoming confused in his mind.

The pain of not having Keeley was unbearable, but the pain was in the wrong place. Trevor looked up and discovered it was not Keeley resting on top of him, but a woman, yet somehow not a woman. Sitting on his chest with her back to him, she lifted her arms high in the air. She held a red glowing stick and slowly inserted it into his leg.

Trevor screamed. She turned and looked back at him, never moving from his body. Only the head swiveled. It smiled a toothless grin at him as a long purple tongue dropped down. Its barbed tongue crawled toward his leg. Its eyes were sunk way back into a pointed head. He couldn't see a nose. The loose green mouth worked into a smirk and then gave him a sinister half-smile. The purple tongue reached out for his leg again and very slowly inserted barbs into the wound as pain surged deep into his body.

Trevor screamed as he tried to fight the thing, but he was having trouble moving at all. He was aware that he still sported a hard-on from Keeley's touch. The bitch on top of him moved seductively, keeping him in that condition. He couldn't believe he was becoming aroused even more by it. He didn't know which was more painful—the sucking motion from the barbs in his leg or his engorged penis that cried for Keeley and was now being abused by this bitch on top of him. He couldn't move to stop what was happening. He screamed for Keeley and because he was unable to stop the pain.

Trevor woke in a sweat and clutched his hands to his chest. There was no one sitting on top of him. No barbs of a purple tongue were inserted in his leg, but his leg was throbbing and blood was trickling from the bandage. He looked around. Tommy was sleeping against the front door, his rifle secured across his lap. Elliott lay close by him. Bentley stood quietly in the corner of the room. The horse lifted his head and whinnied softly to him.

Trevor scrambled to get up and immediately decided it was a big mistake. Pain ran all the way up his leg and clutched his body, paralyzing him. He trembled as dullness filtered though his brain, he burned with fever and he couldn't think.

He looked down to see that he was still rock hard. His erection had not gone down one bit. *Great! I'm hard for Keeley and afraid to close my eyes because my hallucinatory bitch might reappear.*

Trevor wanted to get himself outside. He needed to take the problem in hand, but found he couldn't move that far. He realized that he was badly hurt, the kind that Doc needed to take care of.

Trevor chuckled. "God, another long session of needles."

Trevor longed to see Keeley and his family. He hoped he'd live long enough to get back to them. He certainly wasn't getting any better. Every day he felt worst. He knew the answer…the only answer was to go back, but he also knew that they were close to finding the right place. He needed to hang on for another day or two. *I can do this. I have to do it for Keeley and for Sam.*

Trevor knew he was going to have a son and Sam was going to give him another brother. He was that sure both babies were boys. He took the aspirin bottle out of his pocket. It was almost empty. He shook out the last five pills and downed them. Chewing the aspirin made him smile. He'd gotten used to the bitter taste.

It was almost dawn, but Trevor would wait another fifteen minutes before he woke Elliott and Tommy. It gave him time to let the aspirin work. It didn't do much for the pain any more, but it kept the fever down to a reasonable level so he could function. He groaned as he pulled himself up to a seated position. He waited another few minutes before forcing himself up. His leg almost collapsed under him. Limping over to Bentley, he moaned and held on to his mane for support.

"Hey big fella," he grimaced with pain. "Looks like I'm really deep shit this time."

Trevor put his arms around the horse's big neck. Tears he couldn't stop fell from his eyes. "It hurts so damn much. God, Doc, I'm sorry. If I don't make it, take care of Keeley and my baby."

Elliott stood a few feet away looking at Trevor. "Trevor?"

"Yeah," Trevor straightened. "I'm good. We need to get on the road. Wake up Tommy."

Elliott eyes trailed down Trevor's leg. It looked red and swollen under the bandage, but Trevor insisted that they continue on. Once they were all up on Bentley, they headed west. Elliott was behind Trevor and lightly placed his hand on his back. He was hot. "Trevor, we need to find a town."

"Why?"

"Maybe we can find a pharmacy and get some pills for your leg. You're hot and Doc always says when you're hot, it's fever."

"Don't know where there's a town around here, bro."

Trevor was having trouble speaking. He felt weak and dizzy, his head throbbed, and his thoughts were confused. He leaned forward, resting against Bentley's neck. Elliott was right, the infection raging in him was threatening to take over and he was losing the battle.

Elliott pointed to a small building across an open field and made the decision to stop. Trevor protested, closing his eyes. "We need to go on."

"Not today we don't. You can't go any farther."

After Tommy and Elliott swept the building, they led Bentley into the house with Trevor still leaning across his back. Elliott handed Tommy the led rope and moved Bentley as close to the long couch as he could. They eased the now half-conscious Trevor off the horse and onto the couch. He hit it hard, screamed, and grabbed at his leg.

Tommy went on a search of the farmhouse and brought back bandages with antibiotic ointment he'd found. "Think it'll help?"

Elliott looked defeated. He was scared for Trevor. "Tommy, I've got to take Bentley and find a pharmacy. I'm not going to let my brother die because of a fucking infection. You stay here. Watch him and keep him safe."

Elliott moved closer to Tommy and whispered. "You shoot anything that doesn't look right to you. Don't hesitate, just shoot. Try to keep Trevor quiet. Force water down him if you can. I'm gonna leave right now. We've wasted too much time already."

"Where are you going? How long will you be gone?"

"I don't know. West. I'll keep going west. I'm bound to run into some town. I can make it faster alone."

Tommy looked from Elliott to Trevor and slowly shook his head. "I'll take care of him. I won't let anything get us."

Elliott put his rifle down and hugged Tommy. The frightened little boy returned his embrace. "I'll be back as soon as I can. If Trevor dies..."

Elliott stopped. He almost couldn't say the words. "If he doesn't make it and you're sure he's gone, don't wait for me. Go back home and tell Daniel. I'll stop back here. If I don't find you..." He heaved a big sigh. "If you're not here, I'll bring Trevor home with me," he said in a hushed voice.

Tommy's lip trembled and he nodded. "Okay."

Elliott went to Trevor. He put his hand on his chest and felt the intense heat radiating from his body. "Don't you die on me," he whispered. Elliott threw his arms around Trevor, hoping to give him some of his strength. "I promise I'll be back for you and I'll find something to help you. You need to hang on and wait for me, ya hear?"

Elliott kissed Trevor's cheek. He wiped the tears from his eyes and picked up his rifle. After he led Bentley out to the porch, he climbed up on the rail to mount him.

"I'll be back as soon as I can, Tommy," he said as he gently eased the big horse forward.

# 16

Elliott didn't like leaving Trevor and Tommy behind, but he felt that there was no other choice.  He followed the trail west as planned.  Once he found medicine to help Trevor, then he would go back.  He tried desperately to push the horrible thoughts that plagued him out of his mind.  Elliott felt the need to hurry and gently urged Bentley to move faster.  The big horse quickened his pace, but instead of going west he turned south.

"Why not?"  Elliott gave Bentley his head, relaxed, and followed the horses lead. They covered almost seventy miles before Elliott felt it.  He'd been half dozing when it struck as a slow warm feeling running throughout his body.  He became instantly alert.

The canyon just seemed to appear out of nowhere.  It was hidden from view by a large stand of trees cresting over a sloping hillside.  Bentley seemed to know exactly where he was going. The rocky outcrop on the other side of the hill opened into a green-blue valley.

Elliott laughed.  If you didn't know where it was, you'd never find it.  It would have been easy to miss. He moved Bentley down an overgrown winding trail that went into a thicker stand of trees. On the other side of those trees was a small, deep blue lake, surrounded by several cabins.  They looked old, like they hadn't been occupied for a very long time.  Elliott wanted a closer look and rode cautiously to the nearest one.  As always, he held his rifle ready as he eased down from Bentley's back. He approached the cabin with extreme caution.

Elliott was very aware that he was alone. There was no Trevor there to cover his back. Once inside, he searched quickly and found that it was empty. All the other cabins were also deserted. Elliott tried to relax a little, but was finding it impossible to do. He knew that he had to stay alert at all times. The back of his neck itched and sweat ran down his back.

The cabins weren't big, but they would fit the family nicely. There might be some problems, but nothing they couldn't work out. The electricity was still working in most of them. They each had several large fireplaces, one in each room, and there was some kind of generator attached to each cabin.

"Maybe Trevor can get them to work."

Elliott felt a pain go through him. "Trevor."

Elliott fell his knees, bowed his head, and quietly mumbled a prayer, asking God to help his brother. Please don't let him die. Keep him and Tommy safe."

A smile crossed Elliott's face. He felt Trevor and knew that somehow he was still alive. He slowly got up and continued his search through the cabins.

"This is going to work. It's secure and safe."

Elliott was about a hundred miles from where he'd left Trevor and Tommy. Now he had to find places for the family to stay on the way to their new home. It would probably take a few weeks to make the move, but first he had to find a town. Elliott moved Bentley over to the porch and jumped onto his back.

"Let's go, fella. We still need to get some medicine for Trevor."

Elliott decided to circle and go back a different way. He headed due west in hopes of finding a town where he could get the medicine he sought. He urged Bentley into a gallop and covered another thirty miles before riding into a town or better said—the remains of a town. Most of the buildings had been burned to the ground, but the few left standing were in ruins. He rode slowly through the former main street and to the north where he encountered more burned out buildings.

"Fuck this!"

Elliott had come across this before because many of the towns they'd gone through were in ruins. The total downtown area had been destroyed by fire and it appeared to have been purposely set. It was a study in total destruction. He wondered if anyone had survived the devastation. He saw no bones of the dead. It was as if no one had actually lived here. It appeared that a great fire had ravaged the town to remove everything so it wouldn't be discovered that the town had died deserted. Elliott shrugged his shoulders. He wasn't going to figure out this mystery.

"Reckon we'll never know the truth."

Elliott pushed Bentley forward and then turned south where he found more burned out buildings. He moved on past the destruction until he reached the edge of the town where he came across a house that appeared to be untouched. He raised his rifle and squeezed his legs to move Bentley forward. He stopped in front of the house and eased down from the horse's back. Cautiously, he went up the steps to enter through the open front door.

Once again, Elliott was acutely aware that he didn't have Trevor behind him. He felt the now familiar stab of pain that went with that thought. Carefully, he moved one step at a time, stopping to look and listen for anything out of the usual quiet that greeted him. Swiftly, before he lost his nerve, he went from room to room to make sure he was alone. He brought Bentley into the house and closed the door behind him. It was getting dark and they'd need to stay the night here.

Elliott watched as darkness approached. It was going to be a long night because he was spending it alone. The thought chilled him and he shuddered. He took Bentley into the front room and got him settled. He found logs next to the fireplace, so he started a fire. Soon the room started to warm up, throwing soft glows of yellow and red into the gloom. Next, he searched for the medicine he desperately needed to help Trevor. In the bathroom, he came across six bottles of medicine with strange sounding names. He took them, held them in his hand and examined the names on each bottle. He sighed deeply. "I don't have a clue."

After raiding the kitchen, Elliott went back to join Bentley by the fireplace. He had found two cans of tuna and four cans of warm beer. "Not one of Sam's meals, but it'll work." He ate the tuna and drank one of the beers before settling down on the couch, placing himself adjacent to the door. He kept his rifle against his side and yawned. He didn't realize how tired he was and how the beer would affect him. It took only minutes before he drifted into a deep sleep.

Elliott was not alone in this town of Ghost Hollow. The town had been established in 1878 and it died four months ago when the good citizens burned it to the ground. The town had been invaded by the Beast's monsters—the ones Elliott called Flower Balls. The colorful bunches had literally rolled into town. The entire population of seventy-four came out to fight them. In the end, the Flower Balls captured every townsperson that hadn't been killed in the fight. Twelve year-old Jacob Handler's father, Thomas, gave him ten cans of gasoline and orders to burn the town. Thomas took the East side and Jacob the west. Sixteen Flower balls burned along with it. Sixty-two townspeople also perished, along with Jacob and his father. The remaining twelve were taken to the Beast's camp. Only seven of them survived. None of the seven were what the Beast needed. They were all young children.

The other five had been injured by the tiny pellets shot by the Flower Balls. They hit vital areas, imbedding in their bodies. Leaking sores of purple and blue pus caused high fevers that eventually killed them.

The town of Ghost Hollow died that day and became an actual ghost town. Three days later Elliott arrived and the next morning so did the five escapees from the Beast's camp. Neither group knew that very soon they were about to cross paths.

# 17

Bentley reared up and screamed as the dark figures entered the room. The big horse quivered and snorted, pawing at the floor. Elliott jumped up, but was surrounded before he could get off a shot. He struggled, but it didn't matter because too many hands grabbed him. He was unable to move.

Elliott bucked, arched his back and kicked to get free. He screamed in frustration, spewing obscenities at the hands that held him. "Get the hell off me, you assholes! You goddamn sons of bitches!"

"Let him go, but keep the rifle," a voice said.

Elliott jumped up ready to fight, but with the moon still missing, it was so dark that he wasn't able to see anyone clearly. He briefly wondered when the last time there had been a moon that lit up the night skies. He tried desperately to adjust his eyes, but couldn't see his attackers. The only advantage he had was that he was pretty sure they couldn't see him clearly either. They were so close to him that he could smell them and almost taste them.

Bentley continued to snort his displeasure and thumped the floor. Elliott felt an involuntary cold shudder go through his body as he backed up into Bentley. The horse quivered and moved against him. He put his hand gently on Bentley's big body to steady not only the horse, but himself as well. He was scared, but ready to fight as he raised his hands.

"Relax, kid," a deep voice said. "We're not with the Beast and we mean you no harm."

The only sound left in the room was the labored breathing of Bentley and Elliott. The horse moved nervously and Elliott grabbed his halter to steady him.

Robert Lawson lit a match and showed Elliott his face. He was amazed to see the big horse standing behind the little boy. He hadn't seen any animals since the Beast and his armies first invaded the earth. He grinned at Elliott and shrugged, calling to someone behind him. "Let's find some candles to light up this place so we can reassure our new friend here we mean him no harm."

The kitchen had a junk drawer where they found five candles of various lengths. Robert picked them out and lit two as he made his way back to the front room. Elliott hadn't moved. He stood close to Bentley, talking softly to him. Robert handed some of the candles to a young girl next to him. She lit them and then held one up so Elliott could see them.

Elliott retreated slightly when he realized there were five people in the house—people he didn't know or trust.

"You're just a kid. Relax," Robert said. "We're harmless."

"I'm not a kid," Elliott snarled. "I'll be nine soon."

Robert Lawson's brown eyes flared and then he chuckled. He had a soft, warm smile as he extended his hand.

"Robert Lawson, escapee," he said, still smiling.

Elliott looked at the extended hand and stepped forward cautiously. He took Robert's hand carefully. Robert shook and held out Elliott's rifle which he grabbed and retreated back against Bentley. The horse accepted his familiar body gratefully as he shifted slightly backwards.

"You always keep your horse in the house?" Travis asked with mild curiosity.

Elliott didn't answer. He just looked from one kid to the other, studying them. Other than his family, he hadn't seen anyone new in a very long time. He found the newcomers frightening and unsettling. Rose marched over and got right up in Elliott's face and looked him over. Her big brown eyes went up to Bentley and she smiled. "You might as well talk to us. We're not going away. I haven't seen a horse in like forever. He's real pretty."

"Hey, I found some food," Harlan called to Robert.

Billy and Harlan came from the kitchen with a handful of cans. They dropped everything on the floor and went back for the case of soda Elliott had missed earlier. They dragged it into the front room.

"Light a fire, Harlan."

Harlan got a fire going and then held up a screwdriver with a bent tip. "Couldn't find an opener, but this should work."

Rose looked at Elliott. "Why don't you join us?"

Elliott gave Bentley a reassuring pat and approached the others with caution. He sat down next to the one called Rose and slowly held up a can opener. They all laughed.

"Well, I'll be damned," Robert smiled. "Thanks."

Elliott took the soda offered and a can of soup. He ate slowly as he continued to study the new group. He needed to get away from them and back to Trevor and Tommy. He needed to know if Trevor was still alive. Elliott lowered his head and softly whispered. "Trevor."

"Who's Trevor?" Rose asked.

"My brother," Elliott said quietly. "I have to get back to him. He's been hurt. Do you know if there's a medical office or a pharmacy around here that isn't burned?"

"We don't know this town," Billy Layton said. "We've been on the run from the Beast and haven't taken time to look around."

"The Beast?" Elliott shivered visibly. "I know of the Beast."

"I guess we all do," Robert took over the conversation and explained to Elliott about the Beast's camp and their escape from it. He told of the people left behind and the ones who didn't make it.

Elliott nodded. "You're To-Pans. I know of you and the Exposers too. Y'all escaped from them?"

"Were you at the camp?"

"No, but I've seen them. Rusty does too." Elliott said this with no emotion, making it a flat statement.

Billy Layton jumped up and grabbed Elliott, throwing him against the wall. Elliott threw a right cross at him, but he was so much smaller than Billy that it didn't hit its mark, although he did manage to rock the boy backwards.

"Get off me you asshole!"

Robert pulled Billy off of Elliott. Elliott quickly got to his feet and lifted his rifle squarely at the boy as he scrambled away from the group.

Robert shook Billy. "Stop it. Right now!"

Billy's face constricted into an ugly grin. "He's a half-one. He knows about the camp. How would he know if he wasn't there? Kill him, Robert!"

The group of five turned to Elliott who froze and backed up until he was once again leaning against Bentley. "I didn't ask you here. Y'all found me. I didn't go looking for you. I'm not a half-one, but my brother's killed one. Me and Bentley will be leaving in the morning and we'll be out of your lives. Y'all go your way and I'll go mine. Until then . . . BACK OFF!"

"He's not a half-one," Robert said. "Relax, all of you. No one is going to kill anyone. Billy put that rifle down. God, there aren't enough of us left to fight among ourselves. I think introductions are in order."

Robert went over to Elliott and stood in front of him. Gently, he put his hand on his shoulder. Elliott froze under Robert's touch.

"What's your name?"

"Elliott...my name is Elliott."

"Sorry, I know you're probably scared of us and I don't blame you. We do sort of outnumber you, but we're just like you and I'm scared too. This whole thing is one scary nightmare."

In that instant, Elliott knew that he could trust Robert. It was Billy he'd have to watch and find a way to warn Robert that he shouldn't be trusted. Somehow Elliott knew the kid wasn't what he wanted them to think he was. He was a coward and would never back them up. He might even turn on them to save himself. He felt it all the way to his toes, but he wasn't one of them. He was the outsider from this group. He stayed silent. He'd keep an eye on Billy and if necessary, he'd kill him.

Rose interrupted Elliott's thoughts. She was shivering from the cold. "We need clothes. Do you know if there's any place we can get warm clothing?"

Elliott shrugged. "Try this house. Someone had to live here."

Rose immediately went to search the bedrooms. Ten minutes later she returned her arms draped with clothes. With the exception of Robert they all found something to wear. Most of the clothes were ill-fitting at best, but it didn't matter because they would be warm. Rose struggled into pants that were too big for her and gave Robert a look of concern.

"There just isn't anything big enough to fit you, Bobby."

Elliott eyed Robert. He was almost as tall as Daniel, but not as big. Where Daniel was muscular, Robert was slim. Elliott looked into the other boy's warm dark brown eyes and smiled. His hair was the same color as his eyes. Daniel had black hair and blue eyes, but they were both big guys.

Elliott pulled a blanket from the couch, took his knife and cut a hole in the center. He found a rope in the junk drawer in the kitchen. "We can make a poncho out of this. Wrap the rope around your waist." Elliott grinned. "At least it'll keep you warm."

Robert quickly threw on the blanket and tied the rope tight. He hadn't realized how cold he was until he felt the blanket's warmth surround him. He turned around several times for Rose's approval and they both laughed. Their laughter startled Elliott who seldom laughed. He'd almost forgotten how.

# 18

Travis and Harlan stretched out on the floor next to each other and went to sleep. Rose said she was tired and made herself comfortable on the couch. Billy leaned against the door, eyes closed, but alert. Elliott realized he wouldn't be able to leave without Billy knowing he was gone. *The asshole might even shoot me.*

Elliott's eyes wandered over the other five children. "Robert, I need to talk to you in private. It's important."

Robert took two sodas out of the box and handed one to Elliott. He pointed to the kitchen table where they both sat down across from each other.

"I'm leaving tomorrow morning...early, right after sunrise if possible," Elliott said and took a long pull on the soda. He decided to tell Robert more. "My brother's hurt and I need to get back to him. We had an encounter with a Rhythm Maker Teddy and he got hurt because of me. He could die."

At Robert's puzzled look, Elliott explained about Rhythm Maker Teddies. "Tomorrow, I'm going to check for medicine in town and then I'm out of here."

"Which way are you headed?"

"East. Got to go back more than fifty some miles cause that's where I left him. What about you guys?"

"Haven't given it much thought. We've just been running."

"You should make a plan because you can't just run. Sometimes you have to rest and hold up. Daniel calls it the ease down time."

"Who's Daniel?"

Elliott briefly explained his family to Robert. When he was done, Robert sat quietly for a very long while just staring at the little boy. He'd known there were other people, but didn't know of any large numbers of them like Elliott described. With the exception of the camp, he'd encountered only a few kids at a time and no adults.

"Can you take Rose with you? I don't want her with us when we go back."

Elliott looked at him in disbelief. "You're going back? To the camp? Why?"

"I have to. Maybe we can get some others out. Disrupt the Beast and kill the three that are incubating. Stop him from getting any of us to breed. We plan to get weapons, attack swiftly and be as deadly as we can. We just need enough firepower to make it work. We have to find weapons and try to surprise the Beast. He won't be expecting us to return."

Elliott thought about all Robert had said before he spoke. He'd learned a lot about the Beast and how to fight it. The other boy sat quietly and waited.

"There's a town not far from where we now live. There are all kinds of weapons. I can show you, but first I have to go back for Trevor. Rose can come with me if she wants. My family will welcome her."

What Elliott didn't tell, what he wouldn't tell, was that the family was moving. He planned on keeping that information to himself. "Robert, you need to watch out for Billy."

"What does that mean?"

Elliott got up to leave. "I've just got a bad feeling about him. Don't trust him and don't turn your back on him. He's a coward. I think he's evil and would give you up in a heartbeat."

Elliott went back to Bentley and bedded down next to him. The big horse nudged him. He gently patted his nose. "It's alright boy. I know you're missing Trevor. So am I."

Elliott was up early with the first light. There was still frost on the ground when he led Bentley out to a small patch of grass so he could graze before they left. Travis and Harlan joined him. Travis plopped down on the wet grass.

"How far to where you left your brother?"

"Fifty miles or so."

Travis squinted up at Elliott. "We'll help you look for the medicine if you can tell us what to look for."

"I don't know the names. Daniel would 'cause he's a doctor. Just grab anything in a medicine bottle. That's what I've been doing."

"Not too many houses still standing so it shouldn't take that long," Harlan said as he got up. "Be back soon."

The sun came up and it felt good—bright, warm and comfortable. Elliott sat down next to Travis and they both watched Bentley eat. Neither boy spoke, comfortable in their silence. It was over an hour before Harlan returned and handed Elliott a bag containing twenty bottles of assorted pills. In another bag, there were several guns that he'd found. The weapons were all handguns. Each boy took one. Harlan offered Elliott one of the pistols, but he refused. He was accurate with a rifle, but a handgun was too heavy and awkward to suit him. Rose was offered a gun and she took it. Robert tucked the extra gun into the bag for future use.

"I'm heading east..." Elliott stopped dead in his tracks. Billy had raised his pistol and was pointing it directly at his heart.

"We're taking the horse," he said with ferocious intent ringing in his voice. "Travis, Harlan, help me."

Elliott could barely contain his rage. His eyes grew cold as he deliberately walked up to Billy and placed his body against the pistol he held.

"Guess you better pull that trigger, asshole, because you'll only get Bentley if I'm dead."

Billy Layton was five years older than Elliott and stood five inches taller, but the smaller boy didn't back down. His eyes burned with the anger he felt. Billy pulled back the hammer on the gun.

Robert pushed Elliott out of the way and took the gun from Billy pushing him in the opposite direction. "What's the matter with you?" he yelled at Billy and then turned to Elliott. "And you...are you crazy? He could have killed you."

"Then I'd be dead," Elliott said mildly, "but he'd still be an asshole."

Billy's eyes glared at Elliott as the smaller boy turned his back on him and went to Bentley. "He's a half-one," Billy sneered.

Robert got into Billy's face and stared him down before he spoke again. "You listen to me. That boy is no half-one and the horse is his, not yours or mine. You get out of line one more time and I may let Elliott finish this. Trust me when I tell you that kid will kill you and never look back."

"Count on it," Elliott said coldly, his eyes never leaving Billy. "Killed worse than you."

"Knock it off!" Robert yelled. "I told you we need to work together."

Elliott calmly led Bentley over to the porch where he jumped up to get onto his broad back. "You want to ride with me, Rose?"

Rose gave Elliott a big smile and pulled herself up behind him. She was still tired and very happy to ride behind Elliott. She wrapped her arms around him and hugged him to her.

Elliott was surprised how good it felt to have her warmth next to him. He really liked Rose. Her smile gave him comfort and soothed him somehow. She was open and honest with him and he didn't worry that she would shoot him.

Rose sighed. The escape, the running, and the long walk to this town had been exhausting for her and the chance to ride came at just the right time.

Elliott moved slightly and signaled Bentley to go. He felt an urgency to hurry and the others would just have to keep up. That morning Robert told Elliott he had formulated a plan. Elliott didn't ask about his plan because he had one of his own. It was simple: He would get Trevor and take him home to Daniel. He prayed that Tommy was still there and he prayed that Trevor was still alive.

# 19

Tommy placed another cool cloth on Trevor's forehead, then got up and started to pace. Trevor looked terrible and had been going in and out of consciousness ever since Elliott left. He would moan, fall into a deep sleep, then wake screaming in pain. There was no more aspirin. There was nothing to help him. It not only scared Tommy, it made him want to leave and run away, but he knew he couldn't. He would never leave Trevor alone.

Tommy knelt down and started the task of unwrapping Trevor's leg. It was an ugly color; he used warm packs, hoping that it was doing some good and then he used the last of the antibiotic ointment on his wound.

"God, Trevor, please don't start screaming again."

Trevor slowly opened his eyes and looked up at Tommy. He began to shake uncontrollably, his teeth chattering.

"Cold," Trevor moaned. "So damn cold."

Tommy went to the bedrooms and collected the rest of the blankets. He covered Trevor and built up the fire in the fireplace, then sat down next to him on the floor. He put his head on his knees and cried. In his nine year-old mind, Trevor was already dead. How would they tell Keeley?

It was dusk when Tommy heard the unmistakable scratching noise again. He froze, waited, listened, and then heard it start again. "Trevor, did you hear that?"

Trevor didn't answer. Tommy glanced at him as he bent down to pick up Trevor's rifle. Cautiously, he crept over to the window. He leaned his rifle up against the side of the wall as he raised Trevor's. He couldn't see much, but he heard plenty as the scratching noise became louder, and sounded closer. Tommy trembled with each sound he heard. He stood motionless against the wall.

Trevor moved slightly and let out a deep moan. Tommy ran back to him and bent over putting his hand across Trevor's mouth.

"Be quiet! If they don't hear us, maybe they'll just go away."

Tommy sat with his hand over Trevor's mouth and his gun ready. If anything came in, he was prepared to kill it. It was a long two hours of waiting before Tommy started to relax slightly. He hadn't heard anything in over an hour. The scratching had stopped and Trevor was quiet again.

Tommy got up and went to look out the window, but all he saw was darkness. He eased down against the door putting his head back into his hands.

"Damn it, Elliott, where are you?"

It was almost dark the following day when Tommy heard Bentley's soft neigh. He jumped up, bolting for the door and swung it open. Elliott burst into the room leading Bentley behind him. He quickly hugged Tommy. "How's Trevor? Am I too late?" he asked looking down at Trevor's still form.

Tommy gravely shook his head. "He's still alive."

Elliott went to Trevor and touched his chest to make sure he was breathing and then he felt his forehead. A bolt of fear hit him. "He's really hot."

"I know and he's been out of it pretty much ever since you left." Tommy said as he looked at the other children entering the room. He quickly backed away and moved closer to Elliott.

"I brought a bunch of pills," Elliott said, turning the bag over and spilling its contents. "I just don't know which one is right. I figured Trevor would know."

Rose went over to Trevor and placed her hand on his cheek. "He's burning with fever."

80

"I've got to get him home. Tommy, we have to get him to Daniel before it's too late."

"Give me the bottles and maybe I can recognize something," Rose offered.

They passed the bottles around to see if anyone recognized an antibiotic. Tommy watched as the bottles went from hand to hand. Tommy whispered to Elliott. "Who are they?"

"Later."

"Here," Robert held up a bottle with six pills in it. "This one looks right."

When they tried to get Trevor to take the pills, he choked and gagged on them. Finally Rose managed to get him to swallow two of the pills. She sat down putting Trevor's head in her lap and smoothing her hand across his head as she spoke softly to him.

Elliott directed his attention back to Trevor, his color was grayish and he seemed to be having trouble breathing.

"Oh God," Elliott shuddered. "Tommy, we have to go home. Go get Bentley."

Tommy looked out the window. "It's almost dark."

"I don't care. I won't let him die here." Elliott grabbed Tommy. "These damn pills won't do any good. Look at him!"

"Elliott, we can't! You know we can't. They're out there. Trevor wouldn't let us go out in the dark no matter how sick he was. We wouldn't stand a chance against them with Trevor hurt like he is."

Elliott shook his head. He knew in his heart they couldn't leave right now. He screamed in frustration. "Okay. Okay, but at first light. Let's get everything ready to leave." As they packed and everyone settled in for the night, Elliott explained to Tommy about the other children and how he found them.

Elliott knelt down and leaned against the couch close to Trevor. He listened to his harsh breathing and took Trevor's hand in his. He wanted to cry.

"God, Trevor, I'm sorry. Rose, can we give him another pill?"

Rose felt Trevor's head again. He was still hot and after seeing his leg she wondered if he would even live much longer, so more of the pills couldn't hurt him. They managed to get more pills down him.

"Trevor, don't you die on me."

Trevor briefly opened his eyes, saw Elliott, and attempted to smile at him. His voice was slurred and barely more than a whisper as he looked up at Rose and smiled.

"Keeley, what are you doing here, Darlin'? God, I've missed you. Hold me and don't let go. I'm trying hard to stay with you."

Rose looked at Elliott, but didn't hesitate with her answer. "I'm right here and won't ever let you go. I wouldn't go anywhere without you."

Trevor closed his eyes. "I love you, Darlin'. How's our baby?"

"The baby's fine. I love you too, sweetheart."

Rose cooed softly as Trevor lapsed back into unconsciousness. Elliott sat down and gathered Trevor into his arms. "Keeley's his wife. She's pregnant," he mumbled. "He thought you were his Keeley." Rose leaned over and embraced both Trevor and Elliott.

The sun had just risen when Elliott brought Bentley to the porch. Robert took Trevor under one arm and Billy went to take the other. Elliott's eyes grew cold as he pushed Billy away. "Don't you touch him. Tommy, help Robert get Trevor up on Bentley."

As Trevor was lifted onto Bentley's back, the big horse turned his head around and called softly to him. Rose got up behind Trevor, put her arms around his chest and leaned him back against her. Tommy placed himself in front so he could help support him. "You can lean him against me, Rose."

Elliott led Bentley as the rest of the group fell in step. He closed his eyes and fought the tears that burned in him. They walked most of the day, but were forced to stop for the night as the sun began to set. It would be another day before they got Trevor home.

Elliott searched for a building to spend the night in and found a barn visible in the darkening twilight. It had several boards missing on all sides, but seemed sturdy enough.

"Tommy, we need to check it out."

The two boys went into the barn; one left, one right, and then came out to bring the others in.

"We'll need to keep Trevor warm," Rose said as she shimmied into the blanket next to him. Trevor rolled over to her and she put her arms around him. Tommy crawled in on the other side and leaned against his back.

Elliott took up position at the front door of the barn while the others found spots to sleep for the night. Robert joined Elliott and stood quietly watching him. "Are you planning on spending the night here at the door?"

"Yep."

"Why?"

Elliott turned slowly to Robert. "You don't know? They're out there. It's not just the Beast, but all the things he controls."

"Will they come this far?"

Elliott's voice was laced with anger and pain as he answered what he considered to be a stupid question. "Look at Trevor. He didn't do that to himself. Who do you think burned that town?"

"I'm sorry about your brother. I understand about the watching. Let me help."

"I'll do it. You just keep an eye on Billy. I think he's dangerous. There's something wrong with him. I swear that boy just isn't right. He'll get someone killed."

# 20

Elliott heard them before he saw them. They made the same scratching noises Tommy had heard two nights before. What Elliott was actually hearing was the flutter of the monkey bird's transparent wings. The large hairy, orange, red, and blue bodies hovered over the barn in a circle like vultures.

Elliott listened carefully to determine just what the noise was and where it was coming from.

"Do you know what it is?" Travis asked.

Travis and Harlan were standing next to Elliott, handguns ready. Billy had stepped back out of their sight, hiding behind the barn's door. *Let those assholes get killed. I'm out of here if there's too many.*

Elliott shook his head and whispered. "Go wake up Robert. I'll get Tommy."

Elliott bent down and spoke quietly. "Tommy, get your rifle and join the others. Rose, watch Trevor and if anything comes near y'all, kill it." Elliott handed Rose the extra gun that Robert had given him earlier in the day. "Shoot the red eye, otherwise they get up again."

Tommy stood his ground, but was visibly shaking. "They were here before. I heard them the night before you came back, but I never saw anything, just heard them."

As Robert joined them, six monkey birds attacked, swooping down and breaking through the door. Elliott swiftly went down on one knee, took careful aim, and there was one less. Robert hit the next one and watched it fall to the ground. The monkey bird suddenly jumped up again.

"Shoot the red eye!" Elliott screamed.

Robert took careful aim and the monkey bird fell dead. Travis screamed as a claw caught his arm. Harlan shot it, hitting the red eye on his first shot. The monkey bird fell dead at his feet, but not before leaving its long claw in Travis's left arm. Rose lay in the blanket with Trevor, shaking with fear. She'd never seen anything so hideous.

"Give me the gun, darlin'," Trevor said calmly and relieved Rose of the pistol. He was having problems focusing his eyes and swiped his hand across them. When he looked up again, he saw Elliott drop to the ground with a monkey bird standing over him. It had swooped down hard, hitting Elliott's back.

Trevor didn't hesitate as he pulled the trigger. It screamed with its death. Elliott struggled to his feet and managed to kill another one, which left only one unaccounted for. The monkey bird screamed in a high-pitched whine and went straight for Elliott. A long claw found its mark.

Robert and Trevor shot at the same time and the monkey bird fell. Elliott grabbed his head where he was struck and went down to the floor, but he quickly recovered and was on his feet again. Robert pulled the little boy to him.

Elliott gasped. "I'm okay."

"Bro," Trevor called weakly, dropping the gun.

"Thanks for getting that monster off of me."

Trevor grinned. "Got to protect my little brother's back. Damn, Elliott! You're bleeding, bro. Doc's really going to give us hell. Neither one of us will escape his needles this time."

"It's nothing, just a cut over my eye. Tomorrow we'll be home and Doc will fix you right up."

Trevor grinned and went into a coughing fit. "Don't think there will be needles for me, bro. I'm hurt bad. Elliott, you tell Daniel to take care of Keeley and my baby." Trevor reached up and touched Rose's cheek. "Don't cry for me, Keeley darlin'."

Elliott became furious. "You stop that! I'm taking you home and you're going to be there when the baby's born. You hear me, Trevor? Damn it! Don't you dare die on me!"

"Stop swearing." Trevor said as he collapsed onto the barn's floor. Elliott threw back his head and screamed. He couldn't stop the pain he felt for Trevor that burned inside of him. Ignoring his own pain and the blood dripping into his face, Elliott picked up his rifle and went to the nearest dead monkey bird, shooting it again and again until he ran out of bullets.

Elliott tossed the gun to the ground and went over to Bentley. Tenderly, he put his arms around the big horse's neck and Bentley instinctively moved his head down. Elliott buried his face in his mane and shuddered. He was exhausted and now he was hurt. It was still dark out, but he knew they had to leave. He could feel the sticky blood running into his eye. He moaned, sliding down to the floor and leaning against Bentley for support.

Elliott viciously swiped at the blood dripping into his eye. "I'm not waiting to let it happen. I don't give a shit if it's still dark."

Elliott hesitated for only a moment and then he got up and yelled for Tommy. "We're leaving right now! I'm taking Trevor home before he dies. I can't let that happen. Let's get moving."

Tommy looked from Elliott to Trevor. His stillness shook him.

"Okay."

The last thing Billy wanted was to go outside where the Beast's monsters roamed around at night. "You're crazy," Billy screamed. "In the dark?"

Elliott's eyes turned cold. There was a large blood stain on the front of his shirt where he'd wiped the blood from the gash on his forehead. "Yeah, in the dark."

"Elliott, you're bleeding," Robert said as he moved to help him. "We need to look at that."

"Forget it. I'll live. Help me get Trevor onto Bentley."

Robert reached out for him. "Elliott, you can't."

Elliott turned, picked up his rifle, and shoved it into Robert's stomach. He spoke through gritted teeth. "I'm not discussing this anymore. It's what I'm doing. You can come with me or you can go your own way. I don't give a shit, but me and Tommy are leaving. We're taking Trevor home."

"Okay," Robert said. "We'll all go, but first let's look at your injury and get it wrapped up."

Elliott looked closely at Robert. He knew he was right. His wound needed to be dressed. He spoke his next words quietly. "I've got blood in my eye."

Elliott let Robert tend to him. He would need all his strength to make it home. His head was still seeping blood and it throbbed terribly. He searched his pockets, but didn't find any aspirin.

Robert knew there was no way he could stop this stubborn little kid. After taking care of Elliott, Robert tended to Travis's arm and then helped everyone prepare to leave. He looked into the darkness beyond the barn's door and shuddered.

"God help us."

# 21

It was at least three hours before dawn when Elliott carefully led Bentley out of the barn.  He held a flashlight and was watching every step the horse took so he wouldn't slip.  It was so dark the boys had to hold on to Bentley's tail so they wouldn't get lost from each other.  Rose, Trevor, Tommy, and the injured Travis rode Bentley.

Elliott's head burned where the monkey bird had clawed him, but he ignored the pain.  Robert caught up to him.  "You should ride.  You'll never be able to keep up this pace."

Elliott ignored him and continued walking.

Hours later, dawn started to break with the yellowish sun trying to sneak between the gray of the day's beginning.  Robert didn't like the way Elliott was weaving as he walked.  The kid was pale and sweating even though it was cold out.  He looked like a miniature drunk.

Elliott didn't look at or acknowledge Robert's presence.  His rifle dragged on the ground as he forced himself to march forward.  Robert leaned down and took the rifle, handing it up to Tommy.  Elliott just continued walking at his drunken pace.  Finally, Robert picked up the little boy.  Elliott sighed, putting his arms around Robert's neck.  "I can walk."

"Sure you can, but you need to rest for while, so let me carry you, buddy."  Robert looked up at Tommy.  "Point the way."

## 22

"Daniel, Daniel," Emma yelled as she saw Bentley walking toward the house. "Brady, go Daniel. Bring Sam."

Emma jumped off the porch and ran to meet the group. She took Bentley's lead from the large boy carrying Elliott.

"Is he dead? Is he bones?"

The boy who was carrying Elliott shook his head. Just as they reached the porch, Daniel and Sam came out. He took one look and went to Elliott, lifting his head off of Robert's shoulder.

"Trevor's hurt bad," Elliott mumbled weakly. "Tell Keeley I'm sorry."

"Hang on, Elliott. Sam, take Elliott to our bedroom and put him on the bed. I'll get Trevor. Tommy, are you alright, son?" Daniel asked as he eased Trevor down into his arms.

"Yeah Doc, I'm fine."

Trevor let out a groan and briefly opened his eyes. "I give up, Doc." He tried to laugh, but it came out as a cough.

"Relax, son, I've got you."

"It's too late. I'm already dead."

Daniel could tell Trevor was in bad shape just by his coloring and the heat radiating from his body. He hurried to get him into his office where he immediately began stripping off his clothing as he yelled for Sam.

"I'm in here with Elliott."

"Strip off his clothes. How does he look?"

"Conscious. He has a head wound, but the bleeding seems to have stopped."

"I can't leave Trevor. Take his temperature and pulse. Call it out to me."

Daniel had already started two IV drips on Trevor and left those wide open. He wanted to get as much volume in him as possible and as quickly as possible. He stripped off the bandage on Trevor's leg and knew immediately it was infected. He added a broad spectrum antibiotic to the IV.

"Sam, talk to me."

"The temp's okay. Pulse 150."

"Is he conscious?"

"Yes."

"Elliott, you rest easy, son and I'll be there soon. Sam, get Brady and Emma to watch the little ones, then take Katie to Keeley and keep her busy. I don't want her in here until I stabilize Trevor. Keep Rusty out."

Sam put her arm on Daniel's as he worked on Trevor. Tears formed in her eyes as she looked down at her son. "Will he be alright?"

"Don't cry, Sam. Don't let Keeley see you cry. I'll make sure he's alright."

Daniel never stopped working on Trevor while he continued to give orders. "God, he's hurt bad this time. I need to cool him down. Go get the girl on the horse to come in here. Soak some towels with cold water and have her bring them to me. Make sure George takes care of Bentley."

Sam left and sent Rose in with the towels. "Sam sent me. I'm supposed to give you these wet towels."

"Okay, sweetheart, bring them over here."

Daniel took the cold towels and put them around Trevor's body draping the last one over his chest. "When his body warms the towels, get more cold ones on him. I've got to look at Elliott. I'll be in the next room. Call me if anything changes."

"Alright."

Elliott was pale and his breathing rapid. Daniel sat down and took Elliott's hand in his. Elliott's voice shook with the effort to talk. "Trevor?"

"Stable," Daniel said quietly. "Let's see what I can do for you. Are you hurt anywhere besides your head?"

"Just this cut on my head. It burns and my head hurts."

"I'll bet it does." Daniel quickly examined Elliott. "You relax. I'm going to check Trevor and I'll come back with my magic to fix you up."

Elliott grabbed Daniel's arm. "Don't let Trevor die. I couldn't get him home any faster. I need to see him."

"You're not going anywhere for while and don't make any fast moves or you'll start the bleeding again. It'll also make your head hurt like hell. You can see Trevor later after you've gotten a little rest. I'll be right back."

Daniel went back to Trevor. He actually looked a little better and there was a hint of color in his face, the fluids were doing their job. He touched the girl's arm.

"Rose, is it?"

"Yes."

"Would you go sit with Elliott? I'll be in soon."

"Of course."

"Doc," Trevor's voice was barely audible.

Daniel reached over and took his hand. "Hey, tough guy. Don't talk right now. Save your strength."

"Keeley?"

"Keeley's fine. I'll bring her in soon. I just wanted to make you a little more presentable."

After Daniel settled Trevor again, he went back and hit Elliott with a round of antibiotics and then convinced him to stay in bed.

"I'll be back later and check on you."

Daniel walked back into the office as Keeley walked in and went directly to Trevor, gently kissing him.

"Doc?"

"I'm doing everything I can for him. He's young, he'll fight, and he'll need you to help in that fight."

Keeley put her hand to her belly. Tears were streaming down her face. "I can't lose him."

Daniel folded Keeley into his strong embrace. "I know. If you do exactly what I say, I'll let you stay with him. We want to protect your baby. You can't overstress him."

"I understand." She took a deep breath. "I just want to be with Trevor."

"I'm going to move the chair over so you can sit."

Daniel moved the chair and covered Keeley with a blanket, checked Trevor, and went back to check on Elliott.

"Doc?"

"It's me."

"Trevor got hurt six days ago. He wouldn't come back, so I went ahead alone and I found us a new place. We got some pills in him. Rose said they were the right kind."

Daniel lifted the little boy gently into his arms. He hugged Elliott to him, rocking him slowly. "Elliott, I don't want you to lay here and worry. Trevor is holding his own. You've had a tough time of it. Relax and let your body heal. You took great care of Trevor and now it's my turn to get both of you well again."

When Daniel checked on Trevor, both he and Keeley were fast asleep. "I can stay with them and come get you if anything happens."

Daniel turned to see a lovely, young girl. Rose had sat down at Daniel's desk and he'd forgotten she was there. He grinned at her.

"I guess we haven't been officially introduced. I'm Daniel Bryant."

"Georgia Rose Starling, but I'm just called Rose. I'd know you anywhere, Doc. Trevor spoke of you when he was shaking with fever. He called to you and kept saying how sorry he was. He loves you very much," she said shyly.

Daniel gently took Rose into his arms and hugged her close. "Thanks for all your help, sweetheart. I love him too."

## 23

Daniel went looking for Sam. He checked the family room and was about to go into the kitchen to see if she was there when a small voice stopped him.

"Are you the doctor?" the voice asked.

Daniel looked over at a young boy. His brown hair was shoulder length and his brown eyes were intense. The child looked from Daniel to the little boy sitting on the floor next to him.

"I'm the doctor. My name is Daniel."

"My friend Travis is hurt."

Daniel bent down to the child. There was a bloody shirt wrapped around his left arm. He touched the boy's face. "Travis?"

Travis raised his head. Daniel saw dull pain in his eyes. He pushed back a lock of blond hair to get a better look. "Let's go have a better look at you."

Daniel picked up Travis and leaned him against his shoulder. "I'll take care of him and be back to talk to you. Go sit down and get comfortable or if you're hungry, go into the kitchen. There's always someone there who can make a sandwich. This is going to take a little while."

Sam ran into Daniel in the hall. "Who's this?"

"Another victim. "I'll need some help."

Daniel had Sam clear his desk and then he placed Travis on top of it. The wound was an open laceration that ran from his elbow to wrist. It needed to be cleaned and stitched.

"How's the pain, Travis?"

"Hurts, but not so bad now."

"Okay, here's what I'm going to do."

Daniel explained exactly what he was going to do while Travis listened carefully, nodding his head. "I understand. I'm really tired. Would it be alright if I just close my eyes for awhile?"

Daniel took the boy's hand in his and felt his pulse while he talked quietly to him. Sam brought a pillow and slipped it under Travis's head.

"You just relax." Daniel smiled down at Travis as he pointed to Trevor. "Nothing for you to worry about, I've had a lot of practice patching him up."

Travis gave Daniel a crooked grin. "Trevor told us about the needles." He closed his eyes while Daniel sutured and bandaged his wound. He kept up a steady stream of conversation telling Travis everything he was doing. He always believed it was easier for the patient if they knew exactly what was happening, but he wasn't sure whether or not Travis was listening. The boy didn't talk and never moved.

Keeley was sitting in the chair. Tears were still streaming down her cheeks. Daniel picked her up and sat in his chair securing her in his lap. He didn't say anything, he just held her. After a few minutes he whispered softly in her ear. "He's doing better."

"He's so still," Keeley sniffed. "I had to touch his chest to make sure he was still breathing."

"His body is using every resource to heal itself and to fight the infection. I'm going to help him win this fight. It's only been a few hours, so you need to give him more time. We'll make him better because you need him, his baby needs him, and so do I. Trevor saved my life more than once and sure as hell, I'm not about to give up on him."

"He wants to die." She started to cry again and Daniel tightened his arms around her. He closed his eyes. "It's just the pain talking, Keeley, nothing else." Daniel lifted Keeley's face up to his. "Will you do me a big favor?"

"Anything."

"I want you to go to bed and stay there for awhile."

Keeley started to protest, but Daniel calmly said, "You need to do this for yourself and your child.  If anything happens, I'll come get you, but I give you my word that nothing will happen to him."  Reluctantly, Keeley agreed and did as Daniel asked.

Elliott was awake when Daniel went to check on him.

"How are you feeling?"

"Better.  How's Trevor?"

"Resting.  Elliott, can you tell me what happened?"

Elliott told Daniel the entire story from the time they left until they returned home, and then he told him the location of the new place he had found for them.

"Doc, don't trust Billy.  I got a bad feeling about him."

"I haven't really met the new group yet.  Maybe it's time for me to check them out."

George came into the room, went over to his brother, and sat down next to him.  Lightly, he touched the large bandage across Elliott's head.

"You okay, Elliott?"

"Headache is all."

"I was afraid for you.  When Robert brought you in, you..." George stopped and hugged his brother. "I was afraid."

Daniel left the two brothers.  They had a lot to talk about.  He shook his head.  They fought like cats and dogs, but when it came down to the important things, they defended each other to the end. George needed to be sure that Elliott was alright.

Daniel stepped back into his office with the intention of fixing his desk, but stopped dead in his tracks. The one person he didn't want to see Trevor in his present condition was standing right next to the exam table.  Her lips were trembling and tears streamed down her face as she patted Trevor's hand.

"Buppy," he said warmly.

Rusty turned to him, her eyes showing the agony she was feeling for Trevor. Next to Daniel, Trevor was her world. When she couldn't find Daniel for comfort, she always turned to Trevor. She would ask him endless questions and he never tired of answering them. She followed him around like a lost puppy. Now she stood before him, devastated by what she saw. Daniel swiftly walked over and scooped her up. She buried her head in his shoulder, sobbing with grief. She tightened her grip around Daniel's neck.

"Daddy! Daddy! Daddy!" she sobbed louder.

"I know, baby, I know."

"Trevor's bones. My Trevor's all bones."

"Shhh. Trevor's not bones. He's very much alive."

Once again Daniel went to his chair, but this time it was to console his child, who he cuddled tightly against his chest. He let her sob until she hiccupped with it. He took her chin in his hand and lifted her face to his. He kissed her cheeks, then tucked her head against his chest again and held her there. As he rocked her, he made sure her ear was against his heart. It always seemed to have a calming effect on her. When things were too much for her to cope with, when the demons came to close and nightmares invaded her sleep, she always sought him out. Daniel felt her little body start to respond and relax.

Daniel watched Trevor as he let Rusty's pressure and tension unwind until she leveled out, her breathing deepening as she went limp. He'd let her sleep for awhile and when she woke he'd explain about Trevor injuries and reassure her that he was not dead.

Sam came to see if Daniel needed any help and found him with his arms encircling Rusty's small body. She pulled up the desk chair and smoothed back Rusty's hair from her forehead. "Tough day?"

"I found her watching Trevor and crying. One of her toughest days. She's so young and she doesn't even begin to understand what has happened to her world. Here, take her. I need to make rounds and check on all my patients."

Sam changed places with Daniel and made herself comfortable.

"Where's Katie?" Daniel asked as he checked Trevor's IV.

"Emma and Brady took charge of her. God, Daniel, we have five more children now."

Daniel didn't answer, only grunted as Sam told him what she knew about the newcomers. "I'll meet them later. I'm going to check the rest of the children's injuries. If Trevor wakes or anything changes, holler. I'm moving Elliott in here on the extra bed."

Daniel was concerned about Keeley. Her pregnancy hadn't been and easy one and now she had the added strain of her husband lying wounded on the exam table. She was an emotional wreck.

When Rusty woke, Sam convinced her to go with her for a sandwich. She agreed only after Sam promised she could come right back after she ate. Before she left, Rusty tenderly kissed Trevor's hand. A lot of bargains were being struck that day.

When Daniel placed his hand on Trevor's forehead, he opened his eyes. "Welcome back," Daniel said warmly.

"Hey, Doc," the words came with much effort. "I hurt."

"I know. Be right back."

"Don't go."

"I'm not going anywhere. I just need to get you some medication."

"They got me in the leg again. Damn it! I'm getting real tired of this crap."

Daniel shook his head. "Didn't I tell you to duck?"

"Yeah, you did. Sorry, I just seemed to be jinxed."

Trevor groaned and Daniel hurried back to him, gently putting his hand on his chest. He shook his head. "Relax, tough guy, don't be in such a hurry to move."

"Am I dead, Daniel? I sure feel dead."

"After all the work I did on you? Do you think I'd let you go and die on me?"

"I'm going to die," Trevor said with no emotion. It was just a statement.

Daniel leaned over Trevor and put one hand on either side of him. He spoke very softly. "You are not going to die. What's going on, Trevor? Don't you believe your physician?"

"I'll always believe in you, Doc. It's just that I hurt so damn bad."

"I'm going to take care of that right now."

Daniel prepared the injection and jabbed it into the IV. He threw the syringe down in anger. An unexpected tear fell from his eye as he silently prayed for his son. He had a horrible feeling in his gut that Trevor may be right.

"You listen to me, son, and listen good. I'm not going to let you die. I will not let it happen! You're staying right here with all of us. We need you. I need you, and in about four months your baby is going to need you. Keeley needs you now. Do you understand me?"

"Keeley?" Trevor said softly.

"Yes, Keeley, she's lying down in the other room. Rusty stood here and cried for you. She needs to know her big brother is going to be alright. She desperately needs you, so you forget about dying because it's not going to happen."

"Okay, Doc," Trevor said weakly. "Don't get in a snit. I give up. I won't go and die on you."

"Also," Daniel tried to smile as his voice cracked. "I'm having one hell of a good time making you all better."

Daniel held up a needle so Trevor could see it.

"Just how many needles have you used?" Trevor's half-laugh turned into a moan.

"It's not the ones I've used that should worry you, it's the ones in your future." Daniel whispered.

Trevor groaned again. "Easy, son, you just let the medicine do its job and I guarantee the next time you wake up you'll feel better."

"It's bad this time, huh Doc? Hostile little assholes almost got me. Thought they did."

"It's the infection. Only thing you should worry about getting you is me. You're past the worst of it and they didn't get you. Now close your eyes and stop talking. I'm going to get your wife. She needs some reassurance that you're alright."

Before Trevor drifted into his drug-induced sleep, he asked about Elliott and Bentley. Daniel assured him that Elliott was fine and George was taking good care of his horse.

# 24

Sam and Daniel spent the next hour getting the children settled in for the night. Daniel made another check on Trevor, Elliott, and Travis before he went to join Sam for coffee. Robert came in with Keeley, George, and Rose.

"How are you feeling, sweetheart?" Daniel asked as he took Keeley's hand.

"A lot better now that I know Trevor's going to be alright."

Daniel smiled at her. In his heart he'd been praying for Trevor because he wasn't as certain as Keeley. He had a long way to go and the infection in his leg was quite serious.

Robert had been standing back, studying Daniel closely. He was amazed by all he'd seen and also puzzled. He had quietly watched the family all night and now he had questions.

"Doc, can I ask you a few questions?"

"What's bothering you?"

"Well, ah, are all these children yours? I mean are you their father?"

Daniel laughed and then explained his family. "We all came together at different times and places. Are these children mine? You bet your life they are. We all were brought together somehow and now we belong to each other. Just as he finished one the littlest members showed up and crawled into his lap.

Rusty made herself comfortable and stuck her thumb in her mouth. Daniel gently removed it. "How come you're not in bed, young lady?"

Rusty yawned and moved his arm so she could get more comfortable. Daniel unconsciously wrapped his arms around her.

She closed her eyes and settled in. The offending thumb went back into her mouth. Rusty was content. She felt safe.

Robert stared at Daniel and Daniel smiled back at him. "Problem?"

Robert smiled widely and shook his head. "No problem at all that I can see. I guess I'm just a little overwhelmed by all of you."

"Tell me about your group."

Robert shook his head and told Daniel his story of the camp and how he was contemplating going back for a rescue mission. "I have to go back. I have to try and get the other people out." Robert lowered his head. "There's another reason. There are three more of them—the Beasts, and right now they're incubating. I have to destroy them before they hatch or whatever they do to be born." Robert hesitated before continuing. "Daniel, I've heard of you, in the camp. There's always talk. The Beast knows about you and your family and they're searching for you. He'll never give up until you're found. That's why they're coming this far. It's you he needs."

Daniel gave Robert a long look before he spoke. "You're sure?"

"Yes sir, I'm as sure as I'm sitting here. I was in the camp for a long time. You listen, observe, and you hear things. I learned a lot. There's no doubt that the Beast knows about you and Trevor. Actually, he has knowledge of everyone here. He wants to use you and Trevor. You're going to be forced to impregnate the women he holds. They want the babies for a food source. They live through our blood and there just isn't enough to go around. He made one big mistake when he killed off most of the world's population. I'm hoping that until the Beast can get enough food sources, he can't hatch those others. Unfortunately, that that means he has to find us. He'll never stop."

Daniel let out a soft whistle. He thought that the Beast was after them for a reason, but had never wanted to believe it. Now, he had to be a believer. Now, he had the answer to why they were being hunted so intensely by the Beast.

"He also has things called 'half-ones,'" Robert continued.

"We've met those," George interrupted. "Ethan was one."

Daniel explained about Ethan/Patrick, how he had first come to them as a little boy, been taken over by the Beast, and later came back as another boy—a half-one. He also told Robert how Trevor had been forced to kill him and how the Beast had almost killed Trevor in the process.

"Sounds like Trevor had a rough time of it all the way around. The half-ones," Robert said softly. "There aren't a lot of them—maybe six to ten. It may not be safe for you to stay here much longer."

"We were planning on moving," Sam sighed. "I'll miss this place."

"Don't wait too long," Robert said as he took Rose's hand in his. "They may be closer than you think."

## 25

A few days later, Elliott announced he was ready to get up. He'd begun to feel like he'd been in bed forever. Daniel slowly shook his head, refusing to let him out of bed. "You need at least another week."

Elliott didn't like being confined, so they compromised and he was allowed to perch on the couch in the family room. Another bargain struck. Daniel could tell Elliott was better because he was arguing regularly with George. That was a sure sign he was on the mend.

Trevor would take a longer to heal. Rusty peeked in at Trevor. He was lying quietly with his eyes closed. She padded over and leaned against the bed, watching him as he slept. Trevor was still in Daniel's office on the spare bed Elliott had occupied before him. He wanted him close so he could keep an eye on his progress. He also didn't trust him to stay in bed since he was staring to feel better.

Once his crisis was over, Trevor began to heal amazingly fast. While he felt better, he still needed more time and Daniel knew he wasn't good at staying in bed no matter how many times he was lectured about it. It was a constant argument between them and one Daniel intended to win this time.

It was after six and Rusty had waited just about as long as she could before sneaking in to see Trevor. She went over and looked in the open door leading to Daniel and Sam's bedroom. They were both asleep. Spot, Rusty's constant companion, jumped up and made himself at home on the bed next to Trevor.

Rusty eased up on the bed, being careful not to touch Trevor's injured leg. She laid her head on his shoulder and threw her arm across his chest, gently patting him. Trevor eyed the little girl.

"Good morning, Rusty."

Rusty giggled and squirreled closer to him. "I missed you. I needed to hug on ya," Rusty whispered and placed a kiss on his shoulder.

He grunted. "Thank you. I needed a hug."

"Spot told me you did."

"Smart cat."

"Are you still hurtin?"

"Some."

"Why?"

"My leg aches. Let's not tell Daddy or he'll never let me out of this bed."

"Daddy can fix you."

Rusty sat up and tried to do her best imitation of Daniel. She lowered her voice and tried to look stern, squinting up her eyes and huffing. "Rusty!" she said, raising her finger and pointing. "You have to remember what Daddy said…if you are hurt, or sick, you need to tell me."

Trevor laughed at her antics.

"I'm glad you didn't go away, Trevor. I wouldn't see you anymore if you was bones." Rusty's little bottom lip quivered. She put her hands on Trevor's chest and lowered her head as she sobbed uncontrollably. "My Trevor!"

Trevor was horrified. "Baby, don't cry. I wouldn't leave you." Gently, he took her little hand in his and kissed it. "I'm not going anywhere."

Rusty continued to cry. She threw her arm across Trevor's chest and sobbed as if her heart was breaking. He put his arms around her, but didn't know what else to do. She wasn't listening to him. He felt helpless.

Daniel was standing in the doorway. He'd slipped his jeans on when he heard Trevor and Rusty talking. He was about to join them when Rusty began her uncontrollable crying.

"I'll handle this one."

Daniel sat down on the edge of the bed and reached over, pulling Rusty into his arms. He sat her on his lap and folded her arms under her so she was flush against him. He spoke to her soothingly, lowering his voice into an intensely gentle tone. He controlled her movements, so she couldn't pull away from him while he settled her.

Trevor was amazed, but then realized Daniel always had a way of doing this. He couldn't begin to count the times he too had been calmed by that smooth, soft, deep voice of his. The man had a special talent and he worked it like magic. Rusty sighed deeply and snuggled closer to Daniel as he gently rocked her and rubbed softly across her back.

"Is she asleep?" Trevor asked softly.

"Almost, give her a few more minutes."

"I have to remember that method."

"She's calmed by listening to the beat of my heart and the quiet in my voice. Sometimes it's the only way to handle it. Works great."

Daniel took a clinical look at Trevor as he rocked Rusty and noted his color was still not a hundred percent. Pain showed on his face when he moved. "How bad is your pain?"

Trevor gave him his typical answer. "I'm fine."

"I heard the part of your conversation with Rusty about not telling Daddy. Well, Daddy's here. You shouldn't confide in five year-olds because they always tell."

Trevor grimaced. "I hurt."

"How bad? Try on a scale of one to ten with ten being the worst."

Trevor was reluctant to answer, but he knew Daniel wouldn't let him up unless he did. He decided to lie.

"And don't try lying to me."

"Do you read minds?"

Daniel smiled. "One to ten, and if I don't like the answer you'll be in that bed for a month."

"I hate it when you smile at me like that. Eight," he said in a hushed voice. "I suppose that confines me here forever."

"Not quite that long, but you stay put until I give the okay. I may have to put a guard on you. How about a pain shot?"

"No more needles. I'm just really tired. Never felt this bad. Doc, I'm really worried."

Daniel raised his eyebrow at Trevor. "Worried about what?"

"Keeley. She just looks...I don't know."

"Relax. Keeley's doing fine. You need to let me worry about Keeley and if there's a problem you need to worry about, I'll let you know. Your job right now is to get better."

Daniel had been rocking Rusty the entire time. He looked down at her. She was sleeping peacefully. He tucked her in next to Trevor. She snuggled against his chest and continued to doze.

"I want her to be with you when she wakes up, so she knows that you're alright."

Daniel got pain medication for Trevor and came back with a syringe. "Lean over a little so I can get this into your hip."

Trevor gave him a look and then closed his eyes.

"Thanks, Doc. As always, it's a pleasure letting you stick it to me."

Daniel took a blanket and covered both of his children. He leaned down and kissed Rusty on the forehead and then kissed Trevor.

"Sleep, and next time, don't get hurt."

# 26

They moved silently and stopped just inside the wooded area next to the house. There were eight of them. Sixteen beady eyes looked greedily at the front of the house. None approached, they just stood and watched. Of the sixteen eyes, eight left ones were red and eight right ones were brown. They were anxious and each large throat gave a deep, low rumbling growl. The sun fell low in the sky—only twenty minutes to complete darkness. They came because they were part of the Beast. They had found their prey and now it was a waiting game.

Robert had an uncomfortable feeling, something that slid throughout his entire body and he couldn't shake. Rose was curled up by the fireplace next to him. The gentle crackle of the roaring fire transfixed them. Robert enjoyed its warmth, but he still couldn't ignore the feeling that they were being watched. He shivered despite the warm glow from the fire.

"What's wrong, Bobby?"

"Got a bad feeling."

Rose took his hand and leaned over to kiss him. "Everything seems quiet."

Robert shook his head, smiled, and pulled Rose closer. "You're beautiful."

"I think you're pretty beautiful yourself," Rose laughed. "I like it here and I love Daniel's family. It's been a wonderful month. It's the most comfortable I've been in a very long time."

"Sam said to tell you that it's time to eat," Emma announced.

Dinner was a quiet event, it turned out to be one of those nights where everyone was tired and soon most of the children started to drift off to bed leaving Daniel, Sam, Rusty, Robert, and Rose. Rusty lay contently in Daniel's arms as he and Robert discussed the impending move.

"We'll leave as soon as Trevor can travel. Keeley's almost six months and I don't want to wait any longer."

Daniel looked over at Sam and smiled. She was going into her third month. "The trip will be hard enough on my girls and we'll be able to take only a limited amount of supplies. I want to be set up in time for Keeley's delivery. I don't want to be forced into delivering a baby out in the open. We would have left sooner if all this hadn't happened."

Robert made a quick decision and looked over at Rose. "I'll help you move before I go back to the camp. A little longer shouldn't matter. Can Rose stay with you? I don't want her in this."

"We'll be glad to have Rose," Sam said quickly.

"Bobby, I'm going with you."

Robert turned to Rose and took her hand. "No, I want you safe. I'll be running back to you as fast as I can, but I need to know that you're safe. This is something I have to do alone," he said softly.

Robert and Rose stared at each other. She knew he was determined and nothing was going to change his mind and it scared her deep down in her soul.

Daniel broke the tension. "This little one is done in. Sam, are you ready for bed?"

Rose's terror showed on her face. "Bobby."

He put his finger to her lips. "Shhh. Come with me. We need to talk."

They made their way back to the fireplace. Rose was content to lie on the big rug in front of it tucked safely into Robert's arms, it made her feel better.

"Rose, how old are you?"

"Fifteen. Why?"

"Old enough," Robert sighed. "At least in this world."

Robert pulled Rose closer and whispered, "I love you and I may not be able to come back," he admitted sadly. "I'll try, but. . ."

Rose looked up at this man who just professed his love for her and felt the sting of tears. "I love you too."

"I want to make love to you, but it has to be right for you too. You should be sure you want me."

When she didn't answer, Robert reached over and kissed her, exploring her, tasting her. She responded immediately to his gentle probing. Robert slowly opened her blouse and pushed his hand against her breast, squeezing lightly. He moved his kisses down her throat. She responded by pushing her hips into his throbbing hardness. They got naked on the rug as he ran his hand up her body and back down between her legs.

"Try to relax, it'll make it easier," he whispered.

Rose held onto Robert desperately as they made love. Afterwards, they laid together, holding onto each other. Neither spoke for a long time. Finally, Robert found his voice. "Are you all right? I didn't hurt you?"

"I'm fine."

"I love you Rose. I didn't realize just how much until this very minute. All we've been through together..." Robert stopped, gripped by an emotion he didn't know was there.

"I've always loved you," Rose said softly. "From the first time I saw you in the camp."

Robert felt elated. "Are you okay with this? With me?"

Rose gave him a sly smile. "Let me show you how okay I am."

From the other room, a shadowy figure watched as Robert and Rose consummated their love. Billy laughed to himself, if Robert could impregnate Rose, the Beast will have his breeder.

There were too many to fight with this family, but that just meant lying low and staying with them until he could find out where they were going—information he could put away for future use. He hated all of them. They thought he was a coward. Soon they would find out he was so much more. There were six more like him and being a half-one had its advantages. They had been infiltrated into the camps to get information from the captives and try to find out about future breeders. *Did these assholes really think it was that easy to escape from the Beast? Fools!* Tomorrow night he'd have the Beast's friends outside give them all a run for their money. *Maybe I can eliminate a few. Good thing they've been so busy with the injured because they haven't paid much attention to me.*

Billy thought about Rusty. The brat seemed to know something. It was the way she looked at him. *I'll just have my friends take care of her tomorrow.*

"Enjoy yourselves, kids," he laughed. "Tomorrow it's all over for you." Billy giggled and disappeared into the shadows. *Tomorrow would definitely be an exciting day.* Billy continued to giggle as he made his way down the hall and into his assigned bedroom.

# 27

Dinner was a bedlam of confusion the next day. Trevor had been allowed out of bed to dine in the kitchen with the family and newcomers. Everyone spoke to him at the same time, each wanting his attention. It had been a long time since they'd all been in the same room together.

"One at a time," Trevor laughed and winced as pain shot through his leg.

Sam gave Trevor a sympathetic look. "Daniel, are you sure he's up to this?"

"He loves it. Just look at him. It's good for all of them."

The kids couldn't do enough to make sure that their injured brothers were comfortable. They all surrounded Trevor, Elliot, and also Travis.

"Tell us again what happened," asked George.

"Daniel, maybe you should save Trevor from all that smothering affection."

Daniel laughed at Trevor's obvious discomfort at being the center of attention. "Let his brothers and sisters fuss over him, Sam. They almost lost him."

George got up and picked up his rifle. "I'll be right back," he called over his shoulder.

"Just where does he think he's going?" Sam fretted. "It's almost dark."

George made his way over to the house two lots away. He retrieved a cane he'd seen when he was searching the houses. He was almost back to the main house when he stopped. He'd heard a strange noise. He stopped and then slowly raised his rifle as he scanned the surrounding area. When you live in a world that is absent of noise, the slightest change gets your undivided attention. After a few minutes, he heard nothing, shrugged, and relaxed slightly. Once on the front porch, George turned and again scanned the area. He let his eyes drift across the open land and then over to the small lake. Nothing. He stared into the woods and listened carefully, still nothing. He shook off the uneasy feeling and went inside to join the others.

George walked into the dining room carrying the cane which he proudly presented to Trevor. "I thought it would make it easier for you to walk. I remembered seeing it when we searched that big white house over yonder."

Trevor looked from the cane to George and smiled shyly. "It's great. . . thanks."

Everyone had to try the cane. They laughed at Tommy's dance routine that involved some pretty good footwork. Sam decided to bring out the cake she had baked. She was delighted when she found the box of cake mix, but decided to for a special occasion. Having her boys safe at home again certainly qualified. The kids ate the entire cake. They even pressured Daniel into having a piece.

## 28

Billy quietly slipped away from the group. He wasn't missed as he stepped onto the front porch and signaled his friends. They became instantly alert with red eyes glowing in a now darkened sky. Billy smiled as he stepped back inside and quietly closed the door behind him. When he turned around, Rusty was staring at him. The little girl looked at the door, then back at Billy.

"You're a bad boy."

Billy reached out and grabbed Rusty by the arm. He swung her around to face him, snatching her arm behind her back and drawing quickly away. He clamped his hand over her mouth. "Rusty, I just want to talk to you." Billy tried to be soothing in his speech, but the sound was grating to Rusty. He smiled a smile that became a sneer. She bit down on his hand and he let go.

"Daddy!" she screamed and fell backwards as the front door burst open, ushering in the wolves.

Hearing Rusty's scream, Elliott instinctively went for his rifle and ran toward her. The wolves approached on silent padded feet, moving slowly and deliberately. Rusty screamed again as she looked down the throat of a wolf that appeared to be nothing but big yellow teeth. Behind her, Elliott went down on one knee, carefully aimed, and hit the wolf's red eye. The huge animal fell forward, dead.

Elliott lost his balance. The pain from his not quite healed wound made him cry out as he sprawled on the floor. He quickly scrambled forward on his hands and knees, reaching out for Rusty. Once he had her in his arms, he dragged her backwards with him.

Robert went for Elliott's rifle as the next wolf approached. He picked it up and fired at the large wolf. The four remaining wolves loped into the room just as George threw Daniel his rifle. Robert fired again missing one that was steadily moving forward.

Trevor sat motionless at the table, his face calm and expressionless, and his rifle raised and ready for use. Rose, Keeley, and Sam had gathered the small children together and stood behind Trevor. Travis and Harlan stood to the left and right of Trevor with the only available weapons they had—knives hastily picked up from the table.

Robert dragged Elliott and Rusty out of the path of two of the wolves moving toward them with lips curled back, eyes glossed over, and teeth barred. He raised the rifle to fire but it jammed. He turned the rifle around to use it as a club.

Rusty scrambled away from Elliott and ducked under the dining room table. The larger of the two wolves had Robert in its sight. It was backing him into a corner of the family room. Robert went behind a chair, grabbed the lamp from the table next to him and broke it, intending to use the jagged edges as a weapon. He knew the wolf outweighed him by at least a hundred pounds. The thing was huge. It jumped at him, hitting him in square the chest.

Robert slashed at the wolf, but it had landed against his chest and knocked him off his feet. Its teeth sunk deep into his arm. He was screaming and striking at the wolf when a gunshot went off so close to his head that his ear rang with the sound. George stood over them. The wolf was dead. George gave Robert a brief glance, nodded, and then went after the next enemy. Robert fell back with the wolf's weight directly on top of him.

Trevor hit the glaring red eye just as the wolf jumped for Travis. The boy had stood his ground with the knife raised to strike.

Daniel killed the wolf that approached Rusty as she lay trapped under the table. She'd put her head down and curled into a ball. The last remaining wolf was killed by both Trevor and

George. It jumped up on the table and lunged at Trevor and both boys fired at the same time.

## 29

Billy could hardly conceal his anger. He couldn't believe these morons had killed all of his wolves. He quickly blended into the pandemonium and picked up a knife from the table so no one would suspect that he'd tried to do anything but help.

"Settle down," Daniel yelled above the noise.

"I think that's it, Doc," George shouted. "I don't see any more." He turned to the two new boys and said, "Travis, you and Harlan come help me. Grab a rifle and we'll make sure there aren't any others."

Daniel put his hand on George's shoulder. "Wait a minute. Is everyone here? Is anyone hurt?"

A loud cry came from the other room. "I'm in the family room and I could use some help."

Harlan and George ran into the family room where Robert was trapped under the body of the wolf. They pulled and Robert pushed until he could slide out from under it.

"I got bit," Robert grunted. "It hurts."

Daniel checked Robert's arm. "We need to clean that up. You'll need a tetanus shot and some antibiotics."

Trevor was standing with his back to them watching the front door where the wolves had entered. He chuckled and called back over his shoulder. "That's right, Doc, don't forget the needles."

Everyone laughed except Rose. She started to cry. Robert put his good arm around her and pulled her close to him. "It's not bad."

George looked down at the dead wolves with disgust. "After we check outside, let's get these things out of here."

Daniel took care of Robert's wound and then came back to help with the removal. After they had disposed of the bodies he strolled over to where Elliott was quietly talking to Trevor.

"You all right, son?"

"Guess I shouldn't have moved so fast. I thought I was feeling better. It hurts some, but I'm okay."

"Trevor?"

"I'm fine. Where's Rusty?"

"She was with me by the door when it started." Elliott said. "I think she went under the dining room table."

They found Rusty under the table still curled into a tight ball. Daniel coaxed her out by reaching underneath and gently pulling her into his arms. Rusty's terror became frantic as she thought she felt the wolf's hot breath and felt the piercing of yellow teeth. Her eyes were wide with fear.

Daniel put his hand over her eyes, leaned down, and spoke softly to her. It took almost fifteen minutes before she'd calmed enough to collapse against him, totally exhausted. Her breathing was ragged and tremors shook her body. When her tears finally subsided, she rested her head against his chest and put her thumb in her mouth.

Rusty knew that Billy had brought the wolves and that he was like Ethan. She had seen the red eye that no one else saw and he had teeth like the wolf. Rusty lifted turned her head slightly so she could glance at Billy across the room. He was staring at her. She shivered violently and shut her eyes tight. She wanted everything else go away from her, but she could still see Billy's piercing red eye. He had fangs and a purple tongue. She alone heard the low growls he emitted. She still saw him licking his lips when he looked at her. Billy wanted her dead and she knew it. Rusty tried to tell Daniel, but the words wouldn't come. She poked him and then pointed across the room. He looked to where she pointed, but there was nothing there.

Billy was sitting just outside the front door deciding on his next move. He snorted. "That damn Rusty! She knows, but it won't matter. She'll be the first one I kill. It's time to contact the Beast."

# 30

Daniel and Sam had been arguing back and forth for over an hour. "Honey, there's no choice. We need to leave here and we have to go as soon as possible."

She looked at him with concern. "Why now? Trevor isn't well enough."

"Trevor can ride Bentley with Elliott. Elliott won't be able to walk far. After what happened today, we have no choice. We have to leave."

Sam put her arms around Daniel and looked down at Rusty. She was trying to rest, but every few minutes the little girl shivered slightly. Daniel tightened his arms around her, leaned down and spoke softly.

"Will she be alright?"

"I don't know. We have to hold our children close right now and Rusty the closest. Christ, why wouldn't she be frightened half to death, she was almost eaten by a wolf."

Daniel shifted positions. He was tired, truly tired, and his arm was starting to go numb with Rusty's weight. This world they'd been thrown into made him tired. His children being hurt and scared made him angry. Fighting the fear and the daily fight to stay alive made him even angrier.

Daniel leaned back and let his mind drift. His thoughts led him to Molly, his beautiful wife of long ago. She never made it to this new, difficult and demanding world. Molly and his little girl, four year-old Sally, had been rushing home to him on the day they died. He'd lost them because of a senseless car accident caused by a drunk driver. It seemed so very long ago. They'd been married six years. Molly was only twenty-four when she died. He'd never told anyone about them—not even Sam. They were a secret he would always keep in a special place in his heart. He hadn't thought about them in a very long time.

Rusty reminded him of his Sally. He moved her slightly to ease the pain in his arm. She was helpless, totally dependent on him and he'd vowed to never let anything hurt this child. She was his and he was prepared to protect her with his life. He wanted to cry with her, but it was time to pull it together. There was a lot to be done and not much time left to do it. The first thing was to get everyone on the move because he feared the Beast knew where they were. He felt the Beast was close—too close.

Daniel got a blanket, swaddled Rusty in it, and then settled her into Trevor's lap. Trevor leaned down and nuzzled Rusty's ear speaking quietly to her. She reached up to gently pat his cheek.

Daniel bent down and he kissed Sam. "I love you."

Daniel called a meeting to announce that they were leaving as soon as possible. "Everyone get your backpacks ready. Take only what you can carry. By the day after tomorrow I want to be packed up and on the move." He patiently answered all their questions and tried to calm their fears. The meeting lasted an hour and then the children were off to bed. Within fifteen minutes, Sam managed to get all of them tucked in. Katie was the only one who was uncooperative. She decided to be fussy and refused to sleep. It took Sam another hour to calm the baby before she finally fell into a gentle sleep.

Trevor had asked to speak to Daniel privately. "Keeley, I'll be back."

"Don't be too long."

Trevor carried Rusty with him. He limped over to the fireplace and sat down. Daniel eased into the chair across from Trevor's without saying a word. He watched the quiet interplay between his children. Trevor held Rusty with a tenderness reserved only for her. He used the gentle tactics he used on Bentley when he needed to quiet the big horse. Speaking softly, he whispered words meant only for her. She responded with a sigh and slipped her thumb into her mouth before rolling her little body toward him.

Trevor looked up at Daniel and smiled. "I'm getting almost as good as you at this. I hope to one day do this for my child, but if I can't, I trust you'll take my place."

Daniel was instantly alert. He felt deep concern over Trevor's blatant statement and it made him cold inside. *Why does he think he won't be holding his child?* The thought was disturbing. He thought he'd made it clear to Trevor that he was recovering nicely. Trevor took a deep breath, looked down at Rusty and tightened his grip.

"What's bothering you, Trevor?"

"Do you think the Beast knows where we are?"

"I think the wolves were from him, that's why I don't want to wait any longer. You were right when you said we should leave. We don't know what will be coming for us next. We were fortunate that only Robert was slightly injured."

"How are we going to do it? I can't even walk and Elliot isn't in much better shape than I am."

"We'll manage," Daniel said mildly.

"I've given it a lot of thought. You have to leave me behind. When I'm better I'll—"

Daniel was on his feet in a flash, towering over Trevor. "STOP RIGHT THERE!" His eyes flashed with the hot anger that was coursing through him. "No one stays behind. It's not open for discussion. You're coming with us if I have to carry you."

"Doc, listen to me."

"NO! You listen to me!" Daniel leaned over the chair, one hand on each side of Trevor. "I will *not* leave you behind. It would be a death sentence—or worse. We all go and if it takes a few more days, weeks, or years, I don't care. That's the way it is. I will not leave you or anyone else behind."

Rusty looked up at Daniel with tears in her eyes. "Daddy, don't yell at Trevor."

Daniel softened immediately and looked at the little girl. He wiped her tears with his big hand. "Baby, I'm not yelling at Trevor. I'm just telling him how much I love him." He knelt down and kissed her. "I'm glad you're back with us. Did you have a good nap?"

Tears welled up in her eyes. "I wanted to tell you something, but I can't 'member it now."

"It's okay, Buppy. We'll think about it tomorrow."

Rusty grinned. "Hey, Trevor."

Trevor leaned down and kissed her nose. "Okay, Doc, you win as usual."

Daniel took Rusty and leaned her against his shoulder. She yawned and settled in, draping her arms around his neck. He watched as Trevor struggled to get out of the chair. He closed his eyes and let out a low grunt before he made it to his feet.

"Guess what, son?" Daniel said casually.

"What?" Trevor asked cautiously. He didn't like the grin that accompanied Daniel's question.

"We're going to put Rusty to bed."

"Can I sleep with you?"

"I would be honored," Daniel replied and Rusty heaved a little sigh of relief.

"And for your bedtime pleasure, Trevor, I have a little medication."

Trevor raised an eyebrow. "Needle?"

"Needles," Daniel agreed.

"Swell, I was beginning to miss them."

# 31

The next day was hectic. There were more kids to move this time and more things to consider. This move was going to take longer and would be more difficult. When Trevor was on his feet too long, his pain forced him to stop. It made him angry, which concerned Daniel.

Elliott had a two-fold problem. He still had discomfort from the head wound and he had not recovered from his last encounter with the Beast's monsters. He was having nightmares again.

Travis had his stitches out and Daniel put an ace bandage on his arm for support. Robert's wolf bite was healing nicely, but he also was experiencing some lingering pain. They had two pregnant women and an uncooperative cat. They were not in the best shape to be taking on this move.

Sam managed to organize all the children and supervise their progress. She made sure they packed only necessary items while Daniel gathered the medications and medical supplies. Bentley would carry as much as possible along with his passengers.

That night, Daniel, Trevor, Robert, George, and Elliott sat at the big dining room table. Trevor took out one of his many maps and laid it out the table. "I only got this far," he said, pointing to the map. "There are enough houses and barns along the way for shelter at night, so that's one less worry. Elliott went the rest of the way and found the new place. You're on, little brother."

Just as Elliott was about to show them the way, Billy walked in. Elliott didn't know why, but a chill went through him and he stopped his finger in mid-air. He didn't say a word.

"What's wrong?" George asked.

Elliott shrugged. "I need a minute to remember. It's not right in my mind."

"Hurry up, you baby," George teased.

Elliott immediately saw red and jumped up, hitting George with a body slam. He realized his mistake and curled into a ball, pain lighting up his head.

"Damn it!" Daniel roared.

Elliott couldn't move. The pain shot through his head in waves, bringing tears to his eyes. Daniel reached for him and gently rolled him onto his back. "Lie still and don't try to move. If you do, I'll have George sit on you."

George looked like he wanted to cry. "Elliott, I'm sorry."

Elliott ignored his brother and pulled Daniel down to him. "Billy!"

Daniel looked up at Billy who looked bored by all that was going on. He spoke quietly to Elliott as he examined him. "You need to get a handle on your temper, son, we've talked about this."

"Let me up, I'm okay. The jolt just hurt some."

"You're far from okay. You need more time to heal and unfortunately we can't give you that time. I want you to be in the best shape you can be for the move tomorrow."

Elliott leaned back and for once did just what he was told to do. Daniel picked him up and escorted him to his bed.

"Now, you listen carefully to me. You are to stay in this bed all night and no wandering around. In the morning we'll see if you're okay to travel."

"I will be."

"I'll decide that. Now, stay put!"

"Don't trust Billy."

Daniel sat down on the bed. "Why? What's the problem between you and Billy?"

"There's something wrong about him. That's why I didn't say where the new place is. He's a coward and I don't trust him."

"Tell me where we're going."

Elliott gave Daniel a detailed description of the new location and how to get there. He had studied the land and went over it many times before inserting it as a memory.

"Don't write it down. Don't tell anyone but Trevor."

"You get some rest and stop fighting with George. If you feel worse, come tell me."

"Yeah, I know. Night, Doc."

Daniel went back to the dining room and was bombarded with questions. "Relax, Elliott's fine. I just want him to get some rest. George, go sit with him. He needs you."

"Me? All he ever does is jump on me."

"If you would stop calling him a baby, he wouldn't," Trevor said softly. "He hates that."

"Guess I'll have to knock that off."

"What now?" Robert asked.

"Hopefully, we leave tomorrow as scheduled. Everyone, go get a good night's rest. Trevor, you wait. We have few things to discuss."

"Aw, Doc, not more needles?"

As the boys filed past Trevor, they laughed at his dread of having to deal with Daniel. He waited until they were all out of earshot.

"Honest, Doc, I'm really getting tired of those damn needles."

"Forget the injections for now. Elliott is leery of Billy—almost afraid of him. He doesn't trust the air the kid breaths."

"He never said anything to me."

"Elliott can't say exactly what bothers him about Billy. What's your impression? Do you think he's as dangerous as Elliott does?"

"I never thought much about him. He's different... quirky...standoffish. He doesn't really mix with the rest of us. Now, that I think of it, he's kind of weird.

"Weird how?"

"Like Ethan weird, maybe. He never contributes and seems to be constantly watching everyone. Doc, what if Billy is another Ethan?"

Robert shook his head. "The Beast has searchers out there looking for your family. He infiltrates them everywhere. Billy was in the camp with us for about three months, but that doesn't mean he's..." He hesitated for a moment, thinking about what he'd just said. "There's always a possibility he could be one of them. Elliott could be right about him."

Rusty wandered in with her thumb securely in place. She leaned against the doorway and let her body slide down to the floor. Trevor pointed to her. "We've got company."

"Come here, Rusty."

Rusty immediately went and crawled into Daniel's lap. "Daddy, I don't. . ." Suddenly, she froze. Daniel followed her line of sight.

Billy had walked into the room. He was smiling directly at the little girl. He moved closer. "Just thought I'd check to see if there's any way I can help."

Rusty tried to melt into Daniel. She leaned in closer, while never taking her eyes off of Billy, glaring at him.

"I think were done for tonight and it's time to say good night." Daniel turned to Trevor. "Do you need help?"

"I'm fine." Trevor got up carefully and limped over to Rusty. He gently put his hand on her. "Night, baby girl."

Rusty turned back toward Daniel's chest. He lifted her to his shoulder. She whispered. "Billy's bad." Daniel carried her into the bedroom and placed her on the bed.

"What just happened out there?"

"Billy's brought the red-eyed wolves in to eat us."

"Why do you think he did that?"

"He has a red eye, Daddy. I think Spot seen it. You should get Trevor to shoot him dead."

Daniel gathered Rusty to him and wondered if this is where the new world had brought them. A five year-old child thought about eliminating another child because she believed him to be evil. Daniel looked at this sweet child and had no doubt that this was exactly what she thought. Her way of explaining evil was by saying that Billy was a bad boy. He didn't know if Billy was actually of the Beast, but it was clear that Rusty believed it and Elliott probably thought it.

Rusty had been right before about the evil that lurked among them. Elliott was leery of Billy and Trevor thought he was weird. "Rusty, I want you to stay away from Billy."

"What if he won't stay away from me?"

Daniel kissed her on the nose. "Then you come and tell me and if you can't find me, find Trevor."

"Okay. When we get a new home, will it be time for Keeley to have my new brother?"

"I don't think it's going to be too much longer, but what if your new brother is a sister?"

"That would be okay 'cause Sam said she's gonna get me a new brother too."

"It could also be another sister."

"But, Daddy, I have my Katie. It's just gotta be a brother. Maybe Sam could get a brother and a sister."

Daniel shook his head. "I think one at a time is enough. We don't really have a choice and you'll have to keep what you get."

Rusty thought about that for awhile and finally agreed. "Okay, but it's gonna be a brother."

Daniel covered Rusty and went to change. He thought about Billy. They'd discovered Ethan was of the Beast when he did a blood test on him. Ethan's blood showed a strange substance that turned out to be dust particles from the dead. He had infiltrated the family and done a lot of harm. In the end, Trevor had been the one to destroy him. He made his decision. He would test each child's blood again to see if anyone tested differently. There were several new children with them now and he needed to be sure of all of them. If any of them tested with dust particles in their blood, they would be destroyed. The very thought made him feel uneasy.

# 32

When it was time to leave, Sam looked at the house with tears in her eyes. She hated having to move constantly. She'd gotten comfortable here. She felt warm and safe.

"Don't cry, honey," Daniel said as he wrapped her into his arms. "We'll have another home soon." He let his hand slide to her belly as he pulled her close.

"Do you know how hot you are?" Sam giggled softly.

"You're still a hussy, ma'am. Pregnancy seems to bring it out in you." Daniel took her hand in his and gently tugged. "Come on, I need your help to convince Elliott he has to ride on Bentley."

It took another hour before everything was packed and they were ready to leave. Trevor, Elliott, Keeley, Taylor, and Rusty, were on top of Bentley's back with Baby Katie secured in Trevor's arms. The big horse also carried most of their supplies. George, Travis, and Harlan walked along the left side of the horse. Robert, Billy, and Tommy were in back with Billy following slightly behind all of them. Jamie, Emma, and Brady walked hand-in-hand, talking about how they would decorate their new bedrooms. Daniel and Sam walked ahead, leading the big horse. Progress the first day was extremely slow and it seemed they'd gone only a few miles before twilight came. They came upon a forlorn-looking barn with red paint peeling off most of it.

"Hold on. I need to check it out," Trevor called from on top of Bentley.

Daniel turned and glared at Trevor. "You need to stay right where you are."

"I'll go, bro," Elliott said and prepared to jump down.

Daniel nailed Elliott with a stare. "You also stay put."

"Relax, I'll go check it out," George said. He stepped up and put his hand on Elliott's leg. "You stay here and rest, bro."

"I'll cover your back," Robert said quietly. "Let's get it done."

"Robert. . ." Daniel started, but was interrupted immediately.

"My arm's fine and George needs back up."

The two boys started off down the hill. Trevor had been cradling Katie in his arms. She started to cry and he rocked her slightly, but she wasn't satisfied. He looked helplessly at Sam who laughed at his distress. "Do all females make you uncomfortable? Hand her down to me. What she wants, you can't provide."

Sam held up her hands to take Katie. "You're hungry, aren't you, baby?" she said, cuddling the baby.

Sam got comfortable under a large tree. She kissed the baby before offering her breast. Katie was hungry and immediately latched on and started to suckle.

"Easy there, sweetheart. Don't bite."

Trevor watched Sam rubbing Katie's back while she spoke softly to her. He realized he'd never known his mother, nor had he ever had a mother's love before he met Sam. His emotional response struck him hard. Until that moment, he hadn't realized how much he truly loved Sam. He had put his life on the line to save her from Spencer when he attacked her and proclaimed she was his own, but this was different. Tears welled up in his eyes as he thought of Sam's bond of closeness with Katie and how beautiful it was.

"Trevor?"

"What?" Trevor snapped and looked down at Daniel standing beside him. He'd been watching Trevor as he watched Sam. "What's wrong?"

Trevor was unable to answer. He would never admit that he was moved to tears by watching Sam with Katie. He could never tell Daniel because he wasn't sure he could even explain it, so he lied.

"Just a twinge," he said to cover the unwanted emotional feelings.

"Honey, are you in pain?" Keeley asked anxiously.

"I'm fine, darlin'. It's not that bad," he lied again keeping his eyes closed so he didn't have to face them.

"It's okay." Daniel said quietly.

George and Robert returned to say the barn was clean. They moved the big horse into the barn. He stood quietly as Daniel helped everyone down. Trevor insisted he could get down alone.

Daniel looked up at him in disgust. "Don't be stubborn," and helped ease him off. Trevor grimaced with the pain that seared through his leg when he touched the ground.

"I don't need any help, Doc."

"I know, but I do and you're it. Lean against me, tough guy and I'll need to take care of the pain you don't think you have as soon as we get settled."

Trevor was exhausted and actually glad for Daniel's help. He favored his sore leg and when Daniel helped him lay down, he almost moaned with the relief.

"How do you know?"

Daniel grinned. "I'm magic. I'll be back."

"Swell, I can hardly wait."

Daniel went to check on Elliott. The boy gripped his rifle securely to his side. "I'm good, Doc."

"Only good dreams." He continued his rounds and found most of the children sitting together talking quietly. Several had already found spots to settle in for the night. He made his way back to check on Trevor and Keeley. Keeley complained of back pain after the long ride, but otherwise said she felt fine. Trevor flinched when Daniel touched his leg.

"Keeley, would you please go get my bag. It's over by Sam."
Keeley immediately left to retrieve the bag and Daniel returned his
attention to Trevor. He regarded the boy mildly.

"Doc, don't look at me like that."

"How bad?"

Trevor looked frustrated. "I hurt some."

"That's a start. You should never lie to your physician. What
else?"

"I don't want to talk to you about it."

Daniel eased down next to Trevor. "Anytime you want to
come up with a better answer, I'm here. Do you really think I'll
accept that answer? What's eating at you?"

"I don't want to talk about it."

"You can't run from me. Your leg won't let you and I'm not
leaving until you tell me what's bothering you."

Trevor looked carefully at Daniel before he finally spoke.
His voice cracked with emotion and he looked down at his hands.
"I feel like something's going to happen to Sam. It won't let go of
me."

"Sam's fine. I won't let anything happen to her."

"I'm afraid for her." Trevor shutter. "Fear doesn't come
easy to me, but I look at her and feel it. I can feel it creeping right
into me. I can't explain it any other way."

Daniel took Trevor into his arms and held him close. He was
surprised by his reaction. He was trembling. This kid was so
tough he often forgot that he'd been hurt badly in so many ways,
both physically and mentally. The Beast had entered his mind and
he hadn't completely recovered from that invasion.

Trevor's next words were choked. He loved and trusted
Daniel, it was time to tell all of it, but he found it hard to speak.
He had seen the horror of the Beast in both his waking life and in
his dreams. It was always there and the Beast was close to them.
It wanted to invade what little peace they had.

"Doc. . . Daniel," Trevor stammered. "The Beast is close and he'll never stop searching for us. You need to believe that down to the core of your soul. He's after all of us—you, me, and Sam. The only reason he isn't after Keeley is because he probably doesn't know about her. It wants us and our children." Trevor pulled back from Daniel. "Can't you feel it? Don't you know it's all around us? You need to trust me on this. Deep in my heart, I know it's true." Trevor choked back a tear. "Daniel, he's going to win. There are too few of us."

"I know what Robert told us, but. . ."

Trevor interrupted. "I can feel him. This evil is walking our way and it's reaching out. I know you're the prime target here. Above all else, the Beast wants you. He needs you desperately and he won't stop until he has you. Daniel, I'll stop him if I can. He'll have to go through me and I'll die before the Beast will touch us again. I felt him in me for that brief time and it was like a dirty, destructive disease. It wants to enslave us. The camps are nothing compared to what it will do to our souls."

Keeley returned with Daniel's bag and Trevor immediately stopped talking. He shook his head. He didn't want Keeley to be burdened with what he knew about the Beast. He wiped his eyes roughly with his hands and tried to smile at her, but she knew that something was terribly wrong.

"What's wrong?"

Daniel busied himself with his medical bag and let Trevor explain. He kept reassuring her that he was fine and that the Doc was overreacting.

Keeley gave him a no-nonsense look. "Trevor!"

"Darlin', I'm just hurtin'…nothing for you to worry about. You know how much Doc likes to do the needle thing."

On cue, Daniel smiled and held up a syringe. "Okay son, this will make you feel better."

Keeley looked at the dread in Trevor's face and giggled. She patted his arm. "Be a good boy."

"Hip," Daniel said softly. "And we'll finish our little talk after you get some rest."

"I almost miss it when you don't stick me every day. You win this one."

Trevor knew that he needed the pain medication. His leg was killing him and tomorrow would be an even longer day. Daniel put his hand on Trevor's arm. "Want something to help you sleep?"

"Let's not push it. I'd like to keep the needles down to minimum."

Daniel couldn't help but laugh. "Keeley, if he gives you any trouble, I'll knock him out." He leaned down and patted Trevor on the head. "Rest easy. We're safe for now."

Daniel needed to find Sam, but stopped suddenly, turning back to Trevor. He also felt the Beast was near and they were all targets. A moment of fear gripped him. He tried to shake it off. It wasn't easy to close his mind to the Beast, but he managed to get his fear under control. Panic never got you anywhere.

# 33

Robert threw a few more pieces of wood into the pile. The night had turned considerably cooler and it would feel good to have a fire. He had cleared away all the flammable debris and expertly banked the fire. The children settled around and much to his surprise, they were telling ghost stories.

Daniel leaned against the stall, closed his eyes, and listened to them talk. He enjoyed the kids' conversations about Halloweens past. It brought a smile to his face. When he opened his eyes, he caught a figure out of the corner of his eye. Sam was sitting against the wall across from him. At first he couldn't tell what she was struggling with, but then realized it was the glucose monitor. She'd had a sugar problem with Katie's pregnancy and he had insisted she keep a record of her levels with this pregnancy. She was going into her fourth month and he needed to be prepared if there was a problem. He watched as she became more frustrated. She was looking at the small meter as if it was a coiled snake. She didn't move, just stared down at it and then her hands started to shake as she dropped the meter and covered her face with her hands as tears flooded her eyes.

Daniel had seen enough and went over to her, his large frame overshadowing her small one. Kneeling down, he took her hands in his. "What's the problem, sweetheart?"

Sam shook her head and didn't answer. Daniel lowered himself down next to her and took her hand in his. The day had been a tough one for all of them. He gently turned his face toward his and gazed into her eyes. "Have I told you lately how much I love you?"

She closed her eyes. A tear slipped down her cheek. He was trying to figure out what was stressing her so much. She always attacked anything that happened with calm strength, but now she seemed shattered. He sat with her for a long time, saying nothing. Gently, he kissed her. They were all tired and everyone's stress level was up, including his.

Keeley came over and asked if she could do anything. Daniel raised an eyebrow and tilted his head to look down at Sam.

Keeley knelt down holding her large stomach. "Is Sam alright?"

"She will be. She's tired and I think things just got a little too much for her tonight."

Daniel looked carefully at Keeley. She was going into her seventh month and normally a rock, but already this trip had not been easy for her and they had just started. It wasn't fair dragging a seven month pregnant woman across this rugged terrain. "Are you okay?"

"Just a little worried."

"About?"

"Trevor. He seems like he's in a lot of pain, but you know him, he won't tell you until he can't stand it. Is his leg really healing?"

"His leg will heal, but it was a bad wound and neglected for far too long, so now it will take longer to heal completely. Being jostled around on Bentley all day long isn't helping. Don't worry, sweetheart, I can give him more medicine to help the pain. How about you? How's your back?"

"My back's okay, just sore. Bentley's backbone isn't the most comfortable thing to be sitting on."

"If anything doesn't feel right to you—and I mean *anything*, come see me. Any concerns, big or small, let me know."

"I will."

"Can you do me a big favor?"

"Anything."

"Take Katie tonight. Sam needs a little extra care and. . ."

"Say no more. I'll love having the baby to cuddle up with all night."

"I'll be over in a little while to give Trevor another injection. It'll help him get a good night's sleep."

"Oh, he'll love that. I'll get Rose to help me get all these kids bedded down for the night. You stay with Sam."

Keeley was true to her word. With great efficiency, she and Rose had the kids tucked in for the night. She gathered up Katie, placed her with Trevor, and then took Rusty to him. He wrapped his big arms around the little girls, speaking softly as he cuddled them both. Rusty snuggled next to Katie and in minutes they were both asleep. Keeley had hustled the rest of the kids into barn stalls, making sure they were all away from Daniel and Sam. She wanted them to have their privacy.

Daniel gently laid Sam against a soft bed of hay. "I'll be right back." He took his medical kit and went to the stall Keeley and Trevor were occupying. Trevor eyed the medical kit and looked at Daniel with suspicion. He ignored him and went to Keeley. He took her hand and felt for her pulse. She smiled at Daniel.

"You know," she said casually, "I never knew until recently that you were actually checking me out when you held my hand."

"Watch him, Darlin', he's sneaky. Watch your butt."

Daniel glanced over at Trevor. He felt a cold dread wash over him. The Doc was up to something. Keeley leaned over and kissed Daniel's cheek. "Love you, Doc."

"Thank you," he said softly and put his hand on her belly. He was rewarded with a kick. "He's jumping around."

Daniel turned to the sleeping little girls. Katie's mouth was open as she slept peacefully. Rusty was restless and jerked in her sleep. Trevor grinned. "I'll hold her tonight. Make sure she feels safe. She doesn't seem to rest much. She cries a lot in her sleep."

Daniel put his hand on Rusty's back and gently rubbed in a circular motion. She quickly became quiet at his touch. Trevor smiled; he loved how Doc could do that. "If she has problems, have Keeley come get me. And now, Mr. Trevor Scott…"

Trevor immediately lost his smile. "I'm fine. The shot worked. I'm just a little tired."

"I'm going to make sure you have a nice restful night," Daniel said as he took a syringe from his medical bag and inserted the needle tip into a bottle of clear liquid.

"Good God, Doc. I already feel like a pin cushion."

Daniel grinned inwardly. He enjoyed the banter between himself and Trevor. He knew the injections didn't hurt, but Trevor had the same reaction each time. The needles humbled him. He hated the whole idea of the injections. He resolved that when he had time he would work on him and find out why a simple needle disturbed him so much. There had to be a reason.

"Needles! Always needles with you," Trevor complained. "If the world was still alive, I swear you would have the majority in needle stocks."

Daniel couldn't help himself, he laughed. "Trevor, you and I are going to have to explore this problem you have with needles, but for now, turn over. I want to get this antibiotic in."

"I'm fine. Go away."

Daniel decided to let him protest for a few more minutes. He winked at Keeley who was doing her best to keep a straight face.

"If you're fine, a little injection won't bother you."

Trevor sputtered and threw up his hands. "Damn it."

"You can't win."

"I never win with you," Trevor grumbled. He actually needed the relief the pain meds gave him and he understood the need for antibiotics, but he'd never admit it. Daniel took out a second syringe and filled it with a sedative. Trevor needed as much rest as possible if he was going to be able to continue tomorrow. He injected the pain medicine in his hip and Trevor moved to buckle his pants.

"Not yet. Hold still, I have another injection for you."

"What?"

"Hold still and relax, tough guy, you can handle this."

Daniel injected the sedative and gave Trevor a little pat on the butt. He reached over to feel his forehead. He was still warm. The infection was still with him.

Daniel debated if he should call a halt and have them hold up for a few days. Trevor needed the rest and time off his leg, Keeley could also use a rest, and he was worried about Sam, but they also needed to put miles behind them.

"Just what are you pouring into me?" Trevor growled at Daniel.

"Better you don't know."

"Oh, that's just great . . . and reassuring."

Daniel winked at Keeley before bending over to plant a kiss on Trevor's forehead. "Good night, son. Sleep tight."

"Gee thanks, Dad."

"Take care of our babies."

Trevor sobered and turned serious. "Absolutely. I'll keep my eye on all the babies around here."

Daniel returned to find Sam sitting against the back wall of their stall. "How are you feeling?"

"I'm okay now. Where's Katie?"

"Trevor and Keeley are doing Mommy and Daddy duty. Sure you're okay?"

She shrugged her shoulders. "Yes. Pregnant. It makes me little nuts sometimes."

Daniel put his arm around her and gave her a quick kiss. "Let me do the test for you." He took her hand. She didn't resist his offer and sat back, closing her eyes.

Daniel placed the small needle against her finger. He used the meter to determine her sugar level. It was a little high, but nothing to get excited about. He could feel her tension.

Daniel covered her mouth with his and gave her a long, deep kiss. She responded eagerly. He slowly and gently began undressing her and then took off his clothes and covered her with his body. He pulled blankets over them as he gently moved her into position. He gently entered and pulled her closer, remaining deep in her, but not moving as he held her tight. Sam responded quickly and Daniel started to move, pushing gently against her, letting her feel every inch of him as he moved her in a rocking motion. Deliberately, he continued to soothe her with his body until she completely relaxed under him. She clung tightly to him, felt a warm comforting feeling flood throughout her body in waves of pure pleasure. As they made love Daniel controlled every move, giving her every pleasure while slowly rocking her. He wanted to prolong her pleasure, so he continued to softly thrust, gently making love to her entire body.

Sam let out a little cry as her emotions were finally played out. He stayed inside of her, hardly moving, but making sure she was aware of him until he heard her soft breathing as she slipped into a deep sleep beneath him. Very gently, he withdrew and placed another blanket over her. He kissed her and pulled her into his embrace. He slid his hand up to Sam's belly, very aware of the child growing there—his child.

# 34

Daniel woke to a strange noise. It wasn't very loud, but one that woke him from a sound sleep. He listened intently as the noise grew slightly louder. It was coming from the north end of the building. He didn't want to wake Sam, so he carefully slipped his arm from around her waist. He quickly pulled on his jeans and boots, and then his shirt. He went to the front of the barn where George was sitting against the door, facing him. He leaned down and looked into the boy's face.

"I'm awake, Doc. I heard it, but I don't know what it is. Been listening for awhile," George whispered. "It seems distant and it's coming from over in that direction."

George was pointing to the north end of the building. It was still dark outside. There was no moonlight or starlight. They sat together and waited for a few minutes before Daniel decided it was time to wake the others. He touched Elliott's arm.

"I smell them," Elliott said softly. "I'll wake the others."

Daniel nodded at him as Elliott handed him his rifle. He crept over to where Robert slept with Rose. Elliott continued to make the rounds waking Tommy, Trevor, Travis, and Harlan. The boys knew enough not to ask questions and instantly went for their weapons. Seconds later the Neon Monsters broke into the barn.

The neon's green glow was brilliant and blinding as their lights flooded the barn. They stood almost seven feet tall and appeared man-like. They shimmered with bodies that had no distinguishing features except the familiar red eye/brown eye. They had no nose, no mouth or chin. There was nothing resembling a face. The long body cavity shifted constantly with a fluid green liquid. The arms hung down close to the ground. There were no legs, only one tree trunk-type extender that moved them along in a gilding fashion. They were slow and graceful in their movements.

The first victim to go down was Daniel. One of the neon Green Glow monsters turned on him and extended its arm. He instantly fell to the ground in a heap. He never got off a shot. There had been no time to react.

Elliott screamed and raised his rifle, hitting the Green Glow in its red eye. It shuddered once and then its body blinked on and off, shimmered in and out, and then flopped to the ground, dissolving into a pool of green/yellow watery gel before it just disappeared.

Elliott jumped over to the other side of an unconscious Daniel and knelt down next to him. He swore as he turned to face another Green Glow. "Come on, you bastards."

The Green Glow headed directly for Elliott who raised his rifle and took aim. There were four more Green Glows moving forward, two glided with raised arms throwing puffs of air from their long stubbed hands. Their hands had no fingers—just rounded stubs attached to long arms. Travis, Sam, and George were hit simultaneously by the air puffs and dropped like Daniel had. Elliott looked around for Trevor. He needed help protecting Daniel.

Keeley let out a scream as Trevor raised his rifle to dispatch yet another of the Green Glows. He placed himself between the now unconscious Sam and Keeley who was clutching Katie to her chest. The baby didn't move. Elliott raised his rifle, but the Green Glow sent one of its puffs at him before he could fire. He staggered for a second before falling backwards. He was draped over Daniel as he fell into unconsciousness. Rusty ran forward to kick at the Green Glow that had wrapped its long arm around Daniel's leg. There was anger, fear, and fury in the little girl's face.

"Rusty, come back!" Trevor screamed. She ignored him as he lunged for her. Rusty threw herself onto the Green Glow and sunk her teeth into its tree trunk leg. The monster that held Daniel under one arm reached down and wrapped it other arm around Rusty. She let out a scream of terror.

Trevor knelt down, but couldn't get a clear shot as the Green Glow casually picked up Rusty and threw her away from its leg. She landed hard against the floor and laid still. A small pool of blood oozed from underneath her head.

Trevor quickly took a shot, but missed his mark. The bullet ended up striking the thing in the chest. It had no effect as the bullet was absorbed into its body and spit back out.

Robert was close behind Trevor and moved in for his shot and another Green Glow turned to watery gel. The two remaining Glows turned and locked into the minds of everyone in the barn. All movement stopped when puffs from extended arms reached each child. They fell to the ground. Only Billy remained unaffected. He smiled as his monsters dragged Daniel away. When he looked around at all the unconscious children, a bubble of laughter escaped from his lips.

*It worked! The Beast would have Daniel and soon the rest would also be enslaved. The Beast's Green Glows had done their job well and they had Daniel secured. With him gone, there was no hurry about gathering the others.*

Billy snorted. He would wait for reinforcements and take his time bringing in the rest. He decided to stay with the remaining family and keep track of where they went until they could be gathered and taken back to the camps. He would talk to the Green Glows and have them make contact with the Beast for assistance. If the Beast decided he wanted to end it now, Billy would be informed. The Beast would send help to secure the rest of the family and kill those that couldn't be used.

Billy made the decision to leave Trevor behind for now because he was damaged and would only slow the Green Glows down. He could easily be acquired for breeding at a later date.

Billy snickered and motioned for the Green Glows to leave. He went back into the barn and looked down at Rusty. She had been a major problem and a danger to him because she alone knew what he really was. There was a lot of blood around her head, so maybe she was already dead. He wouldn't have to worry about her anymore. She would be easy enough to get rid of. Billy went over to George and laid down next to him. He didn't want them to suspect him of anything, so it was important that he was discovered unconscious like the rest.

The Green Glows turned and slowly left, dragging unconscious Daniel between them. They were cumbersome creatures and traveled very slow. It was almost dawn when they went into hiding to wait until dark.

Green Glows needed protection from the sun's rays that could destroy them because of their liquid base. They were twelve miles south of the barn when they stopped. The mission was a success and the Beast had already been informed that Daniel had been secured, but that it would many days before they could deliver him to the camp. The Beast commanded that the others not be killed. He wanted all of them.

The distance back to the Beast's camp was a good hundred miles and the Green Glows could only travel at night. The monster carrying Daniel deposited him on the floor in the old house they had entered. The Glows were uneasy about the house. Like the rest of the Beast's creatures, they were used to the dark, damp caves they had dwelled in on their home planet and this place was alien and not part of their essential nature.

Daniel lay in a semi-conscious state, not yet recovered from the effects of the Green Glow puffer. He made no movements that would alert them and kept his eyes closed. He had to wait until his head cleared and he could think straight again.

The Green Glows knew they would have to be careful with this human as he was treasured by the Beast. He was the future. He was the one called "the breeder."

## 35

It was several hours before the effects of the Green Glows started to wear off. George was the first to recover. He had a terrible headache and felt weak, like he'd been sick for a long time. He put his hand up to his throbbing head and suddenly remembered everything. He forced himself to get up and look around. The first thing he did was recover his rifle. The others were in various stages of consciousness and like him were slow to recover from the strange puff clouds that had rendered them unconscious.

George staggered over to the barn door and checked outside to make sure it was clear. They were alone. The Green Glows were nowhere in sight, but neither was Daniel. He knew they'd taken him with them. George went to check on Bentley. The big horse nervously paced in the stall and shied away from him, but otherwise appeared to be unaffected.

"Easy son," he mumbled, lightly stroking the huge head.

George went to Robert, bent down and gently shook him.

"What?" the startled boy yelled, jumping up, ready to fight. He grabbed his head, moaned, and then shook it, trying to clear it.

"It's okay, it's me...George. They're gone. They took Daniel."

"Who took Daniel?" Travis asked. He stood on shaky legs next to an equally shaky Harlan.

Trevor woke with his head pounding and his leg throbbing in rhythm with the pounding of his head. He looked over at Keeley. She was sitting up, but looked unsteady. She had Sam's head resting in her lap and baby Katie next to her. The baby was very still and appeared to be sleeping. Trevor pointed to the baby. "Is Katie okay?"

Keeley shook her head slowly, but didn't answer. Trevor crawled over to her and took her face in his hands. "Keeley? Look at me, Darlin'... Are you alright?"

Tears fell from Keeley's eyes as she put her arms around Trevor's neck. He embraced her and reached over to put his hand gently on Katie's chest. He felt the soft breathing and gently shook the baby. She opened her eyes and looked at him. Trevor lifted the baby and enveloped her in his arms. He hugged her before passing her to Keeley. He looked down at Sam and shook her. She didn't respond. He put his hand on her chest and feeling it rise, he shook her again. "Sam!"

Very slowly, Sam came to. "Are you alright, he asked?"

"Yes, I think so. Where's Katie?"

"She's right here. She's fine," said Keeley, holding the baby up so that Sam could see her.

Sam took her daughter and held her tightly. Suddenly her eyes widened in fear. "Oh God! Where's Daniel?" Panicking, she grabbed Trevor. "Where is he?"

Trevor gathered both Sam and Keeley into his arms and held them. He could barely contain his anger. "They took him, Sam, but I'm going to get him back," he said in a loud whisper. "I promise you, I'll get him back!"

"Trevor! Over here," Elliott yelled.

Trevor looked over and saw Elliott leaning over Rusty's small form. There was a large pool of blood under her head. "Don't move her!" Trevor called as he limped over to them.

"There's a lot of blood." Sam handed Katie back to Keeley and went to help. She moved Rusty's head very carefully to see the extent of her injury. There was a large gash on the back of her head and a huge lump. Her left eye was already turning black. She was unconscious, but alive.

Sam went to work and started to clean the blood away from her cut. "George, bring me Daniel's bag, please."

Trevor shuddered and fell back, sitting down hard. He grabbed a rifle and started to examine it as he kept his eyes trained on Rusty. "How bad?"

"I don't know. She doesn't look so good."

"She's got the kind of hurt the Doc needs to fix," Elliott muttered."

"I'll do what I can," Sam said. "I wish Daniel was here. She's so pale and there's a lot of blood."

Trevor looked down at Rusty and couldn't stop the tears that stung his eyes as he fought to keep his voice from cracking.

"She tried to help Doc."

Trevor gently put his hand on Sam's shoulder. "I'm going to find Daniel. I'll bring him home to you, Sam. You've got my word on it."

Robert came over and knelt down to look at Rusty. "Is she dead?"

"Don't say that!" Trevor said, reaching down to touch Rusty's cheek. "You'll be okay, baby girl. I'm going to get Daddy and he'll fix you right up."

Trevor turned back to Sam and touched side of her face that was bruised and turning black and blue. She'd have a black eye and he noticed there was a large bruise running down her neck. Keeley sat down next to Sam.

Robert glanced at Trevor. "We need to talk. We're in serious trouble here."

Trevor turned to Robert, but didn't answer. His anger showed in his face. Elliott had never seen him like this and took a step back. He'd wait for this to play out.

Trevor needed to think, but his head hurt so bad he was finding it difficult. He grabbed the aspirin bottle he always kept in his pocket and downed four of them. Daniel was gone, taken by those green freaks. He knew nothing would stop him from going

149

after them and it had to be done right now. There was no time to wait. These thoughts were uppermost in his mind because he was sure that Rusty wouldn't survive unless he could bring Daniel home to help her. Elliott was right—she did need Doc's kind of help.

*What if we can't find Daniel? What will happen to him? Will he wind up in the camps, forced to impregnate the women there?* Trevor didn't even want to think about it. *Hell, if they didn't rescue Daniel, their survival was also in question because the Beast would be after them next. The bastard would never give up and because of all their injuries, they were severely handicapped. It would be easy for the Beast to acquire all of them. They needed to go deep and hide.*

Trevor found he was having a hard time standing up on his own and at this rate it would only be a matter of time before they all were enslaved captives. He looked at the disaster around him and decided they needed to get organized and it had to be done fast. He made a quick decision. There was no time to wait or to even discuss it. They couldn't afford to wait even one more hour.

With the help of his rifle, Trevor was able to support his bad leg. He forced himself to a standing position. He ignored Robert's questions and turned to Elliott. "Get Bentley ready, we're going after Daniel."

"Wait!" Robert put his hand on Trevor's shoulder. "You can't. Look at you! Look at the shape you're in. You can hardly walk."

"The hell I can't and who's gonna stop me? Get your fucking hands off me, Robert." Trevor's eyes turned cold with anger. "Elliott!"

"I'm here." The boy stepped up next to Trevor and put his hand on Trevor's arm to support him.

"You okay to do this?"

"Yeah. I'm ready to kick some ass."

"Then get Bentley, bro," Trevor said quietly. "George, I need to talk to you."

"Trevor, listen to me," Robert said. "You're in no shape—"

"STOP!" Trevor yelled. He grabbed the front of Robert's shirt. "You listen to me and listen good. Those bastards came in here and took one of us. Look at Rusty for God's sake," he screamed in Robert's face. "Take a good look at her. Look at what that bastard did to her. I'm going to get Doc back because she needs him. I need him. Hell, we all need him. They already have too much of a head start, so either help me or get the hell out of my way."

Trevor's dark brown eyes flared with his seething anger—anger he no longer concealed or controlled. "George! Emma, get me three sticks. Make them as long as my leg and I'll need something to bind the leg so it will hold me up. Cut strips, or rope, whatever I can use to strap it and make it hold."

"Right away."

"Tommy, Harlan," Trevor bellowed. "You two are going to protect the home front. George is in charge. You guys listen to him—no questions. You got it?"

Tommy and Harlan both shook their heads 'yes" but said nothing.

"Robert," Trevor turned and made a concentrated effort to contain some of his anger. "I'd appreciate it if you'd come with us and keep an eye on Billy for me. I don't trust that little bastard and I can't leave him here, so I'll need someone to watch him. Travis, get your rifle, you're coming with us."

Robert shook his head in disbelief but went to get his rifle.

Trevor softened his voice. "Rose, can I talk to you?"

George and Emma came back carrying four large sticks to brace Trevor's leg. "You'll need to sit down so I can work on this support, said George."

While George worked, Trevor spoke quietly to Rose. "I need you to be strong, Rose. I hate putting all this on you, but Sam's hurt and she's pregnant. Keeley's seven months pregnant too, so you'll have to keep everything going and keep the little ones safe. Emma, Jamie, and Brady will help you, but I need to know that you're okay with this."

Rose looked around at the shambles the Green Glow monsters had left behind. Spot wandered over and jumped into Trevor's lap. He put his hand lightly on the cat's head, wondering where he'd been all this time.

"You don't need to worry, Trevor, I'll take care of everything here."

Trevor winched as George tightened the straps around his leg, then let out a long breath as the pain eased.

Rose glanced at Robert. "Please don't let anything happen to Bobby. I...I... love him so much. And I think you should know— I'm pregnant too."

Trevor reached up and gently touched Rose's cheek. "Does he know, Darlin'?"

"No, I haven't told anyone except you. Just a couple of months."

"We'll all come back. You have my word on it and when we do, Daniel will be with us. Would you get me his medical bag, please?"

Trevor watched Rose walk away. She was special and Robert was lucky to have her. "Sam, how's Rusty?"

Spot jumped from Trevor's lap and walked over to Rusty. He positioned his body next to her.

"She's unconscious and has a large lump on the back of her head where she hit the floor. I've got the bleeding stopped, but other than that, I just don't know."

Sam's hands moved nervously. Trevor covered her small hands with his. "And you, Sam? Are you alright?"

"I'll be alright. Bring Daniel back to me...please."

Trevor touched the bruise on her temple and let his hand slide down her face. The entire left side was going to be bruised. She also had a split lip. He felt an ache in his heart. "Don't you worry, that little kid is tough and I promise you that I'll bring Daniel back to you."

He put his hand gently on Rusty's head. Sam cried as she hugged Trevor. He wrapped his arms around her and kissed her forehead. "Don't worry, I'll get us all home safe."

Rose returned with Daniel's medical bag and placed it next to Sam.

Trevor went through the bag and found the pain medication he was searching for. He took a syringe out and filled it to the mark he had seen Daniel do so many times before. He held up the syringe. "Sam, will you do the honors?"

She smiled and pointed to his hip. Trevor sighed as he unbuckled his belt. "We aren't going to tell Doc that I actually asked for this. Sam, fill as many syringes as you can. I may need them before I'm through," he said quietly. "George, I need to talk to you."

George knelt down and checked the splint he'd made. He looked up at Trevor and shrugged. "That's about as good as I can make it. It's tight and should hold you up. How does it feel?"

Trevor looked at George's handy work. "It's good."

"What can I do?"

"You keep everyone safe. I figure y'all will be safe here for awhile, but if we're not back in two days, you'll need to get the hell out of here. I don't know how you're going to do it. I reckon you'll have to carry them if there's no other way. You're in charge and it's up to you to keep our family safe. I hate it that I have to take Bentley, but I'll never make it otherwise. Don't wait too long to leave. Take care of our girls." Trevor lowered his voice. "If we don't make it back, it's all up to you, bro. You're the next oldest. Sam, Keeley, and Rose are all pregnant. Make sure nothing happens to them."

George didn't question anything. He took a deep breath. "You know I'll protect them with my life. Y'all hurry and come back to us. Take care of my little brother."

Sam appeared with the filled syringes that she'd wrapped in a cloth. She handed them and a small bottle to Trevor. "I found some antibiotics. Make sure you take them."

"I'll never stop, Sam. I'll never give up until I find him."

"I love you. Make sure you all come home safe to me."

Keeley went to Trevor and sat next to him. He embraced her and put his hand on her belly. "Take care of our little one," he said, kissing her cheek, her forehead, and then her mouth. "I love you so much it hurts."

"You make sure that you get yourself back here to me in one piece. Our baby needs his father."

Trevor moved away from her and smiled. "Don't I always come home to you?"

Keeley didn't answer. She grabbed him and pulled him to her. "I love you. Don't go."

"I have to."

"I know."

Emma, Brady and Jamie all went to Trevor; each little girl hugged him and told him to be careful. Brady and Jamie went to help George, but Emma stayed behind and took Trevor's big hand in her small one. She fought back her tears.

"I'm counting on you to bring Daniel home."

"When I come back, he'll be with me."

"Don't you get hurt no more. Is your leg going to make it?"

"I'll make it."

Trevor pulled Emma onto his lap and held her. They'd been through so much together and he knew she was hurting. Flashes came to his mind of the tortures she'd endured with a boy of the Beast—a boy called Ethan. He had killed Ethan, but it had been Daniel who really saved Emma. If they lost him, Emma would suffer in a way worse than Sam.

Before they left there were more hugs all around. Keeley, Sam and Rose cried. Sam pulled Trevor to her again and told him to be careful. He held on to her and whispered in her ear. "My word, Sam, I'll never stop."

Trevor embraced Keeley, reassuring her for the tenth time as he kissed her goodbye. "Don't cry. As soon as I get Daniel I'll be running back to you."

From the barn door Trevor glanced over at Rusty. It filled him with anger and rage and he fought to control it. "Yeah, I'll be back. We all will. Let's go, boys. "Let's get Doc back from those bastards."

Trevor and Elliott rode Bentley with Robert, Billy, and Travis walking behind. The trail was easy to follow as it was actually very clear. Rusty had taken a good bite out of the tree trunk leg of the Green Glow, which left them a clear trail of green gel water behind. They had left at mid-afternoon, only a few hours were left until dark. Billy had tried to convince them to wait until morning. Trevor turned his back on him in disgust.

George watched until he could no longer see them before he turned back to the others. "Tommy, Harlan I need to talk to y'all."

The three boys hovered together making plans for their upcoming move. George feared they might not have time later. He didn't know if they could wait even two days.

# 36

It was full dark when Elliott nudged Trevor awake. "We need to stop. There's a building over there about two hundred feet to the north."

"I'm not stopping," Trevor answered solemnly and reseated himself on Bentley.

Elliott knew it was too dangerous to continue so he tried another approach. "You wanna lose Bentley? He can't see in the dark, bro. For crap sakes, I can barely see. We have to stop."

Trevor turned half way around and then quietly agreed. "You're right. Let's stop."

Tommy and Robert secured the building. It was small and they all barely fit. Trevor positioned Bentley in the middle. "Hope the big guy doesn't step on us," Elliott said, looking up at the giant horse. "That would make a mess with his big feet."

Trevor held on to Bentley's big neck and patted him. He thanked him for carrying them this far. He spoke quietly to Bentley for a few more minutes before easing down to the floor with a groan.

"You okay, bro?"

"I'm fine. Those damn things are probably on the move right now and getting farther away. Damn it to hell!"

Trevor slammed his fist down on his leg in anger and immediately regretted the action as pain shot through him.

"Why don't you take another shot?" Robert suggested.

"I'll need it more tomorrow," Trevor grimaced. "Let's try to get some sleep. We'll leave at first light."

Trevor placed himself in front of the door. He would stay there tonight just in case something nasty happened along and decided to try and eat them. Billy smirked at him before going to the corner of the building where he turned his back on them. Robert and Travis were both asleep on Bentley's left side, huddled together for warmth.

Elliott approached from the right and made enough noise so Trevor wouldn't get nervous and accidentally shoot him. He hunkered down and looked into Trevor's face.

"You hurtin'?"

Trevor grunted. "Yeah, a lot."

Elliott eased down, setting his rifle next to him. "Can I help somehow? Maybe if we raised your leg?"

"Naw. Just need to try and not move around a lot. How about you? How's your head? I can share one of Doc's needles."

"No, I'm okay, just hurts a little. Do you think we'll find Doc soon?"

"They got a good head start on us, but we closed off some of that distance today. Robert said were headed back in the general direction of the camp. We're going to have to pick up the pace 'cause we can't let them get to the camp. I don't think we can fight the Beast on his own ground and win. According to Robert, the camps are over there near the Chappy Mountains, southeast of here."

"How far do you figure it is?"

"I don't know, but the camp doesn't worry me. Right now, we have a bigger problem."

"What bigger problem?"

"They may send reinforcements, so we have to get to Doc fast and strike even faster. We won't be able to fight too many of them, not with just the four of us and limited firepower."

"You don't count Billy?"

"Do you?"

"No. I think Rusty's right about him. If he isn't part of the Beast, he's definitely a rotten son."

"I think he's of the Beast." Trevor lowered his voice to a quiet whisper. "I'm going to have to kill him. I just haven't decided when to do it."

"Reckon I could do it for you."

"If it has to be done, it's me that will do it. You better try and get some sleep, bro. You need your rest."

"I'm okay. I can watch for awhile."

"I'll watch. You get some sleep."

"Okay, but if you decide you want to sleep, call me and I'll take over for you."

Trevor watched Elliott make his way back to the end of the building where he hunkered down next to Bentley. He grinned. "Damn, he's one tough little guy."

# 37

The Green Glows pushed Daniel forward. His arms were secured behind his back and balance was difficult for him. He had neither eaten, nor had anything to drink since his capture. His throat was so dry it was difficult to talk. It was also so dark he had a hard time keeping to the trail and not falling flat on his face.

"Hey," Daniel croaked. "Hey, you assholes. If you want me to keep going, I need some water."

There was no response. The Green Glows just kept moving and pulling him after them. Daniel abruptly stopped and sat down. To his surprise the Green Glows also came to a halt. One of them turned its red eye directly at him.

"Water?" Daniel said again. "You stupid sons of bitches, don't you even understand basic needs? I also need to take a piss."

The Green Glows looked at each other, spoke some gibberish and stood looking at him.

"Great!" He spat at them in anger. "That's just great!"

Daniel felt his mind touched. It was just a light sensation at first, but increased to a seeping invasion. What felt like the point of a needle entered his brain and went deep. He shook his head trying to clear it. He tried to dismiss the feeling of fingers probing and touching the inner parts of his brain. They were seeking, exploring, and investigating. He tried to block them, but felt the probe deepen. He concentrated on water and put everything else out of his mind while he forced himself into an almost hypnotic state. He emptied his mind of all thoughts other than water. After what seemed like a few minutes, Daniel felt a pulling back, as if the needle was extracted leaving him feeling dead. He collapsed right before everything went black.

When Daniel woke, the Green Glows were looking up at the sky. He also looked up and was surprised to see it was getting light. He was confused. *Just minutes ago it was dark. How could it be getting light so soon?* He realized it wasn't minutes that had passed, but hours. *Hours of mind probing? God, what did I reveal? The secret of where the family was going? Robert's plans to go back and destroy the Beast?* Suddenly fear crept through him—the fear that he may have betrayed all of them.

The Green Glow lifted him into its arms. He was repulsed by its touch and tried to pull away, but it was impossible to escape it. He was carried into a building and carelessly dropped on the floor. The second one touched the ropes that bound him and he was freed of them. He looked at them in amazement because the last thing he expected was to be released from his bonds.

Daniel slowly got to his feet. He was unsteady and reached for a chair so he wouldn't fall flat on his face. He turned his back on the Green Glows and staggered into a bathroom. Once he closed the door he relieved himself and then took a long drink from the sink. He went through the medicine cabinet above the sink and found a bottle of aspirin. He shook it open and took out three pills. There was a bottle of antibiotics which he opened and took. *Thank God for better living through chemistry.*

Daniel pocketed both bottles and took off his shirt to inspect the long cut across his chest. He cleaned the wound and steri-stripped the deepest parts before applying a makeshift bandage. He seemed to have free access of the house. He went into a bedroom to check out the closet. There he found men's clothing that looked about the right size, so he stripped off his pants and put on a clean pair of jeans. They were a little big, but he adjusted the belt. Next, he removed his bloody shirt and slipped into a flannel one he found on a hanger.

Quietly, he went over to the bedroom window and opened it, but found that he was blocked from using it as an exit. There was some kind of force, invisible to him, but something that was not allowing him to escape. He tried the window in the bathroom and the back door—same problem. He picked up a chair and threw it against the door in anger. "Son of a bitch!"

It was no wonder those green assholes just stood there like guards at a palace door. He couldn't leave because they'd blocked every exit.

Daniel wandered out of the bedroom and went to find the kitchen. He looked around and began opening cabinets. He took out cans of food and snacked on cold spaghetti, pears, and bottled water.

When he finished eating, he felt better and went back to the bedroom, stretched out on the bed and closed his eyes. He took a deep breath and tried to empty his mind, but thoughts of Sam and his family entered. He longed for them and wanted desperately to be with them. He thought about Trevor and knew that even now he would be on his trail. He'd try to make it easier for him to follow and would leave clues. He might even think of a way to slow these bastards down.

Daniel was tired, his head and chest burned, and he found he could no longer keep his eyes open. As he fell into a light sleep thoughts of Sam, Katie, and his family joined him.

## 38

"Time to move on," Trevor whispered as he shook Elliott. The boy was up instantly. He looked up at Trevor with concern and then alarm.

"You okay? You look kind of green."

Trevor held up a syringe. "I will be as soon as Robert injects this."

Robert raised his eyebrows. "You want me to do it?"

"Yeah, I'd appreciate it. It's kind of hard to reach my own butt."

Robert took the syringe and aimed for his exposed hip. "Probably won't hurt as much here."

"Doc always pushes the plunger and lets some out." Trevor instructed as he watched closely. Robert shook his head and injected the pain medicine.

"Lord Almighty! You're worse at this than Sam was. We need to get Doc back before I need another shot."

The boys left right before dawn to continue their search. Ten minutes later they found where the Green Glows had stopped for the night. Trevor's eyes grew dark. "Robert, help me down."

Trevor stumbled through the house checking for clues and found Daniel's discarded clothes. He hugged them to his body feeling pain surge through him. The clothes were no longer warm, but they smelled of Daniel. Beside the shirt he found a note. It said "southeast." He carefully placed the note in his pocket before going to the porch and following the trail southeast with his eyes. Elliott bent down and saw tracks leading in the direction Daniel indicated.

"They're not even trying to cover their tracks," Elliott said, bending closer to get a better look.

"Probably don't expect anyone to follow," Travis said. "Let's get going."

Robert helped Elliott up onto Bentley's back. He'd walked far enough for one day. "I'll do the tracking."

Trevor eased up behind Elliott and let out a moan.

"Maybe you need to rest. Maybe you can't go on and should stay here," Billy said looking at Robert for confirmation. He shrugged, not looking at Trevor. He knew Trevor wouldn't stop until he had no choice and couldn't go on. He also knew that would be with his last breath of life.

Elliott slid down from Bentley and glared at Billy. "Forget it. We stay together. Trevor goes where I go."

"Elliott," Trevor shuddered as sweat ran down his face. The fever left him cold. "I'm okay, let's get going. We've wasted enough time."

Robert boosted Elliott back up onto Bentley behind Trevor. Travis handed his rifle up to him. Elliott put his arms around Trevor and eased him back slightly offering his support.

"I'm too heavy."

"Then just lean a little. I'll let you know when I need a rest."

Travis called up to Trevor. "I'm going to go ahead some and spot."

"Stay in sight."

"I will, don't worry. I'll holler if I see anything."

They spent the day trailing behind the Green Glows, hoping to close the distance between them. When dusk showed in the sky, Trevor was unwilling to stop. Robert gave Elliott a questioning look and shrugged. They continued on. An hour later Trevor gave in and Robert found a house not far from the road they were traveling on.

Trevor leaned back on the sofa. His head hurt, his leg was beyond hurting, and he felt the fever burning inside him. A tear slipped down his cheek and he quickly wiped it away.

"Maybe we should take the bracing off," Elliott said quietly, "Maybe resting it will help some."

Trevor closed his eyes and nodded. Elliott carefully removed the bindings and took out his knife to cut Trevor's pant leg away. His leg looked swollen, red, and was hot to the touch.

Elliott reached up and lightly touched Trevor's forehead. He was running a fever for sure. He knew that wasn't good. He stood watching Trevor and not knowing what to do to help. "It doesn't look so good—a lot like the last time."

Trevor didn't answer. He kept his eyes closed and let out a deep breath. "It'll be okay."

Trevor had taken all the antibiotics they had and now he was sick with fever. Elliott thought for a minute and came up with an idea. "I'll be right back." He went into the kitchen and found a large pot that he filled with water and brought into the front room.

"Robert, make a fire and heat up this water. I'll go find some towels. Travis, keep an eye on Billy," he whispered. "He gets out of line, holler." Travis nodded and went to find Billy.

After the water was heated, Elliott soaked the towels and carefully placed them on Trevor's leg. He shuddered, but remained motionless. The heat felt good on his leg and if the constant throbbing would stop for a little while, he could actually rest.

Robert put his hand on Trevor's forehead. The boys' eyes met briefly and Trevor grunted. "Forget it, Robert. I'll be fine in the morning,"

"He's pretty hot. Got a fever."

Elliott continued to apply the hot compresses to Trevor's leg. "I know, but this should help. Draw out some of the infection. I saw Doc do it."

Travis went into the bathroom and went through all the cabinets. He found several bottles of medicine and brought them into the front room. They all checked them. Robert picked out the antibiotic and gave it to Trevor. He shrugged and downed it, and then chewed three more aspirin.

"Try to sleep," Elliott said as he replaced a hot towel. "I'm fixin to do these hot soaks for awhile longer."

## 39

Trevor felt better the next morning. He downed more antibiotics, several aspirin, and then instructed Elliott to rebind his leg. The swelling had gone down, but the leg was still extremely sensitive. Trevor ignored the pain. He took out the syringe and handed it to Robert.

Robert said nothing as he injected his hip. "You haven't gotten much better and there's only one syringe left."

Trevor looked at his lifeline from pain. "It'll have to be enough. Let's hit the road."

Trevor rode with Elliott behind him. The boy leaned forward to steady him and wrapped his arms around Trevor's waist. "I've got your back," Elliott whispered and tightened his arms. The ride that day seemed endless.

Two hours before dark the boys found the house Daniel was being held in. It was like any other farm house they'd stayed in over the past year—sad and empty, except today was different. Today it had monsters in it.

The boys stayed hidden in a stand of trees, hunkered down into the mud. They were about four hundred feet from the house. Trevor scanned the house and then turned to Robert and Elliott. "It seems that the Green Glows are confident that no one was going to follow them and have stopped for the night," Trevor smiled. "No one following. . . except us."

"I'll shimmy up to the house and have a look, make sure that Daniel's still with them," Travis said impatiently.

"Be careful and be really quiet," Robert cautioned.

"Don't worry. I'll be back before they know I'm even there."

Everyone settled down at the edge of a dense wooded area. Elliott helped Trevor position his leg to keep the pressure off, and dropped down next to him.

"Waiting's a bitch," Elliott whispered. "I'd rather just go in and kill those bastards."

Trevor pulled Elliott to him. "Better to check it out, bro. We don't want them to get the upper hand. You go slow and easy."

Everything went quiet as they waited for Travis to return. Trevor looked up at the sky. It was beginning to turn a light purple pink color with the coming of night. There wasn't a lot of daylight left and if Travis didn't hurry it would be another day of trailing the Green Glows and waiting for another opportunity to strike. They all knew how hard it was to fight at night.

Trevor watched intently and was rewarded when tall grass gently shifted back and forth. Travis appeared to the right of where Trevor and Elliott were laying on the forest's floor. He silently moved into the circle of boys and hunkered down.

"They're in there alright and Daniel's with them."

"Are you sure?" Robert asked.

"I saw him. He's over to the left of the door."

Travis had belly-crawled from the base of the wooded area where they were hidden up to the house. He had silently gone around the back and peered into a window.

"There's two of those Green Glow things standing like statues. Daniel's on the couch between them.

"Is he alright?" Trevor asked, his eyes cold with anger.

"I couldn't tell. He was just laying there, but it looked to me like he was alright. He had his eyes closed and looked like he was sleeping."

"Since daylight bothers the bastards, we go in before dark," Trevor instructed. "They don't move so fast in the light or they'd have been long gone by now. We've got to move while they can't and there isn't much time. They'll be moving out in about twenty minutes."

"Maybe we should wait until they come out at night," Billy injected. "Seems like a better way."

Trevor flashed his rage at Billy. "NO! I'm not waiting any longer. We could lose them. We need to hit them now."

Billy snorted. He wasn't worried at all. He would just have to make the Green Glows aware of the impending attack. All he had to do was find a way to sneak away from the group.

Trevor looked from one boy to another. "We'll need to use a decoy. . ."

"I guess that's me," Travis volunteered. "I'm the fastest. It makes sense." He shrugged and looked back at the farm house. "I'm ready when you are."

Trevor put his hand on Travis's shoulder. "It's dangerous," he said. "They could get to you first."

"I know, but you're hurt. Elliott's too slow right now and Robert, well he's just too big a target." Travis looked over at Billy and back to Trevor. "Billy's not right for the job."

"I guess it's up to you then, bro." Elliott agreed.

"Yeah…me," Travis shuddered.

# 40

George paced in front of the barn door. He felt like ants were crawling through his entire body. That reaction came with the feeling that they weren't safe anymore. Trevor had been gone almost three days and he knew it was time for them to make their move. He went to talk with the others.

"We need to leave. It's time. I've got a really bad feeling crawling all over me and I can't shake it. Trevor and I agreed that we go south from here. He knows how to find us."

Sam looked over at Rusty who lay quietly clutching the teddy bear Daniel had given her. "Rusty can't walk. She's barely conscious."

"I'll carry her," George said. "We need to leave now."

"That could be too jarring for her." Sam shot a glance back at the child. "She has a bad head injury. Moving her could be a mistake."

George looked from Sam to Rusty. Trevor's words rang in his ears. *Take care of our family. You're the next oldest.*

George knelt down in front of Sam and hugged her. "It'll be okay. We'll make a stretcher and move her that way. Tommy, you go and scout ahead. Find a place for tonight, but don't make it too far. Don't go more than a few miles. Be careful and don't take any chances. If anything looks wrong to you, come back here in a hurry—just make sure nothing follows you."

"I'll run like the devil himself is chasing me. I'll be back as soon as I can and I *will* be alone."

"Wait! Take my rifle and give me the gun. Rifle's more accurate for long shots."

Before George let Tommy go, he pulled him into his arms. "Shit, I hate sending you out alone. Be real careful. Don't get hurt."

"I won't. Take care of my sister for me."

Tommy waved as he disappeared through the door. George watched until he disappeared. He had a sinking feeling. He was afraid for all of them.

"I'll gather up everything so we're ready to leave," Rose said.

George went back to Sam. Taylor was sleeping peacefully next to her and Jamie held Katie securely in her lap. Emma sat next to Rusty. George bent down to Rusty. "How's it going?"

Rusty whimpered and closed her eyes. Emma took her hand. She patted her on the back and started talking non-stop to her. "Daddy will be home soon. Trevor went to get him for you. Until then, I'm going to take care of you."

Tommy came back after a few hours. George sighed with relief—the kid was still in one piece. "I found a house about two miles from here."

George and Harlan constructed a stretcher for Rusty and tied her to it so she wouldn't fall off. "Tommy, go help Rose and Sam. Keeley, stay close to me."

George was worried about Keeley. The ground was rough and she was so big with her child he was afraid she'd fall and he knew that would be a disaster. Sam was just starting to show and he didn't want either one of them to carry anything, so he loaded up the stretcher with the few possessions they had left.

"Everyone ready? It's time to move."

Emma and Brady alternated carrying Katie while George and Tommy managed the stretcher. Taylor followed behind Sam, holding onto her. Harlan went ahead and watched everything…and fortunately nothing moved. Their world was silent—a study in stillness.

Harlan was determined that nothing surprised them and remained in front of everyone. The trip was a little easier than George had expected with only one mishap. Sam fell.

Tommy and George eased the stretcher down and George ran to her. Rose was already there, trying to help her up. Sam looked pissed.

"You alright, Sam? What happened?"

"I just got dizzy," Sam replied. "Don't get excited. Just give me a minute."

"You stay put," George ordered. "Tommy, how far is it to the house?"

Tommy came over and hunkered down next to George. "Less than a mile. No more."

"You and Harlan take the rest of the kids to the house. Be careful with Rusty. I'll stay with Sam. Ya'll need to leave Harlan behind to protect the kids and then bring back the stretcher for Sam. We'll carry her rest of the way."

"George, don't be silly," Sam protested. "I can walk." She attempted to get up, but quickly realized she couldn't. Her head was spinning as if she had just gotten off a merry-go-round. George gently put his hand on Sam's shoulder. "Sam, lay back and rest. Get going, Tommy, but leave me a rifle."

Tommy handed over the rifle. "I'll be back as soon as I can."

"I'm fine. I can walk if you help me, said Sam."

George leaned over and looked into Sam's eyes. She looked tired and he knew she'd never make another mile. "You can't walk that far," he insisted. "Doc would kill me if I let anything happen to you and Trevor would gladly help him do it."

At the mention of Daniel, Sam put her head down and started to cry. She'd been trying to be strong, but an overwhelming feeling of dread hit her. She didn't want to think about never seeing him again. Somehow she felt that he was lost to her already.

"Damn, I'm sorry," said George, hunkering down next to her in the tall grass. "Please don't cry. You know Trevor will bring Doc back home."

George put his arms around Sam and leaned her back against him. They were in the same position when Tommy came back with the stretcher. Rose had returned with him. "Don't you look at me like that. She wouldn't stay behind," Tommy said miserably. "I tried."

"You might need my help carrying Sam."

"You're pregnant!" George yelled in frustration. "You can't lift anything. Trevor gave me strict instructions."

"And Trevor has a big mouth," Rose shot back in anger.

"I can walk!" Sam interrupted.

"No!" All three spoke at once."

George, Tommy, and Rose looked at each other and laughed. "Okay," Rose relented. "Let's not fight and I'll help only if it's necessary."

Reluctantly, Sam laid down on the stretcher. George took one end, Tommy took the other. George graciously let Rose carried the rifle.

Tommy groaned. "Glad your light. I'm getting tired of toting this thing."

Sam laughed, but immediately regretted it. Her head was pounding and she felt nausea rise in her throat. "Oh God, Daniel, please be safe," she whispered, trying to hold back her tears.

# 41

The decoy was in place. Travis sat motionless in front of the house waiting for Trevor's signal. Trevor, Robert, and Elliott were positioned so they could get a clean shot at the Green Glows when they came out. Trevor also kept a wary eye on Billy as he said a fast prayer for the plan to work. He was not happy using Billy's help, but they needed to cover all the escape routes and it was necessary. He still didn't trust him, but they'd need everyone to make this work. He hoped he wouldn't regret the decision.

Travis's job was to lure the Green Glows out into the open. If only one came out and not both, Elliott was the backup. He would go through the back and into the house after the remaining one. The rest were going to create as much distraction as possible and try to take the remaining one down. Robert was Elliott's backup because Trevor just couldn't move fast enough. Billy was supposed to cover Travis.

When everything was in place, Trevor took a very deep breath and yelled out the signal. Travis jumped up and began calling out. "Daaaaaaaaaaaniel. Oh, Dannnnnnnnnniel, can you come out to play?" he taunted as he jumped up and down like a lunatic wild child. He continued to wail, rocking and howling at the top of his lungs like an escapee from a mental institution. He bellowed at the top of his lungs until his throat hurt. Travis was playing his role for all it was worth.

The Green Glows instantly came alive inside the house. They faced each other, looked down, and Daniel found himself once again bound tightly. One Green Glow floated toward the door while the other moved slowly behind him.

Daniel struggled against his bonds, but he couldn't budge them. He recognized the voice calling to him and knew that he was no longer alone. He couldn't help himself. He grinned.

The second Green Glow stood over Daniel while the first one crossed the porch toward the wailing child. Travis jumped up and aimed his gun, but the Green Glow was faster and felled him with an air puff extending out of its arm. Robert aimed, shot and missed his target.

Billy crept around to get behind Robert. Silently, he moved closer to ensure his shot before raising the gun at Robert's back. Elliott and Billy pulled their triggers at the same time. Robert fell back and hit the ground hard while Elliott's shot hit Billy in the neck. His body absorbed the bullet briefly and then spit it out. Billy swiftly turned toward Elliott, his hand raised and the gun aimed for Elliot's heart. Billy's red eye glowed.

Billy's red eye burst from his head with what little blood was left in him. Blood spattered across Robert as Billy fell to the ground. In death, Billy's forked tongue fell out and hung in a purple haze. Trevor's shot had been true. Elliott was already moving toward the house. He jumped the banister on the porch. Trevor felt his blood go cold as he turned around as a shadow fell over him. The Green Glow that had immobilized Travis loomed over him. He swung his rifle around and was faster. The red eye burst before it could immobilize him. The monster became watery gel, drenching him as disappeared.

"Damn it! Ick! Slimed by an asshole like that."

Elliott made a quick decision and ran through the front door. He hit hard and fell to the floor as he aimed up at the Green Glow. Elliott wasn't as fast as Trevor. An air puff hit him full in the chest. Elliott lay unconscious at Daniel's feet.

The Green Glow lifted Daniel under one arm and dragged him out the door, heading west. Travis, Robert, and Elliott lay unconscious. Billy was dead. Daniel was sickened by the sight before him. He began to fight, but either the Green Glow didn't notice or it wasn't bothered by the struggling Daniel whose roped hands made everything he tried ineffective.

Trevor watched Daniel struggle to get free of the Green Glow's grasp. "Daniel," he whispered and then ducked his head lower so he couldn't be seen. Tears stung his eyes because he was so happy just to see that Daniel was unharmed.

Trevor was tempted to jump up and shoot at the monster, but he wasn't sure that he could actually get the proper shot at its red eye from this distant. He laid still, waiting for the damn thing to get closer. He was hidden by the trees and the scrub brush he'd buried himself in, cautioning himself to be patient as he watched Daniel continue his struggle. He could hear him swearing as they passed each fallen child. He screamed in anger and frustration, but he was helpless against the more powerful Green Glow.

Trevor still forced himself to wait. He needed them to move closer before he could strike. He was unsure his leg would hold him, so he'd have to shoot from a bent position. He started to crawl forward, but stopped abruptly. He was startled by a small green and black snake that had slithered out of the grass and across his arm. He stared down at it. He never expected to see a snake crossing his arm. He never expected to see a snake at all. Except for Spot, Rusty's cat, and Bentley, his horse, they hadn't seen any other animals since the invasion of the Beast—not a bird or a bug. He didn't count the wolves he commanded.

Trevor was distracted by the snake and watched with fascination as it moved away from him through the dense grass. He briefly wondered if he should get it and put it in his pocket, but maybe there were more somewhere. Maybe it had a mate. He hoped that was the case as he watched it slither away.

Trevor snapped his attention back to Daniel only to discover that they'd passed by him. He was shocked he hadn't even been aware of it because he hadn't heard or seen them go by. Trevor cursed himself and struggled to an upright position. He closed his eyes momentarily with the pain that hit him. He fell back into the cover of the woods and moved parallel to Daniel and the Green Glow. He moved as silently as possible dragging his leg behind as he tried to get the advantage. He had to get in front of them again.

Trevor's leg screamed at him, buckling with the threat of taking him down to the ground several times. He forced himself to stay upright. He moved silently, adjacent to the Green Glow. He ignored the pain radiating up his leg. He ignored the sweat dripping into his eyes and the tremendous heat pouring off his body.

Green Glow was traveling in the wooded areas to keep out of the fading sun. Trevor looked at the sky. It would be dark in less than ten minutes. He had to get Daniel before the damn thing could escape into the darkness. He'd be to slow to follow and the others couldn't help him.

Daniel had stopped struggling and the Green Glow was letting him walk, but continued to push him along. He found it difficult to move quickly because of his bonds and he slipped on the wet grass, falling forward. The Green Glow pulled him up and prodded him forward.

Trevor finally managed to get in front of them. He slid down a bank and into a small gully. He kept his rifle steadied against the bank waiting for the right moment when he could blow the bastard to hell. Sweat poured down his face as his leg continued to throb. His head was pounding to the beat of his heart. He wanted to scream. He wiped his arm across his face. Trevor hated this whole waiting game, but he didn't have long to wait before Daniel and the Green Glow came into his view. He barely dared to breathe. He blinked and waited until he could get a clear shot at the red eye. They came closer and Daniel slipped again.

Trevor held his breath, took careful aim, said a prayer and pulled the trigger. He shot a second time, then a third, and continued until the gun clicked empty. He had hit the red eye three times. The monster fell back, slid down the bank, and ended up in a stream where it seemed to just disappear.

The roar of the Beast came immediately after the Green Glow disappeared. The connection to him had been broken and the Beast reached out to locate its source. Trevor felt its scream snake through his body. It made him shiver as he collapsed against the bank.

"Trevor." A voice entered through the fog in his brain, but he found that he was unable to respond. He was in a warm place, a comfortable place, and his leg didn't hurt anymore. His head had stopped pounding. There was peace. He wanted to stay, but someone kept calling to him. The voice was familiar, soft, and loving. The voice was calling him back. He opened his eyes. He was laying in the gully. His leg screamed and his head pounded, but he managed to smile.

"Damn, Doc."

Trevor couldn't get up, his leg wouldn't let him. It wouldn't hold him right now, so he crawled over to Daniel. "Hold still. Let me cut you loose." Trevor produced a knife and cut the bindings.

Daniel grabbed Trevor and hugged him. "Boy, you look like hell, but you're the prettiest thing I've seen in a long time."

Daniel helped Trevor struggle to his feet. He grabbed him in a bear hug and briefly lifted him off the ground. Later, Trevor wondered how he had the strength. "God, I've missed you."

"We need to check on the others and get the hell out of here. I don't want to run into any unwanted company."

"Hold on a minute." Daniel had been looking at Trevor's jury-rigged leg. It was very swollen and the kid was hot to touch. He slowly eased Trevor back down to the ground for a closer look.

"Doc, don't look at me like that. I'm fine, just help me up."

Daniel lightly touched the stick brace and Trevor grimaced. "I'll help you up, but don't try to convince me your fine. I can feel the heat in you."

Trevor put his hand on Daniel's shoulder. "Daniel, I've gotten this far and I can go a little farther. We need to move fast right now. Let it be 'til later."

Daniel nodded. He would go check the other children, then deal with Trevor. The journey back to the house seemed endless. Daniel finally lifted Trevor and carried him the rest of the way. He eased him down on the porch steps.

"Stay put while I check on the others."

Trevor hadn't protested when Daniel picked him up. He was exhausted and had no intentions of moving anywhere. Gratefully, he leaned against the post as waves of dizziness overcame him. He could finally give in and lie down.

Daniel went to Travis. He was leaning over Robert, holding his handkerchief to his head. The bullet had creased Robert's head, leaving a long red line of blood, but he was conscious and claimed he was fine, except for one hell of a headache.

Daniel took off his shirt, took Trevor's knife, and cut it into strips for bandages. "You okay, Travis?"

"Yeah. Billy's dead, but I think he was a half-one. Beast product for sure.

"Where's Elliott?" Trevor yelled and attempted to get up. He fell back with a grunt.

"Stay put," Daniel said. "He must still be in the house. I'll get him."

"Is he alright?" Trevor yelled again.

Elliott had only the ugly effect of a bad headache from his encounter with the Green Glows. Daniel carried him out to the porch and placed him next to Trevor who immediately threw his arm around the boy and pulled him close.

Elliott looked up at Trevor and snickered. "Guess that plan didn't exactly go right. Damn, my head hurts like thunder."

Trevor hugged him closer. "We got Doc back, bro. That's all that's important. Can you go get Bentley? We need to go home. I'm about done in."

"Wait," Daniel surveyed his rescuers. He looked at all of his children who had just shown him the ultimate expression of their love. "What can I say to you? How do I thank you?"

"You just did," Trevor grinned. "We couldn't leave you to them and you would have come after any one of us if we'd been taken."

Daniel felt tears fill his eyes. "I would have tracked them to the ends of this beaten up world to get any one of you back," he said quietly before turning a critical eye at Trevor. "And now, son, we need to give that leg some attention."

"Doc, it's not that bad," Trevor answered with caution. "In fact, seeing you has made me feel a lot better."

"I insist." Trevor reluctantly gave in. The pounding in his head had become terrible and he could feel the fever burning inside his body.

Daniel carefully probed Trevor's leg. It was obvious he was still in a good deal of pain, but being Trevor he never said a word. "We need to get you some relief from this pain and get some antibiotics in you. I'm going to check the house."

"I'm okay, Doc. Help me onto Bentley and we'll go home. I've got antibiotics in my pocket."

"You've got a high fever."

"Okay my head hurts. I'm kind of dizzy too, but we have to go home."

Trevor noticed the long cut down Daniel's chest and reached out to touch it. "I'm not the only one hurt around here. You okay?"

"I am now," Daniel said.

"Sam was hurt. Rusty too."

Daniel tried to remain calm. "How bad?"

"Rusty was still unconscious when we left. That thing threw her off of it when she tried to help you. Sam may have a concussion . . . her head was hurtin' bad. The left side of her face was turning black and blue. We need to get as close to them as we can before full dark and that's only a few minutes away. Stop fussing with me. I'll make it."

Robert came forward and looked Trevor in the eye. "Give it to him," he said with an amused deadpan expression.

Trevor gave him a look of innocence. "What?"

"Give it up, Trevor. The last syringe. You'll need it before we start out again. You know, the one you kept for the pain you told Doc you don't have."

Daniel raised an eyebrow and gave Trevor the look he knew so well. "Are you holding out on me, son?"

"He's had several shots already. The last one I gave him was yesterday." Robert spoke directly to Daniel as if Trevor wasn't even there. "Yeah, he's holding out on you." They both turned to Trevor.

"Aw hell," Trevor looked at Robert in disgust. "He isn't even any good at injections."

"Don't even go there," Daniel warned. "Give me the syringe."

Trevor produced the syringe. He always knew when he'd lost.

"That's my good boy," Daniel laughed as he injected the medicine.

"You enjoy this too much," Trevor complained. "Now let's get the hell out of here."

"In a minute." Daniel looked at Elliott. He was holding out a shirt he'd retrieved from the house. Daniel struggled into it. "You okay, Elliott?"

"I'm better than okay. Let's go home."

# 42

The next day they traveled until Daniel called a halt shortly before dark. They found a house on a back road called Peak's Crossing and everyone settled in. Daniel went to search the bathroom in the master bedroom. When he came back to the front, Trevor was chewing on several aspirin.

"I found some antibiotics. Stop chewing aspirin. Try taking them with water."

"Boy, Doc, you sure get crabby when you get kidnapped by the creepiest shit in the universe and I get hurt snatching you back."

Daniel watched Trevor down the antibiotic. He made him as comfortable as possible and then went to work on taking George's splint apart.

"It'll probably take us another day to get back to the barn. I told George to head south if we weren't back in a few days. They may not even be there anymore."

"You need to stop talking and rest. Your leg looks like crap. You shouldn't have come—not in this condition."

"Daniel," Trevor said so quietly he almost didn't hear him. "I wasn't going to let those bastards keep you. I would've followed you all the way to his camp if I had to. I'd have crawled there. Hell, I did crawl some of the way."

"Okay, tough guy, let's try to make you more comfortable. While I'm doing that tell me what happened at the barn."

Trevor shook his head. "I don't really know how Sam got hurt. Rusty hit her head pretty hard when she was thrown. There was a lot of blood.  The rest of us mostly got cuts and bruises.  It wasn't good."

"That's the best I can do here.  Does that feel any better?"

"It'll be fine."

"Get some sleep.  Tomorrow will be tougher."

"I'll manage.  Is my Bentley all right?"

"He's right over there, healthy and happy."

Trevor looked over at his horse before he closed his eyes.  He soon fell into a deep sleep.  Daniel eased down next to Trevor, leaned back, and closed his eyes.  Sleep didn't come so easy to him.  He was listening to the night.  There was no sound, nothing there.  It was like they were in a vacuum where noise was not permitted.  Where it had never really bothered him before, he now found it quite disturbing.

# 43

They made it back to the barn the next day and as Trevor had predicted, it was empty. They would head south. He'd told Tommy to mark the houses they stayed in with a big X and then to continue heading in a straight line, always to the south.

Thirty miles to the south and two houses later they were all reunited. Sam, Keeley, and Rose cried. Daniel went to Sam and they embraced for a long time. He kissed her as she clung to him desperately. Daniel grinned down at her as he slowly released her death grip. "You're going to have to let me go so I can take a good look at you."

"I need five more minutes."

Daniel gave her the five minutes and then he went to work. He eyed her face critically. The entire left side was bruised and swollen, but she said her head was better and the ringing in her ears was almost gone.

"It's only slightly painful and the dizziness had passed," she said.

Daniel decided that in time she would heal. Gently, he kissed her nose, her eyes, and her bruised cheek. Next, he turned to his daughter Katie. He kissed the little girl and wrapped her in his big arms, holding her tightly against his chest, rocking her and enjoying the wonderful feeling of having her back in his arms.

"Daniel," Sam rubbed his back and looked down at Katie. "I'm worried about Rusty. She seemed a little better today, but you need to go to her."

Daniel kissed Katie before he hurried down the hall to the bedroom where Rusty was resting. She was motionless with her eyes closed. Her thumb was firmly in place in her mouth. Spot was wrapped in her left arm. He was surprised the cat was still alive given the death grip she had on his neck.

Daniel stood and just observed her for a little while. He watched her slow breathing and the slight jerking motion in her arms and legs. She moaned softly and her eyes fluttered. He went over to the bed and sat down next to her, placing her hand in his. He felt for her pulse. He reached over and released poor Spot.

Rose brought in his medical bag. She gave Daniel a quick hug and smiled. He winked at her, took out his stethoscope, and listened to Rusty's chest, then placed his hand on Rusty's cheek and spoke quietly to her. She opened her eyes. He was relieved to see that her pupils were equal.

"Daddy," she whispered. "Are you bones?"

"No, sweetheart, I'm very much alive." Daniel leaned down and gently kissed her forehead. "It's been a while since I've seen you."

"I waited for you for a long time. Where did you go for so long?" She shuddered and put her hand to her head.

"I was gone a long time, baby girl, but I'm home now and I won't go away again. Does your head hurt?"

"Kind of bad. Daddy, make it better."

"I will, Buppy."

Daniel gave Rusty baby aspirin for her headache and then gently lifted her into his arms. "Let me hold you for awhile. I need you close to me."

After he settled her into his arms, Daniel leaned back on the bed and rocked her like he had Katie. He felt the bump on the back of her head. It was still tender and slightly swollen. He knew she probably had a concussion. She also had a black eye and bruising across her nose. Rusty sighed and kissed Daniel's chest. She fingered the bandage on his chest.

"Daddy, you're hurt."

"I'm fine now that I'm home."

He repositioned Rusty and nestled her closer. "Is Trevor and Elliott bones?"

"I brought them both home with me. They're both fine."

Rusty gently tapped her finger against Daniel's chest in time to his heartbeat. She sighed as she began to relax completely in the welcome comfort of his warmth. He eased her back, keeping her snug in his arms and spent the next hour talking softly to her, reassuring her, and rocking her gently until she'd relaxed enough to finally fall into a peaceful sleep. He placed her on the bed and went to find Sam.

"How is she?" Sam asked nervously.

"Physically she'll be fine, but she'll need some time to put the rest behind her. Her head hurts, but that's part of the concussion and will dissipate. Are you sure you're alright, sweetheart?"

Sam curled into Daniel's arms. "I'm fine now that you're here. God, I was so worried."

Daniel took Sam's face in his hands. "I love you." He said again, placing his hand gently on her belly and kissing her deeply. "Are you sure you're alright?"

"Just some cuts and bruises, but I managed to come out of this pretty okay. What about Trevor? He was hurt so bad when he left here."

Daniel let out a sigh. "His leg isn't good. I need to get some more antibiotics in him. I'd like to put him on IV antibiotics, but right now we don't have that option. Sam, what those kids did for me . . . it's unbelievable."

"They love you. There was never a question of not going after you. Trevor formed a plan immediately and said they wouldn't stop until you were home with us. He almost came to blows with Robert over it. I'd never seen Trevor so angry—or committed. There was no stopping him. He even went so far as to use syringes for the pain so he could keep going. By the way, you're not supposed to get that information."

"Robert told me. I don't know what to say to him."

"Don't say anything. He understands."

Daniel kissed Sam again and pulled her closer. "It feels so good to be here holding you again. I can't believe I'm back with my family. I had my doubts about ever seeing any of you again and it scared the hell out of me."

Sam pressed against him. "We'd never let you go." She smiled coyly. "How about a date tonight?"

"Woman," he laughed, "you haven't changed a bit! You're still a hussy. Right now, dear wife, I have to go check on our kids, but don't go far because I'll be back to take care of you."

Keeley had helped Trevor to bed and now sat holding his hand. She leaned down to kiss him as he reached up for her. "Sorry if I made you worry, darlin'."

"What makes you so sure that I'm not done worrying about you? Trevor, how do you really feel?"

"Lousy."

Trevor gave Keeley a small smile. "You know I had to go after Daniel?" he said quietly. "I couldn't live with myself if I didn't find him."

"I know there was no choice, but you better not scare me like that again, Trevor Scott, or we'll be having this baby tomorrow."

Trevor suddenly turned deadly serious. He barely controlled the anger he felt at that moment. "I won't stand by and let those bastards hurt any one of us or take any of us away."

Keeley and Trevor held each other. She shut her eyes tight and was trying to keep all her fears at bay. She was afraid to let go of him.

Daniel walked into the room, smiled at Keeley, and then sat down next to Trevor. "I'm awake. Can't sleep, 'cause it still hurts too much. Keeley said she was going to get something and here you are." Trevor looked up at Daniel. "Big admission on my part."

"Rest assured that I'll make sure you sleep tonight. Thank you, Trevor. Thank you for coming after me. I really thought the Beast had won this time."

"Never would have happened, Doc. I'd never give up."

Daniel put his hand on Trevor's cheek. "Be right back."

When he came back Trevor's eyes were closed and his breathing slow. Trying not to disturb him, he injected the medication.

"Guess I knew that was coming," Trevor grunted. "Damn, Doc how come you're always using me as a pin cushion? Why don't you practice on George?"

"He doesn't keep getting hurt. This is going to help the pain and make it easier for you to sleep."

"Everyone else doing alright?"

"Everyone's doing fine. A lot of cuts and bruises."

"My horse?"

"Relax, Bentley's fine. George did everything but kiss him goodnight, so stay right where you are. When you're feeling better you can go and see for yourself, but for right now you are not to take one step out of this bed. Do we understand each other?"

"Relax, Doc, I hurt too damn much to move."

"Go to sleep."

Daniel wanted to wait a least a week before they made another move. Trevor, Elliott, Robert, and Rusty needed time to heal. Sam also needed the time, even though she insisted she was fine. Keeley was doing well considering her advanced pregnancy. The kids were emotionally spent and it was the first time so many of them had been injured at the same time.

Daniel spent a lot of time just talking to the children. He made the rounds and spent time with each of them. He kissed all the little girls and reassured them that everything was fine. Emma crawled into his lap and made herself comfortable. He needed to be near them. The children spent their time staying close to each other and no one went anywhere alone.

Several days before they were going to leave, Daniel decided to discuss the coming move with Trevor and Robert. It was going to be difficult with the three pregnancies and all the injuries.

Robert grinned at Trevor, but spoke directly to Daniel. "He didn't want to tell you about the pain medicine. I injected him personally. He's not a good patient."

Trevor snorted. "Yeah, well I got the bruises to prove just how bad you are at it."

Daniel couldn't help but laugh. Trevor still had a problem with needles and unfortunately he was going to have a lot of them in his future. He was feeling better and Daniel was enjoying baiting him.

"You know, son, we really should talk about this problem you have with the injections."

"Aw, Doc, everybody has something that gets to them. That's my something. I don't want to talk about it."

"Seriously, Trevor, I really think we should explore the problem since you're looking at . . . oh, at least one injection per day for the next few weeks—and let's not forget the pain medication that comes in an injectable. You were bad before, but now you're fighting me every step of the way. You're beginning to hurt my feelings."

Trevor looked at Daniel in horror. "Weeks? Why can't I just take pills? I like pills."

"I don't have any pills and we don't exactly have a pharmacy around the corner. We're lucky to have the injectable medicine. It's too bad we had to lose most of our equipment when the Green Glows attacked. What's the problem?"

Trevor looked down at the floor and grumbled. Robert decided it was time to leave and said he was tired. "Night all."

They watched him leave. Daniel turned to Trevor with his arms crossed. "We're alone now."

"Doc, let it go?"

"Talk."

Trevor closed his eyes and leaned back, letting out a deep breath. "It's really simple. I...I spent fourteen months in the hospital when I was a little kid. Every day, it seemed like every hour they were sticking me with needles. There were tubes going in and out of me everywhere. I was in a coma for three months before the torture started. It still haunts me. Hell, I still wake up at night seeing them coming at me with their needles. The pain was unbelievable and for some reason they kept me strapped down most of the time. I guess because I wasn't supposed to move or something. I was a little kid, younger than Rusty. I would scream and no one came. When they did come, it was always with a needle. I had no peace." Trevor's voice was quiet. "I'd never been so alone in my entire life, not even when I was on the road, before I met Uncle. I was alone."

Daniel leaned back in the chair. "What happened that you were in the hospital so long?"

"Car accident. Drunk hit us head on. It's still in my mind, as if it happened yesterday. In the emergency room, I watched my baby sister die. Her name was Josephine Louise. I called her Joey Lou Lou. My Daddy died . . . gone, just like that. My momma died the year before. I slipped into a coma and came out an orphan. I had a long rehab before I could even walk again. They weren't too careful with the needles if you know what I mean. They didn't much care about a crippled up four year old. I was left in bed for days at a time with only them coming in with the needles to break up the day. They threw me into foster care after that and as soon as I could walk, I did. I was seven the first time I ran. Then I found the man I called my uncle. He really wasn't, but he was good to me. Took care of me the best he could, so I stayed with him until the day he died."

Daniel sat back quietly for a long time before he spoke and then he chose his words carefully. "First, let me assure you that you will never be alone again. As far as not having any family, hell, you're surrounded with them. I'm honored to call you my son and I couldn't ask for a better one. I love you. We all do."

Trevor didn't say anything because he didn't want to cry in front of Daniel. Except for Keeley, no one had ever told him he was wanted before, or that he was loved—not even the man he called "Uncle" had ever said that to him.

"I'm sorry, Trevor," Daniel continued. "I didn't understand, so let's talk about how I can make it easier for you? You really need the injections."

"I trust you like I trust no other, but that doesn't make it any easier for me." Tears welled up in Trevor's eyes. "I guess I can stand it a little longer. I'll just close my eyes and try not to give you a hard time. I know you wouldn't intentionally hurt me."

"I'll be gentle with you, tough guy."

"Sure you will," Trevor managed to laugh. "But you still enjoy it too much."

"Now, I hate to ask you this, but could you please turn over?"

Trevor looked at the syringe, closed his eyes and moaned softly.

44

A week later they decided not to delay any longer, they had to move on. It would be a mistake to stay. Keeley was well into her seven month, Sam her fourth. Rose was two months along and they wanted to get settled as soon as possible. There were a lot of preparations to be made before Daniel would be ready to do a safe delivery.

Trevor's leg was far from perfect, but he was doing fairly well as long as Daniel stayed on top of him and made sure he didn't overdo. Elliott had healed and no longer had any pain. Robert was better. Rusty still complained about headaches.

Rusty always stayed close to Daniel or Trevor, and was frightened of everything. She'd gone back to her old habit of waking up screaming when her sleep was disturbed by nightmares. Daniel was trying to find a way to help her deal with it. Rusty had know Billy for what he was, but hadn't known how to tell them about him.

They'd been traveling for five days and the progress was slow. There was at least another fifty miles before they'd reach the spot that Elliott had found so long ago. They were lucky to make ten miles a day and that was on a good day. Most days they stopped early because the children were tired. Katie cried frequently and only Trevor seemed to be able to quiet her. He would spend hours holding her and mumbling sweetly in her ear. Between the gently sway of Bentley's gait and Trevor's constant talking she was often coaxed into a fitful sleep.

When Trevor got tired, Daniel carried his child against his chest to quiet her. This went on for three days and then abruptly

191

stopped as Katie once again became the sweet, cooperative child she'd been since the day she was born. They couldn't explain why it happened, but everyone was grateful for her silence.

Three days later they were all settling in for the night when a fight broke out between Elliott and Trevor. Trevor stood on a shaky leg and towered over the smaller boy. Elliott looked up at him with his stubborn chin jutted out and his hands on his hips.

"It's got to be done and you can't do it, so I will," said Elliott.

"You're not going anywhere alone. I'm going with you," Trevor said quietly.

"You can't even walk right! If we get into trouble, I sure as hell can't carry you."

"Then, little brother you don't go. Stop swearing."

"It has to be done. You know it does."

Daniel walked in on the last part of the argument and stepped between the two boys. "Okay, stop. What's going on? Trevor, sit down right now."

"Elliott's got this crazy idea that he's going to scout out our next location. He also thinks he's going alone and that's not happening. I'm going with him."

"You're not going anywhere. You wouldn't make half a mile." Daniel turned to Elliott. "You're also not going anywhere alone."

The problem was solved when George stepped forward and offered to go with Elliott. Trevor and Daniel both objected.

"Got to be, Doc," George shrugged. "We'll be fine."

Elliott and George left early the next morning. Trevor watched them as they disappeared in the distance. He moved Bentley over to a large boulder and eased onto his back. Daniel helped Sam, Keeley, and Rose up onto the horse. He looked up at Trevor.

"It should have been me, Doc. They're just little kids."

George and Elliott caught up with the family two days later. They'd found a town about ten miles southeast of their present location.

"It's really not much of a town, but it is a town and not far, maybe six hours the way this caravan moves," George said. "We should be able to find enough supplies there to last us awhile."

The town they entered was deserted, just like all the other towns they'd passed through. This town seemed to be little more than a speck in the hillside—another dusty old town that had been beaten to death by the Beast's intrusion. There was evidence that his monsters had been there. Bones from the dead were still scattered in the streets. The entire town sat silent in death. Four buildings were all that was left of Main Street and two of them were boarded up. The other two consisted of a combination grocery and small variety store. Across the dirt street sat two buildings that appeared to be some type of official dwellings. Around the corner, the "City Thrift Shop" stood next to the medical office of Harold Banter, M.D. A lone tavern sat silently at the end of the street.

Sam looked from building to building. "Which one do we stay in? None of them look all that inviting."

Daniel looked at Keeley. She needed to stop and take a few days off from riding Bentley. Sam was showing signs of fatigue and had dark circles under her eyes. Emma leaned against Bentley barely awake. They were all tired and needed to rest. He looked over at Trevor. The boy never complained, but he could see pain in his face as he unconsciously rubbed his leg.

"Is this it?" Trevor asked.

"There's a house. It's not too far, just a few blocks down from here and three blocks over. Me and George checked it out earlier. It still has electricity, gas, and running water. It also has seven bedrooms, so I reckon that would be the best place."

Elliott reached up, took Bentley's lead rope and Emma's hand. He started to walk slowly toward the house. The rest followed at an even slower pace. When they were within two hundred feet of the house Trevor pulled Bentley up. His trained eyes scanned the entire area before he spoke. "We need to check it out again," he said. "I'll go in with Elliott."

"Trevor," Daniel said. "You aren't . . ."

Trevor eased himself down from Bentley and took his rifle. He put his hand on Daniel's chest. "We're all tired, Doc. It's my job, so no arguments this time."

Trevor turned his back on Daniel and limped toward the house. "Let's go, bro."

Elliott glanced at Daniel, shrugged, and followed Trevor toward the house. When they got to the front porch, he stopped, took a deep breath and pointed at the dark house. "Let's do it." They entered the house.

"NO! NO! NO!" Keeley screamed as she struggled to get down from Bentley. Daniel and Robert both reached up for her.

"Doc, don't let him go in there. What if there's something waiting?"

Daniel wrapped his arms around Keeley and gathered her to him. "He's already in. Trevor can handle himself." Keeley closed her eyes and leaned heavily against Daniel.

Robert reached over, took Daniel's rifle, hesitated for only a second and ran up the stairs. He called out. "Trevor! Elliott! It's Robert."

The two boys came from the back of the house. "It's all clear," Elliott smiled. "Let's get settled."

Trevor turned on Robert in anger. "Damn it, boy! We could have mistaken you for something else. Don't ever do that again! You want to get shot?"

"Keeley," Robert said. "She . . ."

Alarm rose in Trevor and he pushed past Robert. He saw Keeley being supported by Daniel and limped over to her. He bent down to look into her face. "Keeley?"

"She's okay, just worried about you."

Keeley turned from Daniel and hit Trevor in the shoulder with all her strength. He didn't move.

"You can't keep doing that," she screamed.

Trevor handed Daniel his rifle and took Keeley into his arms. "Take it easy, Darlin'. Elliott had my back. It's fine. Hey, look at me. I'm fine. Nothing happened. Hell, if I'd let out one scream y'all would be in there in a flash," Trevor grinned. "I can just see an enraged pregnant lady beating the hell out of one of the Beast's monsters."

Keeley started to cry and Trevor looked helplessly at Daniel.

"I'm alright," she sniffed. "I'm just tired. I've spent the last five hours on the back of a smelly horse. I need a bath," she said and then abruptly hit him again.

"Well, there's a big tub in there. We'll bathe together."


Everyone dragged into the house. It took very little time for them to eat the few supplies they had left and stagger off to bed.

Trevor made sure that Bentley was taken care of before joining Daniel, Sam, Keeley, Robert, and Rose. They sat at an antique dining room table that had legs that ended with large lion's feet. Sam had found some stale coffee. They gathered around to talk about their next move.

Daniel gave Trevor a grim look. "Stay put until you're ready to go to bed. I don't want you stressing your leg anymore."

"I can manage that."

"Doc," Robert said softly. "I'm leaving you here. I'm going back to the camps. I can't go on with you any farther and I don't want to know where you're going. That way if things go wrong I won't be forced to tell what I know."

"Robert . . ."

"Daniel, they got you once and if I know where you're going it could put everyone in danger. I couldn't live with that. You hear a lot in the camps. The Beast made a big mistake when he tried to take over our world. I don't think he knew so many would be killed in the beginning. He hurt his own food supply source—mainly us. Now he's getting desperate because he has to feed so many and there aren't enough people left. It's an ugly, harsh, hard fact. I have to try and destroy him if we can. I have to kill the three that are incubating."

Rose took in a sharp breath and lowered her head. Robert reached over and placed his hand on hers, gently squeezing. "It's something I've given a lot of thought to and Rose and I have discussed. I'd like her to stay with you. She needs the family, especially now that she's pregnant."

"We love Rose," Sam smiled. "Of course, she'll stay with us."

"Robert," Daniel said. "What you propose to do is not only dangerous, but foolish. You can't possibly fight the Beast alone. You wouldn't have a chance. You'll become a captive again."

George had been standing quietly in the doorway. "He won't be alone, Doc, 'cause I'm going with him."

Sam felt the shock of George's statement hit her and she gasped. "Oh George, no!"

Now it was time for Daniel to reach out to Sam. He pulled her into his embrace crushing her against his chest.

"I have to," George said quietly. "Travis and Harlan are going with us too. We've got to keep Robert's back."

"We'll need to split here. The Beast can't get information we don't have...in case we get caught," Robert sighed. "It's just the way it has to be."

Rose looked like she wanted to cry. "Excuse me," she said and got up to flee the room. Daniel nodded toward Rose and Sam got up to follow her. Keeley tapped Trevor's arm. "I'm tired. I'm going to bed." She didn't want to hear this anymore.

Robert talked for the next two hours, laying out his plans to the others. They listened intently. It was a good plan, but somehow that didn't make any of them feel better about it.

Trevor sighed. "My leg's hurtin, so I'm going to go to bed." He realized his mistake when he looked at Daniel. "It's not that bad," he said quickly. "Just hurts some."

"I'll drop by before going to bed."

Trevor left, mumbling under his breath. George also left. He wanted to find Elliott and tell him about his decision. He wanted to make sure he heard it from him.

Robert waited until they were alone. "Doc, I need to talk to you about Rose."

"You don't have to worry about her. We'll all take good care of Rose and your baby when he comes."

"I know that. It's just that, well, if I don't come back . . . her being pregnant and all." Robert met Daniel's stare. "I don't think we'll be able to come back. It's a pretty good chance anyhow."

"Are you sure you want to follow this course?"

Robert let out a deep breath. "There's no choice. The Beast must be destroyed or none of us will survive. I have to make sure those other three bastards don't make it out of the incubator. It would be the end of all of us that are left. Doc, it's scary to even think there could be three more of those assholes running around trying to kill us.

This is our future and it needs you here to help it. You need to take care of the babies. If we're to survive, they're going to need you. My baby, I hope I'll see that baby one day. Rose isn't handling this too well, so maybe you can help her after I leave. Don't let her mourn for me if it goes wrong. Don't let her cry for me."

"She will and I can't stop that, but I'll help her if that happens." Daniel put his hand on Robert's shoulder. "You just make sure that you come back. We all need you."

"Do you think we're the only ones left?"

"No. It makes sense that somewhere there are others like us. The Beast thinks that there are others. Emma's supposed to have that information locked up inside of her somewhere."

"She knows where there are others?"

"If she does, it isn't on a conscious level. Yeah, I think there are other people and somewhere there's also other animals roaming around. It doesn't make sense that Bentley and the cat would be the only survivors. I can't explain it."

"There's something else—something only you can do for me."

Daniel leaned back in his chair. "What do you need?"

"If I get caught, well, I'm sixteen. I've impregnated Rose. I won't let the Beast use me and I see only two options. One, I do me if I get caught, but I don't really know if I can kill myself. And two, you can make sure I don't reproduce."

"You want me to sterilize you?"

"Can you do it?"

"It isn't a question of if I can do it. Do you know what you're asking?"

"I've given this a lot of thought. It needs to be done to protect this new world, be it as it is. It may only give you a little more time if I fail, but then again . . ."

"I can do a vasectomy, but I can't guarantee that I can reverse the procedure."

"I'm not asking for guarantees and I'm figuring it won't really matter if I get caught. I can't go there the way I am. It's just too risky. It's a risk I won't take."

"I have to think this through." Daniel got up and started to pace. "What you're asking . . ."

"It's not your decision, it's mine. I know what I'm doing. This was not a snap decision. Please, Doc, it has to be this way. To my way of thinking, there's no choice."

"Does Rose know?"

"No, but she will before we do it."

Daniel nodded. He'd give Robert time to talk to Rose and give himself time to think this over.

# 45

Daniel made a detour. He wanted to talk to Trevor before he went to bed. He found him alone, deep in concentration. He didn't hear him come in, which surprised Daniel. "Hi there."

Trevor turned around with his rifle ready. "Good God, Doc! You shouldn't sneak up on me."

"Sorry, but I didn't sneak up on you...you were lost in thought somewhere."

"I was just thinking about Robert and this plan of his. Somehow it all seems so crazy, but then maybe he's our only chance at true survival."

Daniel sat down, leaned back, and said nothing. He felt that Robert's plan was doomed to failure. He didn't want to lose any more of his sons, but he also couldn't refuse to let them go.

Daniel rubbed his chest and it was his turn to wince with the pain. Trevor looked up with concern. "Doc, are you okay?"

"Yeah, my chest hurts some," he said absently.

Trevor instantly felt alarmed. He'd never heard Daniel say he hurt before. His concern instantly turned to uneasiness. Daniel sat with his eyes closed and Trevor reflected on how tired he looked. Trevor hesitated before he reached over and gently put his hand on Daniel's chest.

"How bad do you hurt?"

Daniel opened his eyes and saw the deep worry lines in Trevor's face. He put his hand over Trevor's and smiled. The boy never called him by his first name unless he was embroiled in his own emotions or worried. That concern was directed at him.

"I'm okay. It's the cut I have across my chest. It still gives me pain at times."

Trevor visibly relaxed. "Maybe you need to rest and stay in bed for a day or two."

Daniel grinned. "Thank you, Doctor, for the consultation, but I'm here to talk about you."

"Oh no, Doc, don't you look at me like that. I really hate it when you look at me that way."

"Trevor, you and I have to come to a meeting of the minds. How many times have you injured your leg?"

"I don't know…a couple. Look, Doc, next time I'll try to get shot somewhere else."

"I hope there will never be a next time," Daniel said seriously. "Right now tell your very tired physician what's going on? How are you feeling?"

"I'm fine and better every day."

"Okay. Then you won't mind if I have a look at your leg."

"Doc, I . . . it's…Damn it! I'm going to bed."

"Not yet," Daniel said and sat up straight. "Off with the pants and no back talk."

Trevor grumbled and complained all the time he was dropping his pants. "There, are you happy?"

"Very," Daniel said as he leaned down to get a better look. "Let me go get my bag."

"Your bag? Why do you need your bag?"

"Stay put."

"That's just great."

Daniel returned and removed the bandage. Trevor's leg was healing, but slowly. There was still redness and it was tender to touch. He was amazed Trevor had ridden Bentley all this way and never complained. It had to be painful. "Okay. You're healing. How much pain do you have?"

"Hardly any."

Daniel knew it was a lie.

"Okay, it hurts."

"Thank you for finally being truthful. How about something for the pain? It will help you sleep?"

"Does that something involve a needle?"

Daniel shrugged.

"I swear, Doc, you have a mean streak in you. You get some kind of perverse pleasure out of this. There was probably some law back in the day to keep . . ."

Daniel laughed. "Are you done or would you like to continue protesting for a while longer?"

Trevor sighed. "How many?"

"Two?"

"Can't you put that stuff together?"

"Doesn't work that way.

A minute later, Daniel said, "Now that that's done, let's get you to bed. Keeley's probably looking for you by now."

Keeley was waiting and laughed when Trevor announced that Daniel had used him as a pin cushion...again.

"Sleep tight and have only good dreams," Daniel said as he turned to Keeley and put his hand on her belly. "It won't be too much longer now...about six weeks." The baby kicked and turned underneath his hand. "He's an active little guy."

"Don't I know it."

"That's good, you want him moving around."

Daniel kissed her on the forehead. "Good night, sweetheart and don't worry. I just knocked him out for awhile. He really needs to stay off the leg for as long as we can make him."

Keeley glanced over at Trevor. He was already asleep. "He's so stubborn, Doc. He has a heart of gold, but . . ."

"I know. I've been patching him up for a long time and it's always a challenge. You need anything, come and get me."

# 46

Daniel performed the surgery on Robert two days later. He wanted him to rest for at least a week before starting out for the camp. It was decided that they'd wait and depart on the same day. Sam was very verbal about George leaving and the other boy's decision to fight the Beast. Elliott glared at his brother, seething inside, but forced himself to hold it in and say nothing. He'd already tried for two days to change George's mind. Rose sat quietly, saying nothing.

Robert, Trevor, George, Travis, and Harlan stayed up late into the night, each giving input on the plans for the attack on the Beast's camp. Trevor asked Robert several times if he was sure he wanted to do this and the answer was always the same. He was committed to striking back at the Beast and killing his embryos. Their world depended on his success. "I'm sure of it, Trevor."

Trevor spoke quietly. "Then keep the plan simple and attack quickly. It's the only way because you're going to need the element of surprise. Don't forget to run like hell when the deed is done."

Sam snuggled into Daniel's lap. "Our boys are going after the Beast . . .what if . . .will they come back to us?"

Sam let her voice trail off. She hid her face in Daniel's shoulder and cried softly. All he could do was hold her and try to give her comfort. He wanted to protect her, but knew he couldn't, not in this. The possibility of them not coming back at all was overwhelming and they all knew it.

"Sweetheart," he finally said. "I can't tell you that everything will be alright and in your heart you know that's true. We can only help them prepare as much as possible and pray they come back to us. We're at war with the Beast. We've been hurt in the past and we're hurt now. We've already lost some of our children to this war and it could happen again."

Sam put her hand over Daniel's mouth. "Don't say anymore. I can't stand to hear it. It's better left unsaid. It hurts too much."

Daniel continued to hold Sam close as he let his thoughts wander. He was tired and right now he felt helpless. Sam was right—there was nothing more to be said.

It was a bright, sunny, peaceful morning and spring seemed to have finally broken free of winter. The peace was quickly broken with a large crash. Daniel, Trevor, and Robert reached the front room together, rifles ready. They found George and Elliott rolling across the floor.

"Son of a bitch! Damn you!" Elliott screamed.

Trevor looked at Daniel and put his rifle down. "I'll take George."

Daniel pulled Elliott off of George. Trevor grabbed George who immediately stopped fighting when he felt his hand on his shoulder. Elliott was so enraged he continued to fight and swear while trying to strike out at his brother. George stood silently next to Trevor, blood trickling down his lip. Elliott screamed and swung at George again.

"Damn you! You bastard son of a bitch!"

Daniel restrained the struggling boy, so he couldn't do more damage to the now bleeding George. "Elliott, Stop it."

Elliott abruptly stopped, but he shook quivering with the anger that surged through his body. His face was red with frustration as he glared at George.

"What's going on here?"

Elliott took a step toward George and Daniel quickly put his hand across his chest. "Stop!"

"Go ahead," Elliott screamed. "See if I care. Get your damn ass killed by the Beast."

Flush with anger, Elliott bent down and picked up his rifle before running out the door. Trevor turned to follow him. "Let him go," Daniel said quietly. "He needs sometime alone. George, you okay?"

George touched his busted lip. "Just the usual. He's mad because he saw me getting ready to leave. I guess he didn't believe I was really going and now he does. I didn't want to hurt him, but I guess I did."

"You're his brother and he's afraid for you. Elliott loves you."

"I can't back away from this."

"I know. Trevor, please go back to bed."

"I don't do breakfast in bed."

Breakfast was made from cans found in the small kitchen pantry. There was no fresh food, but it could have been worse. At least they had something to eat. Everyone went their separate ways after breakfast, leaving Daniel, Sam, and Trevor alone. Sam was feeding Katie since there was no milk available. She had no formula and opted to breast feed to supplement the weak cereal the baby ate. Katie suckled hungrily.

Rusty ran into the room, her blanket trailing after her and Spot running behind. "Hey, y'all."

"Good morning, Buppy." Daniel said as she crawled into his lap and reached up to kiss him. "Thank you. How are you this morning? Does your head still hurt?"

She shrugged and immediately settled back and made herself comfortable. Daniel picked up a bare foot. "Where are your socks?"

"I think Spot is wearing them."

On cue, Spot jumped up onto the counter. Daniel held up the cat's paw. "No socks." Rusty reached up, kissed him again, and giggled.

"Let's get back to your socks. Where are they?"

"They got losted."

"Who lost them?"

Rusty put her thumb in her mouth. Sam and Trevor were trying hard not to laugh. Daniel never gave up trying to get Rusty to do two things—get completely dressed and stop sucking her thumb. He gently removed Rusty's thumb and reminded her that "big girls don't suck their thumbs." *Round 647.* "Buppy, I want you to go find your socks and keep your thumb out of your mouth. You need to finish dressing."

Rusty started to cry. Daniel felt confused and helpless by her reaction. "Why are you crying?" he asked gently as he had so many times before. She didn't answer. He tried again and when that didn't work, he decided to let her cry it out. She quieted as he cuddled her close.

"What's that all about?" asked Sam.

"I don't know. Sometimes Rusty doesn't even know, she just feels upset and needs to cry it out."

"Doc, how soon do you think we can leave here? I'm getting that uneasy feeling. It's time to move on."

"How's the leg?"

"Fine. Damn it, I can ride and we need to leave."

"Relax. We already have all the supplies lined up and Robert's also anxious to leave. We'll get the little ones ready. Let's go look at your progress."

"No needles?"

"Probably not."

"Doc. . ."

"Give up, Trevor," Sam laughed. "You won't win."

"Just once, I'd like to win."

Daniel laid Rusty on the couch and examined Trevor's leg. He was pleased at the progress and felt there would be no problem in leaving on schedule.

Final preparations began. They were leaving the next day and it was decided that this house, this town would be the connection point between them and Robert's group. It was here they would leave information that would lead Robert and the boys back to them. It would be hidden for them to find at a later date.

When the time came for everyone to say their goodbyes and to go their separate ways there were tears all around. Sam wondered if there would ever be a time when they wouldn't have to cry for a missing child. Robert and Rose had said their goodbyes earlier. Daniel pulled Robert into his arms. "You come back to us, son."

Robert looked over at Rose. "I'll try. Take good care of her for me."

Daniel went to each of the other boys, hugged them, and told them to return safe, then he took Rose's hand and held her to his side. She gave Robert one last kiss before turning into Daniel's chest and weeping quietly. She didn't want to watch him leave. Emma, Brady, and Jamie hugged each boy before joining the rest of the group on the porch.

George wrapped his arms around Elliott and kissed his brother. "Don't you worry. I'll be back before you know it."

Elliott held his brother briefly and then turned his back on him and went to join the others. The family watched until they disappeared through the forest.

Trevor put his arm protectively around Elliott. The boy stood motionless watching the empty space where George had been standing before he disappeared from view.

"Come on, bro. Let's go get Bentley."

When Elliott didn't move, Trevor took his rifle and put it over his shoulder and then picked him up. "It's okay, bro, I've got your back," he said softly as he carried Elliott over to Bentley and helped him on. Trevor climbed up behind him and leaned Elliott back against him holding the little boy close. Keeley and Sam rode behind Trevor as they left the house behind. Rose said she preferred to walk.  No one felt like talking about what had just happened, so they went in silence.

Sam put her arms around Trevor pulling him back gently so he could rest against her. They didn't go far that first day and when it came time to check out the house they were to stay in Trevor volunteered to go in alone.

Tommy looked up at him. "I'll go with you."

Daniel shook his head. "NO, I'll go."

Trevor slid down from Bentley, put his hand on Daniel's chest and said, "No way."

Elliott eased down from Bentley, took his rifle, and started for the house. "It's decided," Trevor said limping after Elliott.  They would clear the house together.

# 47

Keeley woke with terrible pain in her stomach. She shook Trevor. "What?" he said, rolling over, still half-asleep. Keeley shook him harder and let out a soft cry. He came instantly awake. "What's wrong?"

"Get Doc."

"Are you sick?"

"No, you dummy! You're about to become a father."

"It's too soon. Go back to sleep," he yawned and started to turn over.

"Trevor Lincoln Scott! Baby! NOW!"

Trevor was suddenly wide awake. "Now? Are you sure?"

"Just wake Daniel and make it quick."

"Okay, don't go anywhere."

Trevor reached over and grabbed his pants pulling them on as he hopped over to the bedroom Sam and Daniel were in. He pounded on the door. Katie started to cry and Trevor swore under his breath. Daniel was up in an instant to join Trevor in the hall.

"What's wrong?"

"Keeley said to get you. Sorry I woke Katie."

Daniel buckled his pants and went directly to Trevor's room where Keeley was doubled over on the bed. He sat down next to her on the bed and put his hand on her forehead. She turned to look at him. "It's time."

"Alright, sweetheart, you just relax. How close are the pains?"

"Minutes," she gasped.

"Trevor, get the OB kit and then get Sam. The kit's next to my medical bag, bring both. Sweetheart, lean back and relax. We'll check you out. Let's bring you down a little on the bed."

Since Trevor couldn't pace, he sat while Daniel and Keeley did their work. It was four twenty-two a.m. when Daniel Trevor Scott entered the world. He was small, only five pounds, but healthy and very loud.

Daniel held the baby close against his heart and started to gently rock him. He leaned down and kissed his forehead. "Welcome to the family, baby. Congratulations, sweetheart! Your son is beautiful." The baby picked that moment to scream. Keeley looked anxiously at Daniel. He laughed at the little scrunched up face. "Hungry already, son?"

"Should I feed him now?"

"Absolutely, this boy is ready."

Keeley looked exhausted, so Daniel leaned down to help her with the baby. He placed Danny next to her and the baby immediately sought her breast, but missed the nipple.

Keeley became anxious. "It's not working."

Daniel sat on the bed next to her. "Relax and just give him a chance to start to suckle. After all, it's his first time too. He just needs a little help." Daniel adjusted the baby's head closer to Keeley's breast so he could find the nipple and instinct took over. He eagerly started to suckle.

"Congratulations, son, I knew you could do it."

Daniel thought how wonderful it was to hold a new life in his arms instead of looking at death. He took Keeley's hand and kissed it. "You did a great job. He's healthy and beautiful. I'll go get his Daddy so he can meet him."

"Doc, how do I ever thank you—for everything?"

"I asked that very question once of Trevor when he came to rescue me from the Green Glows. Sam gave me the answer. She said that I didn't have to thank him because it was a matter of unconditional love. You're my family and nothing else is more important to me. I love all of you. You and Trevor have given me another child to love. I should be thanking you."

Daniel walked out into the hall. Sam was sitting next to Trevor, holding his hand and quietly talking to him. He leaned down and smiled. "Your son is waiting to meet you. They both did well. Keeley is fine and so is the baby."

"My son," Trevor grinned. "My son!"

Trevor got up so quickly that his leg buckled under him. He cursed quietly as Daniel caught him and they hugged each other. Sam jumped up to join them. Trevor limped into the bedroom, sat down next to Keeley, and gently touched the top of his son's tiny head. "I love you, darlin'. Thank you for my son."

Keeley handed the sleeping baby to Trevor. She was exhausted. Trevor moved the baby's little body close to his cheek and felt his warmth. Closing his eyes, he thanked God for this little miracle.

"Have you decided on a name?" Daniel asked.

Trevor's turned and grinned. "Yes, we have."

Daniel went back to Sam and took Trevor's seat next to her. He was tired and really needed to go to bed, but was too excited. He wanted the warm glow he felt from helping bring a new life into the world to last a little longer. It felt good.

"Everything went well? He's a little early."

"He's absolutely perfect, Sam. About five pounds perfect. Beautiful boy. Keeley's tired, but she did fine with the delivery. Let's go to bed. I'm beat and the kids will be all excited to meet their new brother tomorrow. It will start early."

"Do you know what they are going to name him?" Sam asked as they walked back to their room.

Daniel smiled came and his eyes got teary. "Daniel Trevor Scott. They insisted he have my name."

# 48

Rusty was so excited about the new baby she could hardly wait to see him. She jumped up and squealed, "I told you he was a brother."

"You were right, baby girl," Trevor said as he lifted Rusty into his arms. "How would you like to go and meet him?"

"Trevor, are you his daddy?"

"I'm his daddy."

"Can you still be my brother?"

"Baby girl, I'll always be your brother and don't you forget it." Trevor tossed Rusty into the air. She giggled and threw her arms around him, hugging him tightly.

After Danny was introduced to all his new brothers and sisters, Daniel announced that both the baby and Keeley needed some quiet time. "Everyone out."

Sam had put the baby into a dresser drawer they were using as a crib and Rusty leaned down to gently kiss her new brother before she left. The baby made little cooing sounds in his sleep. Trevor kissed Keeley and whispered. "I'm getting out too so you can rest."

Daniel looked down at his namesake. He touched the baby's foot and Danny rewarded him with a scrunching of his little face. He went to Keeley and put his hand on her forehead. She opened her eyes. "How do you feel?"

"Tired mostly, but otherwise I'm fine. He's beautiful, isn't he?"

"Absolutely...and healthy as a horse," Daniel said taking Keeley's hand in his.

"Checking again?"

"Habits are hard to break," he laughed. "I'll need to check and make sure everything is going alright. You rest. I'll be back later."

Trevor had been restless all day. He limped and paced. "How soon before we can leave here?" he asked when Daniel came out of the bedroom.

"Keeley needs to rest and so do you. This isn't such a bad place to hold up for a few weeks. At least it still has electricity and running water."

"We should leave."

"Why? What's the hurry?"

Trevor shrugged. "Bad feelings, I get them sometimes."

"You have them about this place?"

Trevor shrugged. "Hell, maybe I'm just jumpy."

"You're never just jumpy. You're one of the steadiest people I've ever known, so there has to be another reason."

"It's just a feeling," Trevor looked up at Daniel and rolled his eyes. "Damn, my leg is killing me!"

Daniel started to laugh, he couldn't help himself. Trevor had once again made the mistake of telling him he was in pain and the look on his face was priceless. He quickly controlled himself and turned serious. "You want to share that statement with me?"

"No."

"Why didn't you tell me?"

"You know why."

"I'm not blind. I know the limping has gotten worse. Let's go have a look—or do you want me to just make an educated guess?"

"It hurts, but its aspirin hurt, not needle hurt."

"Now you sound like Rusty."

"Doc, it's fine, I just need to rest some. By tomorrow I'll be running races and . . ."

"Are you done or do we continue?"

Trevor stopped pacing and stood directly in front of Daniel.

Daniel gave him a smile and Trevor felt his heart sink.

"Fine! Strip me naked if it makes you happy."

Daniel laughed. He enjoyed bantering with Trevor. Trevor huffed as he unbuckled his belt. He had reason to hurt. His leg looked swollen again and he wasn't going to like the solution.

"But, but Doc," Trevor stammered.

"A full week in bed. Enjoy your son. Spend time with him and no arguments this time. You're never going to get better if you don't take care of your leg. It's swollen. Do you want to lose it? Trust me, it could happen," Daniel said quietly. "Trevor, it's that important."

"A week and the needle? Somehow, that's not very comforting, not when we should be on the move."

"Relax, tough guy, and leave the details to me."

"That's what scares me…leaving the details to you."

"Go to bed."

Rusty peeked into Trevor's bedroom. He was sitting in bed with Danny sleeping peacefully in his arms. She walked over and leaned against the bed, peering down at the baby. "Hi."

"Hi. Come join us, we could use some company."

Rusty climbed up and kissed the baby on the head. "I love him. He's so little and pink. That's almost red you know. Think he'll change to all red?"

Trevor grinned. Rusty always wanted everything red. "I think we'll keep him the color he is. Do you want to hold him?"

"Can I?"

"Here, lean against the wall and I'll put Danny in your arms. Make sure you keep your arm under his head."

Rusty held her new brother, carefully making sure she supported his head. She looked down at him and smiled. "Can we keep him?"

"We'll definitely keep him. He's your special little brother and because he's so special we named him after your Daddy."

"Daddy said you gots to stay in bed."

"Yes'm, a whole week this time."

"Rusty, you need to help Daddy watch Trevor." Rusty was trying to do her best to imitate Daniel by lowering her voice and scrunching up her face. "And we need to keep him in that bed."

"Great, now he has a five year old spying on me."

"I think I'm going to be six."

"Not yet you aren't. Does Daddy know you're running around without your shoes?"

She held up her foot. "Got my socks."

"Where's the other one?"

"It ran away. The baby's heavy."

Trevor took the sleeping baby and rested him in the crook of his arm. Rusty yawned and leaned against him. He put his free arm around her and pulled her to him. "You tired, baby girl?"

"The monsters make me tired. He's still coming after us. He makes my head hurts."

Trevor didn't ask who the monsters were because he knew. "Stay close to me. Close your eyes and sleep. I'll watch out for the monsters."

Rusty gave another big yawn. "Thanks, Trevor."

Daniel went to check on Trevor and found him asleep with Rusty on one side and the baby on the other. Danny started to cry, so he took him and cradled him, rocking him slowly. Trevor rolled over to Rusty and pulled her into his arms. They both sighed.

Daniel went to find to the kitchen to find Keeley because the baby was probably hungry. Sam and Keeley were both in the kitchen. Daniel's presence was announced by a loud wail from Danny. He kicked his little legs in anger at having to wait.

"Someone's hungry, Mommy."

Keeley took the baby, sat down on a chair in the corner of the kitchen and offered him lunch. After a few minutes, Danny stopped suckling and started to scream. Keeley felt the tiny baby shiver and then they heard the low howl in the distance. They all looked toward the window and waited, but nothing else happened. When Daniel turned around, Elliott was standing quietly behind him, his rifle ready. Keeley felt the baby calm.

Elliott reached up and put his hand on Sam's arm. "It's far away. Sounds like the Beast is just pissed off."

"I agree," Daniel said. "I'm going to check on Trevor.

Elliott picked up piece of peach from the bowl on the table. They would soon run out of canned food. "Don't be too hard on him, Doc, you scare him."

Trevor's leg was not healing as fast as Daniel thought it should. He needed good month of antibiotic therapy and rest. It would make all the difference. The constant moving and jarring of his leg had made it more difficult and was adding to the problem. There was also the other problem of keeping him off the leg. The kid had a high pain tolerance.

When Daniel walked in Trevor was deep in a conversation with Rusty. They didn't even notice him, so he waited. "You don't have to be afraid. They're far away from us and we're going to a very safe place where the monsters can't ever follow. It was only noise."

Rusty leaned against Trevor and rubbed her head. "My head hurts really, really bad."

"I'm sorry, baby. We'll tell Daddy and he can make it better."

"No, don't tell Daddy."

Trevor gently lifted her chin and kissed her nose. "Can't we tell Daddy anything?"

"You never tell Daddy when you hurt."

"Well, I should. You always need to tell him when you're hurting."

"Are you hurtin' too?"

"My leg hasn't stopped hurting for so long I don't remember it any other way."

Rusty climbed up on Trevor's chest and straddled him. "Daddy can make it better?"

Trevor pulled her down into his arms and hugged her. "He's been trying." Rusty snuggled next to him and sighed. He lowered his chin and lightly rested it on top of her head as he rocked her. "One day, Rusty, this will all be behind us."

"Hello, you two," Daniel called as he walked over and sat down next to them. He put his hand on Rusty's forehead. "Your head hurt, Buppy?"

"Yes," She started to whimper. "And I can't find my sock."

"Don't worry about the socks right now."

Daniel looked into Rusty's eyes. They were dull and filled with pain. He went and got some medicine for her head and held out the two pills with a glass of water. She took the pills and drank half of the water before curling back against Trevor.

"Don't leave, Daddy."

"I won't. I'm just going to have a look at Trevor's leg."

"His leg hurts real, real bad...like my head. Make him better."

"I know he hurts and with a little cooperation, I will make him better."

Rusty closed her eyes and patted Trevor's chest. "Good."

Trevor let out a little moan. "You've made the kid a tattle tale."

"Never trust a five year old."

# 49

The house was quiet and everyone was tucked in for the night. It was shortly after midnight when all hell broke loose. The house was battered with rain, lightning, and thunder accompanying the winds. Emma, Brady, and Jamie crawled into the same bed and huddled close to each other. Keeley got up to get Danny. She lifted him out of his makeshift bed and cuddled him close. Trevor pulled on his pants and walked into the hall and down to the front room, rifle in hand. Daniel, Elliott, and Tommy were already there.

Tommy grimaced. "It's just a storm, right?"

Elliott nodded. "Yeah, just a storm. I sure hope George is alright."

Sam took Katie and went to join Keeley. She placed the sleeping baby next to little Danny on the bed. Rusty was standing in the corner of the room with a terrified look on her face. Sam went to her and put her arms around the little girl. "Everything will be alright, Rusty."

With the next clap of thunder Rusty bolted from Sam and ran out the door. She ran into Emma's room and jumped onto the bed, pulling the covers over her head.

"I'm going to check on the kids," Daniel said as he handed his rifle to Elliott. He found all the little girls huddled together in one bed. Taylor ran into the room and dove into the bed between Emma and Brady. Daniel winked at Emma. "Stay put. This will be over soon and I'll come back for all of you." He started to leave and go back to rejoin the boys when Rusty grabbed him from behind. He lifted the terrified little girl into the safety of his arms. "You better come with me."

"Did you hear it?" Tommy asked. "The howling's started again."

On cue, a long piercing howl entered the room. Rusty screamed and buried her head in Daniel's chest. She began to tremble uncontrollably. "It's them."

"It's only noise."

"No, Daddy. It's the Beast's monsters. They've come to get you again."

Trevor was the first to hear the low growl and then Elliott turned quickly to the sound. They both raised their rifles and slowly backed away from the door. "Trevor, go to the babies, take Rusty with you. Get all the kids together and stay with them."

Trevor didn't argue. He reached over to take Rusty before hurrying down the hallway.

"Elliott, go help Trevor guard the children. Tommy, keep your rifle on that front door."

Elliott left without a word to join Trevor. The storm lasted all night sending colors flashing in the sky, an eerie remembrance of when everything first started. It was like the first coming of the Beast. The howling continued as did the scratching and beating at the front door. Daniel and Tommy stood ready, each waiting for the unseen enemy. Elliott tapped Daniel on the arm.

"Everyone's okay. Trevor will holler if he needs us."

With the end of the storm, the howling stopped and so did the constant scratching. In the distance, the flashing of the colored lights faded until they were gone from view. Daniel and Tommy stood ready with their rifles trained on the door. Elliott move closer, ready to protect them.

He whispered softly. "Got your back, Doc."

Tommy nodded before he swung open the door and fell back against the wall. There was nothing there—only the morning's soft light filtered in to greet them. The door had several large, deep scratches in it.

Daniel turned slowly and was surprised to see both Elliott and Trevor behind him, their rifles raise to protect him.

Trevor limped over to Daniel and grinned. "You know that bad feeling? I think it visited us last night."

"Okay, we leave tomorrow."

"Good idea."

# 50

Daniel decided it was time to make a professional visit to the Scotts and make sure they were ready for tomorrow. He knocked at their bedroom door and when Keeley answered, she smiled and hugged him.

"House call," he cheerfully announced.

Trevor was sitting in a chair, deep in another conversation, but this time it was with his new son. He looked up. Daniel smiled at him and Trevor felt the old familiar dread fill him as he came over and lifted the baby into his arms.

"Just came by to check on this little guy. Make sure he's ready for the road." He cuddled the baby, speaking softly to him as he checked him over. "He's healthy and very wet."

"I'll take care of that," Keeley said, scooped Danny into her arms. After she changed the baby, Keeley went to the chair Trevor had exited and settled in to feed him. Daniel turned his attention back to Trevor.

Trevor had been watching and waiting for Daniel to turn his unwanted attention to him. "I'm fine," he said quickly.

"Good, can I have a look?"

"No reason to."

Daniel turned to Keeley and raised an eyebrow. The baby was making little sounds of pleasure as he sucked greedily.

"He's lying."

"You really shouldn't lie to your doctor," Daniel said mildly.

"Great, now you're both ganging up on me. Look, we're leaving tomorrow and I will be walking right next to you, Doc.

Then you'll know just how good this leg is. Right now, I've got a million things to get ready. Bentley has to be looked after."

Daniel said nothing and shook his head. "Good God Doc, don't do that…and stop smiling at me.

"Are you done?"

Trevor limped over to the bed and eased down. "You make my head hurt," he mumbled.

"Your head hurts too?"

"Yeah. NO!"

"Yes or no?"

Trevor knew he couldn't lie his way out. His leg was painful and his head did hurt. The last thing he wanted to do tomorrow was get on Bentley and ride another forty plus miles. He actually felt he may not be able to make a whole day on the back of the horse.

"Are you listening to me?"

"Sorry. What?"

"You need to tell me what, where, and how much pain?"

Trevor let out an exasperated sigh. "It's not that bad."

Daniel knelt down next to Trevor. "Don't even think about walking, you'll be riding because there's no other way. Your leg won't last a mile walking and for your own good I'm going to load you up with pain medication for the trip."

Keeley put little Danny over her shoulder. "I'm going to visit with Sam while you two argue this out."

Early the next morning they left the house behind. At Daniel's insistence, Trevor rode. The big horse wasn't fazed by the additional weight.

Three days later they came across a town and like many of the previous ones, it was dead. They found all the provisions they would need and Daniel was delighted to discover it had a small rural hospital that was very well equipped. He restocked all of the drugs he had used. It had everything he needed to set up again, including supplies for the upcoming birth of his next child and Rose's baby. They could come back later for what they couldn't take with them now.

While Daniel went to work checking for the equipment and drugs he wanted, Elliott and Tommy decided they were going to have a look around and see if they could find a grocery store. Everyone was hungry and their supply had dwindled to almost nothing.

Trevor wanted to go along, but Daniel told him it would be better if he rested. He reluctantly agreed and sat down under a large shade tree. As always, he scanned everything around them.

Daniel went through the Emergency room and found a combination trauma and pharmacy set up. He made a quick decision that they should stay here for the night.

The children were tired and crawled gratefully onto the gurneys in the emergency room. Sam put Danny and Katie in a crib she found in a corner of the examination room across from the pharmacy. She placed Taylor on a gurney next to the babies and laid down with him. In a short while they were all asleep from sheer exhaustion. Trevor pulled a chair over to the Emergency room door so he could keep watch for the night.

Daniel went to the pharmacy store room. Rusty followed, deciding that he couldn't possibly do his search without her help. "I'm glad you came to help me," he said, lifting her over some boxes in the store room. He moved from shelf to shelf pulling down additional items.

Tommy and Elliott went to hunt for the kitchen. "Hey, Elliott, where do you think they'd keep the kitchen in a place like this?"

"I don't know. I've never been in hospitals much. We should have asked Doc before we left. Let's go check down this hall."

Tommy peered into the darkened hall. "It looks kind of spooky down there."

"Anything comes along just shoot it. Come on, there's nothing here and everyone's hungry, including me."

"Okay, but most everyone is sleeping so how hungry can they be? Make sure we stay together."

The two boys walked shoulder to shoulder down the hall until they reached a large lobby curling around to the hospital's front entrance. There were three or four small offices off of the lobby which they quickly scanned.

"Nothing here," Elliott said and went over to check the doors at the front entrance. They were locked up tight. He nodded and went back to Tommy.

They walked through another office and found it was some kind of a communications area. There was a large switchboard in the center and through a door to the left of it was the switch room. To the right of that was a larger office with multiple desks. Elliott looked at the six empty desks and wondered if the people who worked at them had just gotten up and left because he saw no bones anywhere.

They continued walking through the office and into a small room at the back. Inside were several vending machines. There was a soda machine and several snack machines. "At least we won't starve, even if it is junk food. You want to break the glass or should I?" Tommy asked.

Elliott raised his rifle and was just about to bring it down on the glass when he heard a noise. It was distant and muffled, but he was sure he heard it. He stopped with the rifle held over his head. Tommy looked at Elliott and was instantly alert. He raised his rifle toward a dark hallway. "What?"

"It sounded like a cry," Elliott whispered. "Come on, Tommy, but be really quiet."

Elliott moved slowly, the tension enveloping him as he entered the dark hallway to the left of the offices. They heard another small whimpering sound float from down the long corridor. Elliott kept his rifle ready as he stepped over a pile of bones.  It was the first they had encountered.  Tommy followed close behind him.

"Elliott?"

"Shhh.  Be quiet and follow me close."

"Got your back."

# 51

Tommy looked behind him just to make sure that nothing was following them, and then moved closer to Elliott so he could keep him in his line of sight. It was darker in this corridor so it was necessary to be as close as possible without falling over each other. The farther in they went, the darker it seemed to get. Elliott was opening each patient room door as they went along, checking to make sure it was empty. He didn't want anything to surprise them. The crying noise was getting louder.

Tommy caught Elliott's arm. "Wait! What if it's some kind of a trick?"

"The Beast doesn't play this kind of trick. Mostly he just tries to kill us out right," he whispered. "Come on. Keep ready."

"I'm scared."

"Me too. Just keep moving."

Elliott and Tommy stood before the door the constant crying was coming from. Their eyes met in the half dark and Elliott nodded, pointing to the door. Together they went in. Elliott's right. Tommy left. They came to a halt and stared at the center of the room. Elliott turned to Tommy.

"Go and get Doc. I'll wait here."

"You'll be alright?"

"Sure. Go on, Tommy, and hurry it up."

Tommy ran down the corridor jumping over the bones that Elliott had stepped over earlier. He circled around the lobby and went back down the second hallway, running right past Trevor and into the Emergency room.

When Trevor heard running noises coming toward him he had raised his rifle. He almost squeezed the trigger as Tommy rounded the corner, but pulled back as he recognized the little boy. "Damn it, Tommy!"

Trevor lowered his rifle and turned to follow Tommy back into the Emergency room. Fear gripped him when he realized that Elliott wasn't with him. He grabbed Tommy when he stopped to look for Daniel. "Where's Elliott?"

"Where's Doc?"

"Is Elliott hurt?"

"No, but we need Doc."

"He's in the back with Sam. Where's Elliott?"

"Down on the first floor in a patient room at the end of the hall. He's with dead people."

Tommy wrenched free from Trevor and ran down to the end of the emergency room. "Tommy, watch the door," Trevor yelled. "I'm going after Elliott."

"Elliott, damn it!" he mumbled as he limped down the hall. *MY frickin' leg is throbbing and now I have to go and find you and your dead people. Damn kid!*

When Trevor got to the lobby area, he looked around and saw the long corridor to his right. "Elliott, where the hell are you?"

"End of the hall. Just keep coming all the way to the end."

Trevor jumped when he felt a hard hand fall on his shoulder. He backed up, ready to fight.

"Relax, it's just me."

"Damn it, Doc, you scared the hell out of me. I'm jumpy enough as it is. Come on. let's go see what kind of trouble Elliott's got himself into."

"Where is he?"

"End of the hall and, of course, its dark as all hell down there."

"Let's hurry, I don't like leaving Tommy all alone. He's pretty shaken. Rose is with him, but . . ."

"I'll go back to Tommy unless you think you need me?"

"Go ahead. If we get into trouble, I'll holler."

"Doc, remember you know how to use that rifle you're carrying."

Daniel cautiously entered the room. "You alright, son?"

"I'm fine, but take a look at what I found."

Elliott pointed to the center of the room where a small brown-haired, blue-eyed child stood looking back at them with wide eyes. He couldn't be more than two years old and his eyes were overflowing with tears. He was dirty and obviously frightened. His little body shook uncontrollably.

Daniel handed Elliott his rifle and leaned down to the little boy, holding out his hand. "Easy, little guy. No one's going to hurt you."

Daniel slowly moved toward the child. He gently put his hand on the boy's shoulder and drew him into his arms. The child didn't resist as Daniel embraced him. He threw his arms around his neck and lowered his head onto his shoulder, putting his thumb into his mouth. He gave a big sigh as his tears diminished into small sobs, hiccupping several times before he became quiet. There was a small pile of bones laying next to the bed. Daniel briefly wondered who's they were. It took only minutes to reach the ER.

"Elliott, go get Sam."

Daniel laid the little boy down on a gurney and started to strip off his filthy clothes. "Where did he come from?" Trevor asked as he looked down at the now contented child.

"Found him in a room next to a pile of bones."

"How the hell did he get there?"

"I haven't a clue, but we seem to have another child."

"I can't leave you alone for a minute, can I?" Sam laughed as she touched the baby's cheek. "Who is this little one? Is he alone?"

"Except for the pile of bones that Elliott found him standing next to…yeah, he's alone. I want to get him cleaned up and exam him to make sure he's not hurt in any way."

"Can I give him a bath first? This little guy looks like he's been rolling in the dirt."

"That should be okay. He doesn't seem to have any obvious injuries."

Sam took the little boy from Daniel. "Oh, you're so tired, aren't you, sweetheart?" she cooed to the little boy. "We'll just get you cleaned up in no time. I'll bet you're hungry too."

Sam gave the sleepy little boy a bath in a sink and then addressed the problem of clean clothes. She went through Taylor's backpack and came up with a pair of pants and a shirt, both were too big, but they would do for the time being. She'd just have to roll up the sleeves and pant legs. She tickled the little boy's belly and told him that at the first opportunity she would go shopping and get him some clothes that fit.

Sam took the boy back to Daniel who gave him a fast once over and pronounced him healthy. "He just needs to eat a little more regularly, but he seems healthy enough. Someone took good care of this little guy. He couldn't have been alone too long."

"Where do you think he came from? And where are his people?"

"We may never know, but we found him and now he's ours."

"We can't keep calling him little boy. Since he can't tell us his name, what should we call him?"

"You'd better pick a name for him before Rusty gets here. We don't want her to name him. He'll wind up with Rover or something else inappropriate."

Sam gave it some thought and said she would like to call him Wyatt after her favorite great uncle.

"Wyatt it is." Daniel picked the little boy up and kissed his little cheek. "You like your new name, son?"

"Who's that?" Rusty asked as she circled Daniel to get a better look. She jumped up to see the little boy.

"This is your new brother. His name is Wyatt," said Daniel, placing Wyatt next to Rusty. I

Rusty eyed the little boy and then flung her arms around him, hugging him to her. "Oh, boy, another brother!"

Little Wyatt was almost as big as Rusty and he laughed, clasping his small hands around her waist. Rusty was small for a five year old and barely a foot taller than Wyatt.

Trevor grinned. "Do you like your new brother?"

"Can we keep him, Trevor?"

That was always Rusty's first question when someone new arrived. "Yes, I think that would be a good idea."

Rusty sat down, pulling Wyatt onto her lap. "Daddy, did Sam or Keeley have Wyatt in their belly? Are you his Daddy or is Trevor?"

"You got some explaining to do, Daddy," Trevor snickered.

The children who were still awake came to surround the newest member of their family. Wyatt took all the attention well and delighted Emma.

"Don't anyone wander off. We're going to eat in a few minutes." Sam said. "Brady, wake up the others."

"Doc, are we staying here?" asked Trevor.

"Sure, the hospital is as good as any other place."

Daniel had a plan for Trevor. He had found IV antibiotics in the pharmacy and would administer them for the length of time they were there. He was very concerned that he hadn't been able to completely clean up Trevor's infected leg and this might make the difference. Now all he had to do is convince Trevor it was the right thing to do.

Elliott brought Bentley into the front lobby and made sure the big horse was comfortable. They used the patient rooms just past the lobby for their sleeping arrangements. Daniel had set up a room where he could treat Trevor and made sure there were two beds—one for Keeley and one for Trevor. He pushed them together. He brought in a crib for the baby. He and Sam would use the room across the hall. Sam put Wyatt in bed with Katie. The rest of the children were in adjoining rooms. As an after-thought, Daniel brought in another bed for Rusty. He wanted her close. She was having nightmares again and the incident at the last house had completely unnerved her. She hadn't spoken much since then—at least not until she saw Wyatt. Rusty was completely taken with the little guy. He wanted to keep them together tonight.

Daniel went to look for Sam. He found her gathering the three little girls and putting them to bed. Rose was going to sleep in with them. "Everyone comfortable?"

"Hi Daniel," Emma called from the bed. "We're all sleeping together."

"Except for Brady, she snores too loud." Jamie poked the girl.

"I don't snore."

They all giggled. Daniel went over and kissed each little girl goodnight, then turned to Rose. "How are you doing?"

"I miss Robert. I worry about him, but I'm okay."

"Daniel," Emma called. He went and sat down next to her. She reached up and kissed him. "Love you."

"Love you too. Have only good dreams, ladies, and I bid you all a good night." Daniel bowed to them as he left and guided Sam out the door.

"I never knew it took so long to get three little girls to settle down," Sam laughed. "Where are our boys?"

"They're all settled in for the night, except Elliott who insisted he has to stand watch. He's on a couch in the front lobby. He said Bentley needed company too."

Daniel pushed Sam against the wall and leaned his body into hers. He kissed her deeply, pushing his tongue into her mouth. She responded and slid her hand down to his crotch. He came up for air and smiled. "God, you feel so good."

"Thank you. How about you and I go mess around?"

Daniel put his hand on Sam's belly. She was going into her fifth month and had a nice little bulge. "I'd love doing it with a pregnant lady, even if she is a hussy," he whispered and squeezed her butt.

"Flattery will get you laid, Doctor."

Daniel sighed. "It will have to wait. Unfortunately, I have to go deal with my other child."

"Trevor? Go ahead. Rusty is bunking with us tonight, as is Wyatt, so no fun and games tonight. Maybe we can sneak away later and find a private room."

"Let me go convince our son to do the right thing. I also want to see how Keeley is doing after that long ride. We should probably stay here for the next few days and rest."

Daniel looked closely at Sam. She had dark circles under her eyes and seemed tired. "Honey, are you alright? Anything I should know?"

"Just very tired."

"Go lie down. I'll be back soon."

Daniel went to Trevor's room and found Keeley alone. She was feeding the baby. "How's everything?"

She frowned at him. "Fine, but this little guy is hungry all the time. All he wants to do is eat."

Daniel chuckled. "That's his job. Where's Trevor?"

"I think he went to look after Bentley. You know how he feels about that big old horse."

"He's supposed to stay off his leg. I'll go find him. I've got a little surprise for him. He'll love it."

"Doc, sometimes I think Trevor's right—you do enjoy this too much."

Daniel went directly to the lobby. Elliott was stretched out on the couch and Bentley stood quietly. Trevor had his arms wrapped around Bentley's neck as he spoke quietly to the big horse.

Bentley moved his big head down and ears forward as he rested his head on Trevor's shoulder and nuzzled him.

"Thanks for carrying all of us today. We wouldn't have made it this far without you."

Trevor buried his face in Bentley's mane and sighed. "I hoped someday we can run together again like before. It felt so good and for just a little while we were free from all of this. I've missed not being with you more. I bet you miss not having other horses around, but even if I can't run with you, I'll always take care of you."

Daniel smiled to himself. Trevor sounded so young, but then he was only seventeen, something Daniel tended to forget.

"Trevor, we need to talk."

Trevor turned around and leaned back against Bentley. Daniel went over and patted the horse, and then put his arm around Trevor. "Come on, let's go make you better."

Trevor held his breath as Daniel inserted the needle directly into a vein and then taped it in place. "Good God, Doc."

"Relax, I'm almost done."

Daniel started the IV drip and threatened Trevor within an inch of his life if he even thought about moving from the bed. He sat with Trevor as he drifted into a drug-induced sleep. Daniel unconsciously rocked him while he said a brief prayer for both of them. He sighed, turned off the light and went back to his room where Sam was fast asleep. Katie looked up at him and smiled. It filled his heart. He was looking at the mirror image of his own smile. He grinned at her and picked her up.

"Maybe I'll use you on Trevor. Why aren't you sleeping, little one?"

Daniel laid Katie's small body across his chest, positioned her ear to his heart and rocked her for a few minutes. The baby yawned and closed her eyes. Her little mouth worked in a sucking motion for a few more minutes, and then she relaxed into a sound sleep. Gently, he laid her in the crib and rubbed her back for a few more minutes as she drifted into a deeper sleep. She stretched, rolled to her side and put her thumb into her mouth. He laughed at his little thumb sucker. He made the rounds checking on the rest of the children. When he came back he stopped at Rusty's bed, she was awake so he picked her up and cradled her.

"Can't you sleep?" Daniel whispered.

She shivered slightly. "Daddy?"

"Go to sleep. I'm right here."

Rusty rolled into Daniel's chest and sighed before surrendering to her heavy eyes. He waited until he was sure she was sleeping and placed her next to Wyatt. Rusty always rested better when she wasn't alone. The little boy was peacefully sleeping and didn't move when Rusty wrapped her arms around him.

Daniel undressed quickly sliding in next to Sam. He placed his hand on her belly and rolled her to him. He was tired and needed a little comfort.

# 52

Daniel felt a little hand traveling across his chest. Sam was gone, Katie and Wyatt were gone, but Rusty had joined him in the bed. He kissed her hand and laid there for a long while just watching her. He stretched and Rusty opened one eye. She looked up at him and grinned.

"Morning, Buppy."

"Hey, Daddy."

"Did you sleep well?"

"Monsters came."

"Is that why you came to join me?"

"I was scared."

Daniel snuggled Rusty, folding her into his arms. He wanted her to feel secure while he talked to her. "I'm glad you came to me when you got scared."

She yawned and played with the hair on his chest, pulling at it lightly. "They want to hurt me."

"Baby, I won't let anyone hurt you."

Rusty choked back a sob. "But they're a lot bigger than you."

"I'm pretty tough."

"They're still a lot bigger. Maybe you could get Trevor to help you."

"I will. Buppy, I don't want you to be afraid when you go to sleep, that's why Sam and I keep you close."

Daniel held Rusty for awhile longer and they talked of monsters. He tried to assure her that they wouldn't be able to hurt her. "I'm hungry."

"We'd better get up and get dressed or Sam won't feed us. Go find some clothes and make sure you have shoes."

Daniel had just slipped on his pants when he heard Emma scream. Dropping his shirt, he grabbed his rifle and headed toward the lobby where the screams were coming from. Emma's face was pressed against the window and her eyes wide open in fear. He looked around and saw only Bentley who stood mildly watching them. Elliott ran in, half dressed, rifle in hand.

"I went to get a clean shirt. What's happened?"

Dragging an IV pole behind him, Trevor limped into the room. Daniel grabbed Emma, turned her around and took her face in his hands. "Stop screaming and tell me what's wrong."

She pointed toward the window. "Out there! Fog stuff! It's all over and they peeked out of it. They looked at me!"

Daniel glanced out the window and into the dense greenish fog. Over his shoulder he called to Trevor. "Sit."

The anger in Daniel's voice made Trevor take a step back and abruptly sit down on the nearest chair. Daniel carried Emma to him and placed her on his lap before returning to the window. Trevor said nothing as he hugged Emma to him.

"Sorry, Trevor," she mumbled.

"It's okay. He's just grouchy in the morning."

Daniel surveyed the surrounding grounds for as far as he could see. The ground was covered in a greenish purple low-lying fog. It seemed to be floating just above the ground, rippling slightly at intervals. A low pitched hum filtered into the lobby. Emma covered her ears and buried her face in Trevor's chest. Bentley stamped his foot nervously. Elliott joined Daniel at the window, slipped his suspenders over one arm and raised his rifle. Tommy appeared next to Elliott.

"Doc, I don't see anything," Elliott whispered.

"Daniel."

He didn't turn around. "Sam, go back into the bedroom and stay there with Tommy. Keep the kids with you. Tommy, go with her."

Tommy nodded. Went and took Emma's hand followed Sam down the hall.

"What is it, Doc?" Trevor asked. He weaved slightly as he stood next to him.

"Damn it, boy! I swear I am going to sedate you for at least a week. Sit down."

"Not until this is over. Right now you need me."

They continued to watch for ten minutes, but nothing was happening. Daniel dragged a chair over and pointed to Trevor. He eased down into it, but kept his rifle trained at the window.

"Doc, please stop grumbling at me. Makes me nervous."

"I am not grumbling."

"There's something moving out there," Elliott said, pointing to the middle of the fog. "Something that looks really big."

The something was moving swiftly. A long thick tube-like neck emerged from the fog and looked around. It was purple and had a spiked head with a large greenish cast to it. What little of the body they could see had scales. Daniel and Elliott both moved back from the window and into the shadows next to Trevor. Suddenly, there were dozens of them poking up at various spots in the fog. Each creature sported a hideous purple tongue with thick red spots. Three barbs protruded from the ends. The hum grew into a high-pitched whine, piercing their ears. Elliott gritted his teeth and raised his rifle.

"Assholes."

"Don't bro," Trevor said quickly. "Let them pass. We don't fight unless there's no choice. There's too many of them."

Elliott swore under his breath. "I'd like to kill all those bastards." He eased back, but kept his rifle ready.

Bentley stamped his foot again and whinnied before going into a half rear. Trevor quickly went to him. He needed to quiet the big horse fast. At his touch, Bentley stopped his restless moving and lowered his head to nuzzle him. "Easy, big guy," Trevor called sweetly.

After Bentley had calmed, Trevor moved back to the window and watched the parade of heads going by. "Ground fog? I don't get it, Doc. There isn't any water around here. Where's it coming from?"

"Who the fuck knows," Elliott snorted. "Beast created."

Daniel shook his head and continued to watch as the strange creatures moved pass the hospital. The fog disappeared with the last creature. The only thing left behind were headaches for all.

"That was fun," Trevor said sarcastically.

Everyone gathered in the lobby and Daniel passed out medication for the headaches they all seem to have. "Sorry, Sam, you're going to have to sleep this off. I can't give you anything because you're pregnant. Rose, you'll have to sleep it off as well."

"I'll take Katie and Wyatt with me. We all need a nap," said Sam. Rose took Wyatt from Sam. "I've got to feed this little guy and then it's nap time for him.

Daniel winked at Keeley "You go lie down. Trevor and I have a date. In fact, everyone should try to rest. It's over. They won't be back."

Trevor was sitting on one of the lobby couches with Rusty secured in his lap. She was in her underpants because she didn't have a chance to get changed before everything happened. She was clutching a very unhappy Spot against her chest. Daniel stepped on something rough and realized he also hadn't finished dressing. He was only in jeans. He took Rusty from Trevor and leaned her back in his arms. "Buppy, how's your head?"

"Hurts. Spot's head hurts too."

Gently he released the poor cat from her death grip. "Let's go take care of that for you. Trevor, would you care to join us?"

"Sure, I'm up for some more torture."

Rusty chewed on the baby aspirin as Daniel handed her a bottle of juice he'd found in a machine down the hall. "Here, try drinking this and then you need to lie down for awhile and let the medicine work."

"Can you go with me?"

"I'll put you in with Wyatt, and when I finish with Trevor I'll come and hold you."

Trevor flinched when he heard his name and while he had the chance, he got up and left the room.

"Okay, Daddy."

Trevor was in bed when Daniel went in to see him. His eyes were closed and he could tell from his deep breathing that he was sleeping. He quietly piggybacked a new antibiotic to his IV and then he loaded a syringe with sedation and injected it into the IV port. It would keep him down for awhile. Daniel reached down and felt his forehead.

"Are you here to torture me?" Trevor asked calmly without opening his eyes.

"Is that how you see it?"

Trevor opened an eye and peered up at Daniel. "No. I know it's for my own good, but I don't have to like it. I'm really sick of the needles."

"I don't like it either. I don't like that you had to get hurt and that I'm having so much trouble knocking out the infection. I also don't like having to keep sticking you with needles when I know how it bothers you, but I don't see how we have much of a choice."

"Yeah, me either."

"Go to sleep. Think about Keeley and Danny. Try to forget everything around us for a while."

Trevor was starting to feel good and he was getting very lightheaded. "You drugged me, didn't you?"

"Sure did."

"Thanks, it'll be nice to not hurt for awhile."

Rusty had crawled in bed with Sam and when Daniel joined them she moved over to him. He pulled a blanket over all three of them and closed his eyes reflecting on how tired he actually felt.

Elliott stood in the dark close to the window. He had accepted the aspirin Daniel offered, but refused to lie down. He reached into his pocket, pulled out three aspirin, and popped them into his mouth. Two weren't enough. He watched closely for any signs of trouble as he slowly chewed the aspirin.

## 53

It took another three weeks before they reached the canyon that would become their new home. It was well hidden from view, just as Elliott had said, but he led them right to it.

"I never would have found it, bro," Trevor said. Elliott smiled at the compliment.

They were all taken by surprise at how comfortable the valley seemed. It was filled with the smell of the coming of spring and shimmered in deep greens and blue. It seemed to welcome them.

The large lake made Sam laugh with delight. The surrounding tall trees on one side of the bank shaded half of the lake.

"It's beautiful."

Elliott pointed to the end of the valley. "Those last three cabins have electricity—or at least they did when I was here before."

"Well then, there's no choice about where we start. Lead the way, Elliott," said Daniel.

"You know, I've been thinking, I bet we could build a covered entry way to connect the cabins. That way we'd never have to actually go outside to get from house to house. Maybe we could also have a garden, if we can find seed. I miss fresh vegetables."

Trevor laughed. "Bro, we need to move in first."

Within a few months the boys had connected all of the houses by Elliott's bridges. Sam, Daniel, Katie, Rusty, Taylor, Wyatt, and the three little girls used the first two cabins while Trevor, Keeley,

Danny, Rose, Tommy and Elliott lived in the other cabins. The children would sometimes roam from cabin to cabin and Elliott decided to bar them from his and Tommy's room.

Rusty always stayed close to Daniel. He'd been working with her to make her more independent and secure, but it was hard for her. She was still afraid of the monsters that roamed in her dreams. Trevor's leg healed, but left him with a slight limp.

Katie came running and headed straight for Trevor. He grabbed her up and she hugged him tightly. She patted his back. "My Ever."

"What are you up to, little one?"

Katie giggled and kissed his cheek. "My Ever."

"Katie, my name is Trevor. Can you say Trevor?" The little girl smiled at him and giggled.

"Aren't you supposed to be taking a nap?" he asked her.

Katie wiggled in his arms and laughed at him again. She patted his chest. "My Ever."

"Well, she almost gets it right," Elliott laughed.

"Yeah, Doc's probably been working on her so he can train her to snitch on me."

"Where is Doc? I haven't seen him all day."

"I don't know, but this little escapee has to be returned to bed. Does your Daddy know you're on the loose?" Trevor asked Katie.

With Katie in tow, Trevor and Elliott walked back over to Daniel's and Sam's cabin.

"How's Sam?" Elliott asked.

"She's fine and so is the new baby."

"I'm glad she had a boy," Elliott said. "I was beginning to feel like we were going to get outnumbered by the girls."

"Elliott, trust me, one day you're going to appreciate having females around."

"I doubt that."

They found Daniel hold up in the back room he was using for an office. One of the first things Trevor, Elliott, and Tommy did was to find Daniel a big overstuffed chair so he would be comfortable when he wanted to read. They had painstakingly transported it from a little town twenty-five miles away. Bentley had not been a happy participant in that adventure.

"Hi Doc," Elliott called.

Daniel looked up from his book and smiled at the trio. Trevor nodded at Katie. "I found an escapee."

"How did you get out of bed?" Daniel asked as he took Katie. Katie pointed her little finger at Trevor. "My Ever. Hurt."

Daniel eyed Trevor and Elliott broke into laughter. "Man, Trevor, you're right, he's made the kid a snitch."

"Damn it, Doc, I'm fine, so don't even go there. Katie, who taught you that?"

Katie giggled. "Ever." She clapped her hands and smiled, leaning into Daniel's shoulder.

"Doc, that's a dirty trick."

"I didn't do it," he exclaimed innocently.

"Yeah, well I'm out of here. I'm going to see Sam and my new brother. At least he can't talk yet."

Trevor turned and limped out the door to the sound of laughter. He strolled down the hall and lightly knocked on Sam's door.

"Come in."

"Sam, should you be up?"

"I had the baby four days ago, I think it's alright to be up."

Trevor moved a chair over to the crib where Sam was standing.

"You should sit down."

Sam sat and told him to join her. Trevor pulled up a chair across from her and took her hands in his. "You look great. How do you feel?"

"I'm fine. How about you? Is your leg bothering you?"

"A little, but not bad. Just don't tell Doc. I really want to stay away from any needles for awhile."

Sam chuckled. "I won't say a word."

Trevor got up and looked down at the baby. He gently lifted him and cuddled him to his chest.

"Good morning, Mr. Matthew James and how are you this morning? Would you like to go for a ride with your big brother?"

"Oh no you don't. This child is not going on that horse at four days old."

"Aw, Sam, I won't take him far."

"Absolutely not!"

Trevor gave her a big grin. "I'm only kidding. He has to be at least two weeks old."

"Give me my baby, Trevor Scott and leave."

Trevor gently rocked the baby and laughed. He handed Matt to his mother and swiftly kissed Sam's cheek. "See ya later."

## 54

The evening sky was a thing of beauty. The setting sun went behind the lake and lit the horizon with colors of pink, yellow, and gold. Trevor was sitting on the front porch. Daniel came out to join him.

"Pretty, isn't it?"

Daniel smiled at Trevor. He wondered how this boy could have gone through so much and remained so strong. The Beast had put him through both physical and mental pain. His resistance seemed to be at its lowest right now, but yet he found beauty in a setting sun.

Elliott walked up from the barn where he had bedded Bentley down for the night. Trevor watched Elliott. He seemed more relaxed and settled. He even laughed occasionally. They never mentioned George because it made Elliott angry and moody. He could feel his sadness at the loss of his brother. He didn't believe Elliott would ever forgive him for leaving. Elliott never realized how much he loved George until the day he watched him leave.

All the children were in bed with the exception of Wyatt and Rusty. Wyatt was snuggled comfortably in Daniel's lap and Rusty in Trevor's arms.

"You reckon the moon will ever come back?" Trevor asked in his lazy drawl.

"I don't know. It's been gone a long time."

"How's Rose doing? When will she have the baby?"

"She'll probably deliver in about four weeks. Baby and mom are doing well. How's Keeley been feeling?"

"Fine. Why?"

Daniel gave Trevor a long look and bust out laughing. "You really don't know?"

"Know what?"

"You, my son, are going to be a daddy again."

"What?"

"In about seven months."

"Does Keeley know?"

"Yes. Why do you think she's been nauseated and vomiting? Morning sickness."

"Damn." Trevor smiled. "Damn. You know, Doc, I think I'll just have to make this porch bigger. Then put up a fence around it with a gate so we can keep all these babies locked up. Another baby."

"Relax, tough guy, you've got a long time to worry about it."

Trevor looked up at the darkened sky. "You know, Doc, sometimes you don't miss something until it's gone. Like the moon not being where it should be." He looked down at Rusty. "This little one's gone. I'm going to take her to bed. Goodnight."

"Goodnight. Only good dreams."

As Trevor left, Sam came out to get Wyatt. "I'll take him."

Daniel leaned back in the chair to watch the night darkness spread deeper into their valley. He wasn't afraid to be out in the dark now...not here. He thought of the children they'd lost. Not only those who were not with them now, but the ones who had died. He wondered about Robert, George, Travis, and Harlan. Where were they? Were they still alive or had they become victims of the Beast? Was the Beast still actively hunting them? Those questions would be answered in the future, but Daniel was not sure he really wanted to face the answers. The valley was well hidden and at least for now they were safe and it was good to feel safe. It had settled them, making them comfortable. He stood quietly watching the blue lake. It didn't even ripple in the darkness.

"It's nice to enjoy the quiet again and not feel the icy fear that's been following us," Daniel murmured.

Trevor reappeared and stood beside Daniel. "I thought you went to bed?"

Suddenly, Trevor wrapped Daniel in a bear hug. "Trevor, what's wrong?" he asked.

He thought back to the day Trevor saved him from the Beast's monster that would have killed him—the first day they met. Trevor was a young boy then and he looked like that boy now.

"Nothin's wrong. I'm just glad that we're here together. I'm glad it was you I met that first day. I know I wouldn't have made it this far without you. I'm scared, Daniel, deep down afraid. The Beast isn't done with us. It's still waiting for us out there. I can almost feel him."

"You may be right. We'll face it together."

ΩΩΩ

If you enjoyed reading

*RUNNING INTO THE FOREVER*

Read on for an exciting look at the conclusion to the

**FOREVER SERIES**

J. W. Becker's

# DEAD IS FOREVER

Coming soon. . .

# DEAD IS FOREVER

## Chapter 1

Daniel stood by the window watching the big chestnut horse as he grazed down by the lake. The rising sun made his coat look like a fiery red blaze. Behind the horse the sun reflected off of the trees and mountain ranges and back into the lake. The day was brisk with changes in the air. Fall was slipping away and winter would not be far behind. Soon the mountains would be covered in new snow and the strong westerly winds would bring colder weather. A lone figure came from behind the horse and wrapped his arms around its big neck. The horse immediately lowered his head to accept him and pushed gently against his chest.

Trevor lay against the horse's big chest for a few minutes. He smiled as Bentley blew into his black hair and shoved at him again. He gently tapped the horse's nose and then turned and ran. The horse looked around at the boy and snorted before he took off after him at a trot. Bentley reached out with his long nose and tapped Trevor in the back before turning and trotting off with Trevor close behind. He pulled the horse's tail and ran in the opposite direction. They were playing a game of tag.

Daniel shook his head in wonder. It might be the funniest thing he'd ever seen. He felt a light tap on his leg and looked down to see his daughter, Katie. The little girl smiled up at him and lifted her arms. She child had his dark blue eyes and black hair. She also had his smile. Katie wiggled in his arms and threw her little hands around his neck. Her soft baby body molded against him.

"How did you get away from Mommy?"

The two and half year old giggled, putting her hands on her Daddy's face. She kissed him and looked deeply into his eyes. Daniel was always taken aback by the way her eyes pooled around him. She had a delightful way about her.

"My Daddy."

"Don't Daddy me, little one, you're supposed to be taking a nap."

Katie pointed out the window, squealed and clapped her hands. "Ever? Entley?"

"That's Trevor and Bentley, sweetheart. They're playing a game."

Daniel looked out the window again. It was a good game and it made him happy to watch. There wasn't enough playing in their lives.

Sam walked into the room with Matt and Wyatt. Matt was fast asleep in her arms. Wyatt trotted close behind her. Daniel had found Wyatt abandoned in an empty hospital room. The little boy was standing next to a pile of bones—more destruction caused by the Beast. They had no way of knowing who the dead person was or where the child had come from. He thought the little towheaded boy was around three years old. There was a scar that ran all the way across his left eye and half way down his cheek. He stood there blinking, his big brown eyes staring up at Sam. He adored her and had become her constant companion.

"She escaped," laughed Sam. "Here switch. You take your son and I'll take Katie and Wyatt back for their naps." Sam looked down at her daughter. "You, young lady, are going to lie down and take a nap."

"Daddy help!" Katie pleaded as Sam carried her out of the room and down the hall.

Daniel grinned and turned back to look out the window. He watched as Trevor played with his horse and smiled. It was good to see Trevor almost well again. Daniel rocked his son and was completely absorbed in the ongoing game. He was startled when he heard a voice behind him.

"Hi, Doc. I have a patient for you." He turned to find Rose walking toward him with Rusty in tow. Rose smiled as she pushed back a lock of blonde hair. She stood only five foot four and at six feet, Daniel towered over her. Her brown eyes sparkled as she tried not to laugh. "Rusty can't attend school today because she claims she's ill, so I gave her the option of school or you."

Rose had started a school in one of the unoccupied houses that surrounded the lake where they lived. Her husband, Robert, had left more than a year before to fight the Beast that threatened them all. He'd taken Elliott's brother, George, and two other boys, Harlan and Travis, with him.

Rose had thrown herself into teaching the children. It was her way of coping with life without Robert. She had the boys make a room where all the toddlers and babies could be occupied in a daycare type of environment while she taught the older children.

Daniel's thoughts went to Robert, George, Harlan, and Travis. All of his adopted sons had gone to fight against the Beast that was determined to capture them and make them slaves. The boys had gone back to the camps where most of the remaining humans were now being held by a creature referred to as the Beast.

Robert and Rose had been among those who lived in the camps and had escaped with Harlan and Travis. The four had joined with Daniel and his family. Robert went back to kill the three remaining unborn embryos of the Beast and help free those who were left. Rose was pregnant with Robert's child when he left. Rose gave birth to their daughter six months later. She named the baby, Riana Ann, but everyone called her Reed.

Daniel smiled at Rose as he looked down at Rusty. She wouldn't look back at him and kept her eyes planted on the floor. She'd wrapped a finger around a blonde curl while shifting slowly from one foot to the other. She hummed quietly to herself.

"I'll take Matt with me and leave Rusty to you," Rose said, reaching for the baby.

Daniel kissed his son and handed the sleeping ten month old over to Rose. She'd take him to the nursery and put him down in one of the cribs. Daniel took Rusty's hand in his and led her into the front room and over to a chair. He sat down and eased her into his lap. He leaned Rusty back in his arms so she was facing him. "Are you sick, Buppy?"

"Kind of," she answered quietly, as her blue eyes pooled with tears.

She wasn't warm, but shivered in his arms. He looked into her eyes and she looked away. "What's bothering you?"

"My head booms."

"Does that mean your head hurts?"

"Uh huh."

Rusty rolled into Daniel's chest, put her thumb in her mouth and clasped the cross around her neck. Daniel had given her the cross long ago and told her it would protect her. It was the day she questioned if she could still be his daughter, the day Katie was born.

Daniel had saved Rusty from the Beast. She wasn't his biological daughter, but his feelings for her were so deep that he'd always considered her his own. She had just turned seven. He carried her into his exam room. Headaches were nothing new to Rusty and she frequently suffered from them. Gently, he placed her on the table. She rolled away from him. He rolled her back and used a small penlight to look into her eyes. She shied away from its brightness. "Daddy no!"

"Sorry baby, here, sit up and tell me exactly where your head hurts."

"All over."

Rusty leaned into his chest. He lifted her into his arms and went to sit in his chair. Unconsciously, Daniel positioned her so that she was resting against his chest and could listen to his heart. She immediately started to relax. She needed his comfort and burrowed as close as she could.

"What has you so frightened?"

Rusty didn't have the words to tell him that her head hurt because she'd been touched by the Beast's presence. She didn't know how to explain the nightmares that came to her every night—nightmares that managed to haunt her even during the daylight hours. In them, large winged creatures came from above to blacken the sky. Even if she tried to tell him, it came out confused and wrong because that's how she felt.

The Beast had reached out to Rusty's mind and touched her that morning. She didn't understand what happened, only that she was frightened. The connection was a weak one. The Beast was searching for Daniel's family and his desperation was felt by Rusty. She tried to blank out her mind, but the Beast still reached in and when she felt his touch, the pain in her head intensified, burying itself deep into her. Violent shivers overtook her body.

"Daddy, make it stop."

Daniel shifted Rusty on his lap, pulling her tight to him and slowly massaging her temples. He spoke softly in his deep calming voice. Of all his children, Rusty worried him the most. She was the most sensitive and emotional, and needed the most protection. She spent too much time alone. For companionship, she turned either to Bentley or her cat, Spot. When she did play with one of the children, it was either Katie or Wyatt.

Daniel waited until she was asleep and then took her and placed her into bed. He sighed, leaned down and kissed his troubled child. "Only good dreams."

As he watched Rusty sleep he knew that her dreams would be anything but good. It would only be a matter of time before she would wake screaming and calling out in terror. The dark things that invaded her unconscious world didn't let her sleep for long. Daniel was at a loss, he didn't know how to help conquer her fears.

## ABOUT THE AUTHOR

J.W. Becker is retired and lives in Henderson, Nevada with her husband, Jeff and two schnauzers, Katie and Dusty Rose. She loves Sci-Fi/Horror. The "Forever series" is her first.

## Books by J.W. Becker

"FOREVER SERIES"
Dust, Bones and the Forever
Journey Toward the Forever
Running Into the Forever